MAKE ME BEHAVE 2

TARA FOX HALL

CONTENTS

MAKE ME BEHAVE

8 spanking-new tales of domestic discipline to whet your ardor...and bring out the submissive within. Join professionals and novices experiencing their first forays into the dance of dom and sub in this sequel to Make Me Behave.

SEVEN STEPS

Lara's boyfriend Mac has schooled her well in being a submissive to his dominant. But he has a seventh lesson to teach her in overcoming her fear of heights in the seclusion of a forest treehouse.

SEVEN STEPS

"How much farther?" Lara called with a slight wheeze, pausing on the dirt path. She wiped the cuff of her rolled up sleeves over her sweaty brow and shifted her daypack slightly.

"Another half-mile," her boyfriend Mac answered with a smirk, looking over his shoulder. "Do you need a break?"

Lara straightened, all thoughts of resting wiped from her mind by her annoyance. She returned his smirk. "No, do you?"

"Always have to make a contest out of everything," Mac teased her. "You're supposed to be having fun and relaxing, Lara. Fresh air, exercise, and each other. That's why we came here to the wilderness instead of going to some faraway destination for our vacation."

Lara sauntered up to him, slipping her arms around his moist neck and giving him her best bedroom eyes. "This is just the first day, Mac. We've got all the time in the world. Just me," she kissed his nose, "and you." She lowered her lips to touch his teasingly.

Mac pulled her close, his mouth devouring hers as he molded her sweaty body to his, his hands sliding inside her short jacket to rub her curvaceous body through the thin material of her T-shirt. "Good. You promised me some time off." He kissed her throat, then bit her skin softly, eliciting a soft cry. "Don't make me make you behave, little girl."

Lara dipped her head, and nipped his cheek, even as her hand ran

3

down to cup his swelling member. She gave it a sharp squeeze, making Mac groan. "You're talking to a woman, little man. Don't forget that," she gave him another squeeze, caressing his erection with her fingers. "I can match you thrust for thrust."

"I think you mean lust for lust," Mac said huskily. He kissed her again, and Lara lost herself in the kiss, her libido rising. *I want him, there's no one around, maybe …*

A sudden crack of thunder above startled the couple, making them stagger apart. "Damn," Mac said, pointing to the south, where a large thundercloud was moving fast. "We'd better find shelter. There's no way we can make it back."

"The last campsite was two miles back!"

The sky was rapidly darkening, the storm system rushing towards them like an inescapable wave. "C'mon, we have to move!" Mac grabbed Lara's hand, pulling her forward along the trail. She raced to keep up with him, as rain began pelting down. Running down the path, the rain became a deluge as more lightning lit up the sky.

"Hey, there's something over there," Mac shouted. He led her down an overgrown trail, to the base of a tree. Another crack of thunder sounded above. "Hurry!"

"Hurry where?" Lara yelled.

"Up!"

Lara's eyes widened as she tilted her head up, following a series of steps complete with railing affixed to the side of a huge tree. A tree house sat above, swaying slightly in the roaring wind. "Mac, I'm not going up there! That's the last place we should be in a storm!"

Mac grabbed a step, shoving into it hard. The stair didn't move. "It's solid." He grasped the railing, then put all his weight on the first step. "C'mon!"

Lara didn't budge, shaking her head, water flinging off her soaked tresses. "You know I don't like heights! That's got to be fifty feet up!"

Mac grasped her by the shoulders. "Do you trust me?"

Lara took a shuddering breath, as thunder sounded again above. "You know I do."

"Give me your pack." Mac shouldered the extra weight, took her hand, then half led/half lifted her onto the first step. Lara grabbed the railing, then began to inch up the stairs, Mac behind her whispering encouragement. Lara began to shake the higher she went, nearly losing her footing when thunder boomed again high above. Mac grabbed hold of her. "I've got you."

Together, they made their way inside the tree house, shutting the door tightly behind them.

Lara sank to the floor, sitting cross-legged, trying to acclimate to the slight swaying. Mac took off Lara's pack and put it in front of the door, wedging it from blowing open. He tapped his phone, then grimaced. "There's a huge system, it's going to be hours before it's through."

Lara forced a lopsided smile. "So much for the weather channel."

Lightning flashed, then thunder boomed again. Mac put his phone away, then took off his pack, and sat down across from Lara. "Are you okay?"

Her lower lip trembled.

He pulled her over close to him, then hugged her tightly. "You know I wouldn't let anything happen to you."

Lara relaxed back against him with a soft sigh of contentment, the solidness of his chest a welcome comfort. "I know. I was just scared."

He kissed her gently, his arms and body a barrier keeping her safe. *But not warm.* Lara broke away gently. "We should get out of these wet clothes. I don't mind being damp, but even my underwear is soaked."

Mac laughed as he stood, then helped her up. "We can't make a fire in a tree, but maybe there's something here we can use." He moved to the far wall, which had a few plastic tubs in front of it.

"This is really well built, actually," Lara said, running her hands over the rough wood. "The roof isn't leaking, and neither is the plastic, or whatever it is in the windows."

"Fantastic!" Mac had opened the tub and produced a thick layer of rolled foam. He cut the tie, then rolled it out. Going to his pack, he brought out a thick fleece blanket which he put over the foam. "Just like home."

"Now all we need is a heater, lol."

"This will help," Mac said, unfolding a wooden drying rack. He put it near the door, as Lara began taking off her clothes, peeling off all the wet layers.

"And I did bring the heater," Mac said arrogantly, producing a small catalytic heater and propane tank from his pack. He turned it on with a click and set it in the corner.

Lara stopped undressing, staring at him. "I'd say you planned this, but I don't see how you did it."

Mac turned to her, his gaze lingering on her prominent nipples straining against her wet bra. "For someone who was so concerned with wet underwear, you seem to be doing a lot of talking and not much taking care of it."

Lara smiled, then reached behind and unfastened her bra, letting it fall to the floor. She stepped over to Mac, then unzipped his pants, stroking his stiffening penis. "I thought you were going to take care of it for me."

Mac pulled his shirt over his head in one swift motion, then grabbed her, his mouth closing over one silken sweet breast. Her nipple tightened further as he sucked and nibbled. Carefully, he lowered her onto the foam, then slid her panties off. He hung them on the rack, then stripped off his pants, letting his erection bob free.

Lara smiled sexily. "So you're ready to make me behave?"

"Aren't I always? Touch yourself for me, angel."

Lara cupped her breasts with both hands, then slid them across her nipples, teasing and pulling. The flesh tightened up once more. Mac tongued one nipple, then the other, as Lara groaned and writhed.

"I want you."

"Not yet, angel. Show yourself to me. Spread those legs wide, so I can taste you."

Lara shuddered, then eagerly spread her legs, her clit already shiny with dew. She touched it in circular motions, the flesh swelling. Mac moved between her legs, then dipped his head. With the first touch of his tongue, Lara arched her back up, crying out softly. Her cries intensified as Mac licked and touched her, slipping his fingers in gently.

"Now!" Lara demanded, trying to pull him on top of her.

Mac stopped, then shook his head slowly, even as his smile widened. He pulled her over his knee, then administered a sharp slap to her still-cold bottom.

"Ow!"

Mac cupped her reddened cheek, then pinched it lightly, making Lara writhe. "Bad girl," he whispered lovingly. "Now recite the seven steps."

"No," Lara said petulantly.

Mac brought his hand down in a resounding whack, and Lara let out a yelp. "Say them! Number one."

"I will not demand, I will ask."

"Two."

"I will touch myself when asked."

"Very good." Mac shifted Lara again in his arms, moving her so she sat in front of him between his legs. He cupped her breasts, then began pulling her nipples. Lara groaned.

"Three."

"I will spread my legs when asked."

"Very good," Mac murmured. "Now spread them."

Lara leaned back into him, widening her legs as his hand slipped down her thigh. Deftly, he penetrated her with his hand, rubbing until she was bucking in his arms, her need to come undeniable.

"Four."

"I ... I will not come until asked."

"And I didn't ask you yet." He kissed her throat lovingly, still touching her slippery womanhood. "Five."

"I will speak my desires plainly, with no hesitation."

"Yes, you will," Mac said roughly. "And so will I. I want to be inside you, Lara, my cock is hard as stone feeling you so wet and ready for me."

"I want you inside me so bad," Lara groaned, trying to turn in his arms. "I want to ride you, and make you come, please!"

"No," Mac said, stopping his hands. "Behave! Six."

"I will not move if I'm told not to, just as if tied in place."

"Yes, that's right," Mac groaned, moving up on his knees. "Get on all fours."

Lara got on her knees, and Mac moved behind her, his thick hard cock sliding into her wet channel as he pushed in to the root. Slowly and deeply he thrust, as Lara groaned.

Mac slipped out, then rolled onto his back, motioning for Lara to mount him. She straddled him, then paused, waiting.

"And finally, the seventh step?" he prompted.

"I will move only when asked," Lara murmured, grasping his penis, and angling it down, as she tilted her hips.

"Move, angel. I want to hear you scream. Come for me."

With a deep satisfied sigh, she sheathed him inside her and began rocking.

Mac grasped her hips, letting her move on him. Quickly she ground to climax, the motion bringing him to orgasm in a shout as he clasped her hips to his, his body pistoning under hers.

Lara collapsed on Mac, both of them breathing hard. He held her to him, as their breathing quieted.

"The thunder's stopped," she said languidly, stretching.

Mac chuckled. "The rain will probably go on for a little while yet, but it's just sprinkling."

Lara reared up atop him, and pushed back her long hair with both hands, letting it fall forward in a luxurious wave, enjoying Mac's instant appreciative hungry look. "So are you going to tell me that you planned this? Finding this treehouse right here with just what we needed is a little too perfect to be accidental."

"I might have," Mac teased, reaching forward to pass his hand through her fall of hair. "Just like silk."

Lara shifted slightly, and her hair enclosed their faces like a curtain, as she kissed him gently. "So what is next? I know you too well to think that you'd go to all this trouble just to have what you could have had back at the hotel."

Mac winked. "You're right." He caressed her naked bottom with his left hand, then spanked her once gently, making her jump. Lara's motion caused an involuntary contraction of her vaginal walls, squeezing his semi-erect penis gently, and making it stir, as he let out a groan.

With a satisfied sigh, he grasped her hips, then lifted her off him reluctantly. "I did have something in mind, but we need to wait for dark."

Lara blinked in surprise, then smiled as she checked her phone. "Okay, handsome, its nearly six, and dark is a good hour off. Plus I have to admit I'm starving."

"I planned for that, too," Mac replied triumphantly, producing a bottle of wine and a wedge of cheese from his pack. He reached into the other plastic tub and brought out a packet of crackers, and two wine glasses. "Do you want to get out whatever you had packed for lunch?"

Lara laughed, then brought out several different kinds of apples, a serrated knife, a hunk of cheese, several chocolate bars, and a small plastic jar. "Deluxe salted nuts, your favorite."

Lara shared the food and Mac poured the wine. The naked couple dug in, Lara cutting up the apples as he sliced her pieces of cheese. "I like to feed you," she teased him, as she brought a piece of apple to his lips.

"I'll be tasting some of your honey later," he said huskily, then snatched the fruit with his teeth.

"Okay but watch the teeth!"

Mac grabbed Lara, tickling her. "Now, c'mon, you like my teeth, when properly applied."

"And you like mine," she replied, undaunted. "And my tongue."

Mac grasped her naked breast, rubbing the nipple between his thumb and forefinger. "I do, sweetheart. And it's finally time." He rose to his bare feet. "Come with me."

Lara stood, curious, taking his proffered hand. "Where are we going?"

"Up."

Her eyes widened. "You're kidding. Mac, we're already fifteen feet up."

"Try twenty-five. Didn't you wonder what that other door was for?"

"What door?"

Mac pushed the two tubs aside, revealing a small lock on the bottom of the wood. He unlocked the deadbolt, then pushed open the narrow door. Moist cool air rushed past Lara, tightening her nipples as she shivered, looking at a narrow stair leading up into the leafy canopy.

Mac went to lead her, but she didn't move, uncertain.

"Do you trust me?" he asked.

"I do," she said slowly. "But you know I'm afraid of heights, Mac."

"I do know, and that's why we're here," he replied. "To conquer your fear."

"I'm afraid," she whispered, clinging to him.

"I'm right here, and I'm not going to let anything happen to you," he assured her.

She clung to him and didn't reply.

"Please do this for me," Mac whispered. "You're right, I did plan this, but I did more than that: I built this house, and what's above, Lara. I built it for you. For us."

Lara bit her lip, blinking in astonishment. "You must have spent hours. Days!"

"Try a week," he chided softly, then kissed her forehead. "I wanted to help you conquer your fear of heights in a safe way. Trust me."

"I trust you," she whispered. "Lead me."

Mac led Lara up the narrow stairs, showing her where and how to grip the handholds he'd screwed into the trunk. They went up another fifteen feet, then twenty, until the stair ended at the last stout branch of the tree nearest the top. A sex swing hung there made of padded leather, securely anchored.

"Fuck me," she said, exhaling loudly.

"That's the idea," he teased. Mac brought the swing closer, then helped Lara buckle herself in. Carefully, he eased her back out into midair.

Lara gingerly leaned back, then relaxed into the leather, holding onto the main supporting straps for dear life.

"You can let go," Mac called. "Swing a little, if you want. I reinforced and widened the padding in several spots so you can do more than just sit, and tested it for five hundred pounds."

Lara hesitated a moment, then began to move a little, testing out the straps. They held her securely as she swung back and forth. "God, it's like flying!"

Mac meanwhile was extending a platform plank in front of the swing. He bolted it in place, then turned to Lara, his cock at rigid attention. "Show off for me. I want to see all of you."

Lara grinned, then tilted her pelvis and spread her legs, flashing the blonde thatch and pink folds of her pussy. She smirked, then closed her legs and tilted her body up as if she were diving, to wiggle her bottom in Mac's face.

Mac grabbed hold of her torso, then pulled her close, delivering a swift whack onto her smooth cheek globes. Lara yelped in surprise.

"What was that for?"

"I said all of you, my little vixen."

Lara stifled a laugh, then began moving in the swing, arching her back as she touched her breasts, scissoring her legs and stroking her clit.

Mac meanwhile touched a control on the top of the swing, and the contraption began to rise, a small motor whirring. It stopped a few feet up, and Lara swung around, her head and body now on a level with Mac's.

"There," Mac said approvingly. "Now come here."

Lara smiled, and leaned back her head, her lips inches from Mac's. He leaned forward and kissed her roughly, consuming her lips with his own, his tongue delving into her mouth to tangle with hers. With a groan and a push, he withdrew, then spun Lara around, grasping her legs.

"Spread them. Now."

Lara spread her legs, stretching them out straight, the shock of his tongue slipping into her making her cry out. Mac nibbled at the tiny pink bud, his tongue circling and circling until her juices flowed freely, and she was whimpering in his grip.

Carefully, he spun her around, then lowered her slowly, sucking her breasts one by one as she writhed in midair. Gripping her hips, he brought her onto his shaft with a grunt, and began thrusting slowly and deeply.

"Say them for me, sweetheart."

"No," Lara said, and gripped his hips, driving herself down on his cock. "You can't make me. I want to come!"

Mac stopped moving and spanked her hard.

"Ow!"

"Do as you're told, or I'll make you."

"No."

Again, Mac spanked Lara, her cry louder this time.

"No!"

Mac withdrew his swollen shaft, then shifted her onto her stomach in the straps. Holding her torso in one muscular arm, he delivered a series of whacks to her swiftly reddening ass, as she flailed and screeched. Finally, she began whimpering, a tear falling down her cheek.

"Shh," Mac said gently, crouching to kiss it away. "Say the words for me, sweetheart."

"I will not demand, I will ask."

"Two."

"I will touch myself when asked."

"Very good." Mac brought Lara into his arms, hugging her. "Three."

"I will spread my legs when asked."

"God, you get me so fucking hot for you," Mac groaned. He slipped his hand down to cup her pussy. Her excitement drenched his hand, as he slipped his fingers inside her. "Just like I get you stoked for me. Four."

"I will not come until asked."

Mac slipped his fingers up to his mouth, tasting her juices. "Better than honey. Five."

"I will speak my desires plainly, with no hesitation."

"What are your desires?"

"I want to taste you," Lara said sexily, batting her eyelashes.

"I'm all yours. Taste what you want."

Lara rolled in the straps, repositioning again on her belly. She reached for his leaking shaft, bringing the tip to her lips, licking away the fluid, then bringing the whole of his penis into her mouth.

Mac's head went back as he fought to stand, Lara's licking and sucking driving him crazy. She moved in rhythm, feeling him readying to come, wanting to make him lose control.

Mac grasped her shoulders, stopping her with a moan of regret and separating. "Six," he managed.

"I will not move if I'm told not to, just as if tied in place."

Mac hurried, working at another control device, as he buckled himself into several straps. "Seven."

"I will move only when asked."

Mac moved closer to Lara, then grabbed hold of her tightly. "Eight."

There had never been an eighth rule for their bondage, but Lara knew what to say all the same. "I will not fear heights."

"Fly for me," Mac said, then pushed them both off the platform.

Lara let loose a screech, holding onto Mac. But the straps held, and they swung gently, as Mac positioned himself beneath her, and she straddled him, sinking down on his member.

"Come," he commanded.

Mac grasped Lara to him as she rocked, panting as her orgasm approached. As she began to come, Mac came loudly, shouting and bucking up beneath her, triggering her climax as she screamed for all she was worth.

Mac sighed happily, then hugged her close, as they swayed gently.

"The rain's stopped," Lara whispered.

"I'm so glad you enjoyed this," Mac said sounding uncharacteristically hesitant. "I really wanted everything to be perfect for you, for us."

"It was perfect," Lara assured him. "And I promise from now on, I won't be afraid of heights, as long as you're with me." She smiled. "But can we get back inside now?"

"Yes," Mac said with a chuckle, helping her to the platform and unbuckling the straps. "I admit, I'm tired now. I want some water, the heater, a blanket … and you."

"I want that, too," she whispered to him, as they descended.

When they were settled below, cuddling and warm, Lara asked, "Why did you want to wait until dark?"

"I thought it would be less scary being up so high if you couldn't see the ground." He looked at her out of the corner of his eye. "For the first time, at least."

Lara laughed. "I guessed you didn't go to all this trouble to use this place once."

"No," Mac said, taking her hand in his and squeezing. "I want this to be our place. I know we said we'd take it slow, and I respect that. This is my way of showing you I'll be there for you, no matter what, Lara. And that you'll always be safe with me."

"I know that," she said lovingly, kissing him and snuggling into him. "But I love you saying it all the same."

THE END

THE CHASE

Katrina always resisted the temptation offered by her best friend Blair, until a weekend getaway with friends lands her smack in the middle of an adult game of Chase. Caught by not only Blair but "almost" lover Terian, Katrina decides to stop running ... and embrace forbidden desires.

THE CHASE

The brindled Pitbull ran yelping across the ragged hayfield, the black and tan coonhound in close pursuit. Katrina turned to her friend Blair with a smirk. "So much for your big tough dog. Sebastian's got him on the run."

"Clark doesn't have to be a big tough dog," Blair said with an easy smile, baring one lithe tattooed bicep. "He's got me."

Katrina's eyes widened. "Is that another new one? What is it?"

Blair moved the neck of her T-shirt slightly, revealing a flash of color. "Maybe I'll show it to you during our trip."

Katrina blushed, and looked away.

"Always so prudish!" Blair laughed. "I swear you were still a virgin if I didn't know better."

Katrina stuck out her tongue at her friend. "You wish you knew better, you mean."

"Anytime, baby," Blair said with a seductive smile.

"C'mon, my dad's waiting for us," Katrina mumbled, flushing. Blair nodded, and the pair were silent on their walk back to the house, the dogs running in front of them, still chasing one another.

Blair's always been blatant about her interest in me as more than a friend. But I've never taken her up on it, since that stolen kiss our first year in college. The New Year's Eve we both turned twenty-one.

Katrina looked at Blair out of the corner of her eye, letting her gaze slide over her friend's lithe form. *Definitely feminine in some aspects, but a lot of power, restrained power. And an air of danger, like a tiger.*

The pair walked back to Katrina's small trailer. Her dad was waiting with open arms near his small house, and the dogs ran circles around him, barking happily, until he let them inside. "Are you girls packed for your adventure?" he asked, shutting the dogs inside. "Good to see you, Blair."

"Hi, Mr. Anderson."

"I'm all packed, Dad," Katrina said, giving her father a hug. "Now you know where Sebastian's food is, and—"

"Get going," Her father said, giving her a big hug. "Sebastian will be fine. And so will Clark. They seem to be as good friends as you two are."

Yeah, but their probably not thinking about screwing each other. Katrina looked over at Blair, to catch her friend staring at her with a knowing smirk. Katrina flushed red, then sat in the driver's seat Blair getting into the passenger seat. They got on the road and headed off.

K atrina went to the kitchen, then began doing the dinner dishes, the few that there were. She snuck a look at Blair, but she was talking to Damian. Damian's boyfriend Tom was looking out on the city lights far below and talking to Gregory.

If I didn't know better, I'd think she was interested in him. Blair and Damian were thick as thieves tonight. Good thing you came here to have fun, not hook up. Katrina washed the last of the dishes and put the last one to dry in the rack.

There was a knock at the door.

"Finally!" Blair said, leaping up. "Guys, I'll need help." She ran for the door and opened it. "Hi, Terian. Hey, you cut your hair."

Terian handed a case of beer to Damian, then a cloth tote with several wine bottles in it to Tom. Turning, he gave Blair a big hug. "Yes, it was time." He turned side to side, showing off his reddish-brown locks. "Do you like the shorter do?"

"Of course!" Katrina hurried over, then gave him a big hug. "I didn't think you were going to make it! I'm so glad to see you, it's been years!"

"I'm only here for the night," Terian apologized. "But I hope I can help everyone relax and have a good time. Who wants a drink?"

"I do," Blair said quickly. "Kat, can you come with me? I have a surprise for Terian upstairs."

Bewildered, Kat nodded and followed Blair up the stairs. *Does she really have something to give him?*

Blair was rummaging in her bag, then came up with several heavy old books, which she handed to Katrina. "Sorry, he heard that the library was selling off some of its collection that no longer gets much use. I have another box here to carry."

And I thought this was a ploy. Boy, do I feel like an idiot. "Glad to help."

Katrina turned to carry the books downstairs, but Blair stopped her. "No, put them in the smallest room with the two twin beds. He's taking the last of the four bedrooms."

Katrina's eyes widened, and she let out a nervous giggle. "But that room is taken already. Where's Gregory going to sleep?"

"I have it on good authority he'll be spending tonight in the master bedroom," Blair said with a grin.

"What?" Katrina whispered fiercely, following her into the small bedroom. "With Tom and Damian?"

Blair nodded, then set down her box of books in a corner. She took the armload from Kat and set them on top. Turning fast, she grabbed Katrina's arm. "C'mere."

Katrina froze, then made herself relax. "What?"

"You didn't say anything on the way up." Blair took a deep breath, then exhaled. She hurried to the door, then closed it. Turning again, she faced Kat. "But before we left your house, I thought you might have been giving me some signals."

Katrina flushed, but didn't speak.

"Were you?"

Gut up and stop being a coward. "Yes."

Blair walked toward her, a predatory sway to her step. "Don't tease, if you don't mean it."

"I'm not teasing. I just ... I ..."

"You just what? Wonder what might have happened if your roommate hadn't come home as we were kissing?"

Katrina flushed deeper. "Yes."

Blair smiled, then edged closer. "I do, too." She reached out and touched Katrina's arm, then ran her fingers lightly down the bare skin. Katrina jumped, then smiled nervously.

"What's wrong? I don't bite."

"You might," Kat quipped, eager to diffuse the tension. "You remind me of a tiger in a cage, acting casual and laid back, but every once in a while, like now, I see your eyes."

"You see what is my eyes," Blair murmured, leaning forward to kiss Katrina's cheek.

"The hunger in them. I see how you look at me, and I know exactly what you're thinking."

"You're right, I am hungry," Blair whispered seductively, moving her mouth down Katrina's throat in soft kisses. "I'm hungry for you, Kat."

I don't want her to stop, this feels too good. But we shouldn't do this.

"Are you hungry for me?"

Katrina shivered.

Blair lifted her head, her lips inches from Katrina's. "Is that a yes?"

"Hey, you in there?" Terian said, knocking on the door. "Can I come in?"

"Yes," Katrina answered, moving past Blair and opening the door. Terian looked at her, then at Blair, who let out a dramatic sigh and raised her dark eyebrows.

"You two brunettes up to some mischief?" he teased, setting a duffle down on the closest bed. "Thanks for getting these books for me, Blair."

"No problem," Blair gave Katrina another smoldering look, then sauntered out.

"I hope I didn't interrupt something," Terian apologized.

"No," Katrina murmured, hurrying downstairs.

For the next hour, Blair seemed to ignore Katrina, teasing Terian and telling stories of her strangest customers at the library. Katrina found herself staring several times, forcing her gaze away. *This power to say yes or no is heady. That with a touch of my hand or a single "yes", she'll likely do everything I was always curious about.* Her nervousness increased until she finally poured herself a second glass of wine.

G od, it's near midnight. I'm having fun, but it's late. Katrina yawned discreetly then went to rise, prepared to excuse herself.

"Now that we're all relaxed and more open minded," Tom said, getting to his feet, "I confess I had a little game planned for this evening."

"Charades?" Damian quipped, and the others laughed.

"Not exactly," Tom said with an odd smile. He reached into his pack and brought out several tails, one orange and furry with a white tip, the others solid and multicolored, like a dog. "Fox and Hounds."

"I never heard of it," Terian said, his brows knitting.

"I have," Gregory said, then burst out laughing.

"What's so funny?" Katrina asked.

"It's a game of chase," Tom went on. "There's usually one person designated as the fox, and the rest are hounds." He smiled wider. "Whatever hound catches the fox gets it."

Gregory laughed. Katrina gaped in shock.

"So who's the fox?" Terian asked. "I'm guessing it's not me, if you weren't sure I was coming."

"I brought two sets, so there will be two foxes," Tom explained, producing the tails. "I'll be one, unless Damian would prefer to be?"

Damian shook his head.

"Katrina, I thought you'd be the other."

"I think we should have discussed this ahead of time," Katrina said delicately. "I'm not sure it's safe to be running around outside with a tail strapped to me—"

"In you," Tom corrected.

Katrina gaped at him. "What?"

"It's an anal plug. I know, it sounds terrible, but it isn't. It just sits inside your—"

"I can guess where it goes," Katrina interrupted, flushing. "But I'm not going to run around with some plug up my butt in the forest."

"Naked," Tom amended. "You're supposed to run around with this in your butt, naked."

Katrina leaned back in her chair and smiled a shark's smile. "Fuck. No."

"Well, you may have to convince her," Tom said, laying the one set of tails down on the table. "Boys, if you'll join me, we'll get our own game underway."

Damian, Tom, and Gregory rose up, and went into the other room. There were shrieks of laughter, then also some curse words and more laughter as the trio disrobed, and headed outside, tails in place. Some howling ensued, accompanied by more laughter. The sounds faded, leaving Terian, Blair, and Katrina alone.

"Sorry," Blair said, raking her fingers through her short hair. "If you don't want to do it, it's okay. It sounded fun."

Katrina wheeled on her. "Anal plugs, are you serious?"

"Not about the tails," Blair said, her tone dropping huskily as she stared into Katrina's eyes. "About chasing you, yeah, I'm serious. But if you won't run from me, I can't chase you." Her eyes narrowed, and she got up, moving upstairs.

"This is not what I thought it was going to be," Terian said slowly, after Blair had left. "I feel like I came to the wrong party."

"You and me both."

"Is it me?" Terian asked suddenly. "Am I the reason you said no?"

He's remembering that week before finals, right before we graduated. We were both stressed; we'd had fights with our lovers. I knew my relationship was over, and I wanted something to make me forget him. So I made a pass at Terian. Initially he responded, but then he felt guilty and stopped me. And I felt so bad about it that I stayed away from him completely after that.

"Katrina?"

"It's not you. It's me not wanting something in my ass. Or up my ass, or whatever."

"How do you know you don't want something in your ass? You might like it."

"Do you want something in your ass? I can probably arrange it."

"What I want to get back is that night with you," he whispered. "And to not say no this time."

Katrina took a breath to tell him the moment had passed, that they couldn't get it back. Then she stopped. *He's not asking for your firstborn, he's asking to play a game. And if you want to have sex. That's all.* "Let me go talk to Blair. Yes, I'm up for a game of chase outside, but no, I'm keeping my clothes on out there."

Terian grinned, then nodded.

Katrina went upstairs. Blair was pacing back and forth, as if she'd wear out the floorboards.

"You planned this?"

"Hell yes, I planned this! I want you, it's not like this is a news flash," Blair said angrily. "What the hell did you think I meant in the bedroom earlier?"

"Why didn't you tell me about this proposed game of chase?"

"I wasn't sure how to. 'Hey, let's bring some sex toys on our trip?' You might have thought I was joking."

"That would have been honest."

Blair turned away. "I thought you would say no."

Katrina laid her hand on Blair's arm. "I would have asked what kind of toys. And told you no anal plugs."

"I know you haven't ever had anal sex," Blair said bluntly. "You've probably heard bad things about it. But I could make it very good for you."

Blair moved to kiss her, and Katrina stepped back automatically.

"Why won't you let me touch you?"

Because you're a girl, too, and a voice in my head is telling me I'm wrong to do this. But it's not my voice telling me that. It's someone else's voice. Someone I don't have to listen to.

Katrina steeled herself. "Go ahead and touch me."

"I'm not going to touch you. You don't want me to, not really—"

"You either kiss me right now, or I'm going to go spend the night with Terian. He wants me and he's not afraid to do something about it."

Blair looked at her in amazement, then grabbed hold of her and kissed her. The kiss was like nothing Katrina had ever experienced before; pure passion, an all-consuming fire that set all her nerve endings tingling.

Katrina slid her hands down her friend's body. *She's so delicate.*

Blair had hold of her now, kissing Katrina's throat, those strong hands fondling her breasts. *It's so different than a man's touch, which is all possessive lust. It's gentle.*

"You'd better run, or I'm taking you right here," Blair said gutturally. "I've waited too long for this."

"Catch me if you can." Katrina ducked out of the room, and down the stairs. Blair went after her, but slipped in her socks, sliding past the stairs to land on her bottom.

Katrina ran to the table, grabbed the foxtail, and ran for the door, evading the sudden lunge from Terian. She slammed it open and ran out into the night, hiding behind a nearby tree.

Terian and Blair emerged, then set off in different directions.

It was going to be hard to evade them both for long. The woods would be full of animals hunting, and the pond would have mosquitos. The best route was probably to head into the shed and hide there.

Katrina hurried to the shed, put her hand on the door, and heard a moan from inside, then low laughter. *Damn it, the gay threesome is already in there going to town!* Stymied, she turned to go, and almost ran into Terian. He made a grab for her but missed, and she dropped to all fours and then lunged back to her feet, sprinting towards the cabin. Blair came around the front at a dead run, and cut her off, determined.

Katrina tried to slip past her but slipped on the wet grass and went sprawling. Blair dropped down on top of her, just as Terian's hand closed over her left ankle.

"Gotcha!"

Blair kissed her on the cheek with a triumphant smile, then got up, offering a hand. Katrina took it, then held out her other to Terian, who was looking unsure.

"Go ahead," Blair said, obviously disgruntled. "Join the party." Then she grinned. "You did drive her right into me."

"Not my intention," Terian replied, but then he grinned too. "Guess we have to share."

Katrina looked from one of them to the other. *Uh ...*

"I'm game. C'mon."

Katrina was led into the house, and upstairs to the master bedroom.

"This is where Damian and Tom sleep."

"Probably all three tonight, but they'll be in that shed for at least another hour," Blair said with a grin, flopping down on the bed. "Come sit, Terian. Let's see what she's got to show us."

Immediately Katrina felt self-conscious, then decided not to. *The hell with shyness.* She began to take off her clothes.

"I didn't tell her to strip," Terian said to Blair.

"I didn't, either," Blair said slowly, her eyes glinting in the dim light. "I guess we'll have to punish her."

Katrina stopped cold. "What are you talking about?"

"Grab her, Terian."

Katrina went to bolt, but Terian yanked her off her feet into his arms. Blair and he quickly arranged her over Terian's lap, Blair pulling off her jeans.

"What the hell do you think—?"

Terian yanked down Katrina's underwear and delivered a stinging slap to her bottom. Katrina let out a shriek of outrage, then began kicking.

"Spank her more!" Blair said excitedly.

Terian paddled Katrina's ass, as she flailed and kicked.

"Ouch, that's enough kicking," Terian said. "She's not behaving, even with discipline. I think it's hopeless, Blair. We'll have to tie her up. Naked."

"Good thing that Damian's got a good stash," Blair joked, bringing a set of leather restraints out of a drawer, and handing a pair to Terian. "Lube, condoms, the works. I think we'll use these; the handcuffs might hurt. You hold her, I'll do her arms." She fastened one restraint around each of Kat's ankles and wrists, then clipped them to light chains.

OMG, this is a bondage bed!! "Hey!"

"Facedown or face up?"

"Hmm. Facedown to start."

Katrina let out a yell, then began kicking again. But Blair operated some crank under the bed that tightened the slack on the chains, leaving her spread-eagled face down on the bed in her bra and panties.

"Oops, you left her clothes on."

"No impediment," Blair said eagerly, taking off her clothes. "Take off your clothes and let's start touching her."

Katrina took a deep ragged breath of fear as she felt the others climb on the bed. But her fear quickly turned to soft sighs as Terian's and Blair's lips began kissing up and down her body, their hands stroking her cool flesh, warming it with the press of their own bodies against hers.

Terian slipped his hands under her bra, cupping her breasts and squeezing hard. "Oh God, I've wanted to do this for so long, Kat." He pulled on her nipples, the sensation wringing a moan from Kat. The moan was swallowed by Blair's tongue, gently tracing her parted lips before licking her gently. Terian shifted, thrusting his hips against Katrina's ass, his thick hard shaft sliding against her bare ass cheeks. She shivered, then gasped as she felt Blair's hand slide up her inner thigh, her fingers massaging her clitoris.

"Oh God …"

"Put the blindfold on her."

Katrina's view was blocked by the whisper of satin as Terian put a blindfold on her. Then both of her lovers retreated. Katrina waited, breathing hard in anticipation.

There was the soft sensation of something touching her ass cheek. "Are you going to behave?"

"Yes," Katrina said instantly.

"Good," Blair said. "Hold still, little fox."

Katrina had a second to wonder what she meant, then felt a lubed finger penetrate her ass. She shrieked and began squirming. A sudden smack of leather hitting her ass cut off her protest.

"Behave. Lie still!"

Katrina squirmed a bit, as the anal foxtail was gently inserted. The feeling was odd, but not uncomfortable. Then she felt someone working under her hips, the soft touch as her inner thighs were parted, and then the shock of a mouth delving into her womanhood.

"Hold it in," Terian said, his words rough with lust. The crop brushed her ass, then patted once.

Katrina had only a moment to realize that it was Blair beneath her before she began crying out, her grip on the foxtail loosening.

Thwack! went the crop into her ass. Immediately Katrina tightened up her ass, holding the plug inside.

Blair licked and sucked on her clit, her every motion distracting Katrina in a rush of pleasurable feelings. Again, the crop smacked into her ass, making her cry out and snapping her concentration.

"Please," Katrina begged.

"Please what?" Terian taunted.

"I'd rather have something else inside me," Katrina said coyly.

Katrina felt Blair slide out from beneath her, then movement. Suddenly there was the snap of rubber, and then a hot phallus grazed her lips. Katrina quickly opened her mouth, tonguing the shaft. Terian groaned, then pushed inside her mouth. Katrina sucked and nibbled at the head, her relentless motion turning her dominant male into a submissive.

"Very good," Blair said in approval. She carefully undid Katrina's restraints. "I'll be right back."

Terian pulled off the blindfold, then turned Katrina on her back, giving her a long kiss. "Are you enjoying this?" he asked huskily.

"Very much," Katrina assured him. "It's like I wandered into a fantasy."

"Good." Terian moved on top of her, spreading her legs. "I'm sorry," he said. "But if you don't let me come once quickly, I won't last. I haven't been with anyone in a long time."

He parted her vagina, then eased the head of his hard cock in her.

"God, you're big," she moaned. "Please don't stop."

"Glad you like it," Terian slowly eased, in then began to move. The feeling was pure pleasure, as he touched her insides, stroking her over and over.

"Please don't come yet," Katrina groaned. "This feels too good."

"You feel good," he moaned. "God you're so tight around my cock, like a glove."

Blair appeared with a strap on. "Are you sure you're okay with this? You said no anal."

She's really going to do what I think she's going to do! OMG! Screw it! I'm having too much fun to balk now. "I also promised to give the winner whatever they wanted. I was caught fair and square."

Terian withdrew, then moved to the side, obviously unsure.

Blair didn't move. "But I don't want it, unless you want it."

"I want it," Katrina said lustily. "I want you. Come here and fuck me for all you're worth."

Terian lay on his back, his rigid cock encased in a condom. Eagerly, Katrina sank down on it, letting out a guttural moan.

Carefully, Blair took up position behind her. Katrina felt her buttocks part, then the tip of the dildo slipping past her sphincter.

"There we go. Let me in, baby."

Katrina deliberately relaxed her muscles, until Blair was fully inside her. She let out a long shuddering breath of anticipation, suddenly afraid to move. What's next?

"Let me do the moving," Blair said. "God, I've waited for this." She cupped Katrina's breasts and began thrusting.

The motion of the dildo sliding in and out of her ass impaled her further on Terian's cock, until she felt his ball sack. Carefully she shifted, and the movement brought her clit in line with his pelvic bone, the gently but insistent rubbing stimulating her clit. Oddly there was also a feeling building in her anus, a stirring of something like the beginnings of an orgasm.

The climax didn't take long to break over her, a matter of seconds. *Holy shit!* "God!"

The orgasm was sudden, intense, and like nothing she'd ever felt before. Katrina came screaming, pleading for God, the Devil, and anyone else that Blair not stop.

Blair moaned her name, clutching her repeatedly. Gently, she kissed Katrina's neck, then eased out.

"Wow," Terian said with a smile. "Let me hear one of those for me, Kat."

Katrina leaned down into Terian, kissing him and touching his chest, as she rode him hard, both of them straining. This orgasm took longer to build, yet it crashed over them with less fervor. Terian began moving almost as soon as he'd stopped, wringing orgasm after orgasm from Katrina. She finally sighed and stopped him, after the third.

"Sorry, but I need to stop, I'm getting sore."

Terian nodded, then gently pulled out. He removed and threw away the condom, handing her a box of tissues with a kiss on the cheek. "Sweet dreams, beautiful." He lay back down with a sated sigh, and quickly dropped off to sleep.

Katrina listened to him snore for a while, then went to the bathroom to clean up. Afterwards, she stood in the doorway for a moment, watching Terian sleep.

He's a good guy, and I'm glad we got this chance. But he's also not right for me. I'm not sure I like being tied up.

Turning, Katrina headed back to her own room, to find Blair waiting for her.

"Forget which room was yours?"

"I came in here to be close to you. You just left."

"You were enjoying yourself. I thought you might want to stay with him the rest of the night."

Katrina crawled into bed, and Blair moved over. "No. This is my room. I want to sleep. And cuddle near you."

Blair didn't say anything, but she put her arm around Katrina, giving her a gentle hug. Together, the two of them dropped off to sleep.

Sometime in the night, Blair awakened, thrashing. In the process she woke up Katrina.

"What is it?"

"A stupid nightmare. I called the police, but they didn't answer. I tried everyone else I could think of, but no one answered their phone."

"Because you were hurt?"

"No, because your arm got hurt when I tackled you outside. I always have stupid dreams like that." Blair came closer spooning her. "Sorry to wake you."

"It's alright. I was awake already."

Blair turned her over. "Something wrong? Are you sore?"

Katrina smiled, stifling a chuckle. "No, I'm fine. I was just musing about life."

"What about life?"

"That the people you care about are the ones that matter. It should be obvious, but it isn't until you're older." *And that the gender of your sex partner matters a lot less than the strength of your feelings for them.*

"I think we know it to begin with," Blair said thoughtfully. "But we're afraid to show it, because we aren't sure of ourselves. In youth, we don't know who we are, much less what we stand for. We're so scared of looking stupid that we act stupid."

"I have been stupid." *Because I've been scared of being myself. And the one that behavior hurts the most is me.*

"Everyone is stupid about something."

"I'd rather not be."

"Then let me go down on you."

Katrina blinked, and looked over at her. "That's your cure for a bad nightmare?"

"Hell yes."

"Okay." Katrina fumbled for her bag. "I brought some of those things."

"I'm so glad you got some of 'those things'," Blair mocked, then spanked Katrina's ass gently. "Roll on your back."

"Be nice. I'm behaving."

"I'm about to be real nice."

Katrina stopped. "No."

"No?"

"Let me go down on you."

Blair raised her eyebrows, then laughed. "You're sure?"

Katrina nodded, a little over vigorously. "Sure. Lay back."

Blair moved back, then pulled her nightgown over her head, revealing her heavily tattooed body, dark thatch, and small breasts.

Nervous, Katrina fumbled with the thin piece of plastic.

Blair watched her for a moment, then motioned for the packet.

"So where's your tattoo?" Katrina said nervously, handing it over.

"You can see it there, on my left wrist, on the inside," Blair said, turning her hands as she unfolded the plastic. There was a small fox there, showing its teeth and snarling.

"It doesn't look happy."

"She doesn't look happy," Blair corrected. "She hasn't gotten laid in a while." She lay back, putting the plastic square over her vaginal opening. "All set."

Katrina moved closer, flushing furiously, aware she had no experience at all. *But I know how a woman's body works, I've masturbated successfully hundreds of times. I have to take cues from her, and not be afraid.* She put her head between Blair's legs, closed her eyes in concentration, then tentatively nibbled.

Blair let out a happy sigh.

Katrina nibbled more, letting her tongue lick carefully, then more forcefully, hearing Blair's increasing sighs. She used her mouth to suck gently, meeting Blair's hips as she began to thrust up in rhythm. Blair began to moan, her thrusts more insistent, and Katrina increased the force of her mouth, deliberately bearing down on Blair's clitoris. With a shout, Blair came, her hands fisting the sheets. Her thrusts weakly subsided, and she grinned.

Katrina waited, unsure of what to do.

"Oh yeah," Blair murmured throatily, taking the plastic square off and disposing of it. Then she lay back, motioning Katrina to come to her.

Katrina snuggled close, holding her friend. "You came fast."

"That's because I've only been waiting for that forever," Blair said contentedly. She kissed Katrina's cheek. "You're a quick study, girl."

"You mean lover," Kat amended.

Blair smiled, then kissed her sensuously on the lips. "Yes, lover."

"And thanks," Katrina said after a pause. "I wanted it to be good for you."

"You know," Blair murmured, pushing back a lock of Katrina's long black hair. "I always felt like you would never find me attractive even if we were both free to pursue something."

"I always found you attractive," Katrina whispered. "I just was afraid to say it."

"Why? You had to know I'd never reject you."

"Afraid of myself, afraid of what people would say, afraid to give myself the label that you've had for years," Katrina sighed. "Lesbian."

"Dyke is much worse," Blair said languidly, stretching. "But you're neither, Sweet Thing. You're bi. Or maybe just bi-curious. You are not a lesbian, though you gave it a good try." She got up from the bed, and grabbed her sleep T, sliding it back on.

"What I am is confused."

Blair grabbed one of Katrina's nighties, and handed it to her. As Katrina put it on, Blair got back on the bed and ducked her head between Katrina's legs. Instead of stiffening up, Katrina relaxed, lying back and waiting.

"I'm glad you're not nervous of me anymore." Blair kissed her way up Katrina's left thigh, then rested her head on her navel, looking up at her friend. "Want some advice? Don't worry about what you are. I'm happy. I'm glad we shared this, and yeah, I want it to happen again, if you want it. Tell me you're happy, because that's all that matters to me."

Katrina ruffled Blair's short hair, then smiled widely. "Get up here."

Blair laughed, then crawled up close, and Katrina nested into her arms. "Yes, I'm happy," Katrina whispered. She gave a contented sigh, then turned and kissed Blair slowly, letting herself enjoy fully the sensuous softness. "And yes, I'd like us to come together again. I like being chased. But I like hearing you come even more."

Blair began kissing her earlobe. "I'll chase you all night long. Just tell me when you want to come."

"A few minutes from now? I didn't want you to stop."

"Come here, my little fox. Let's begin."

THE END

A NIGHT TO REMEMBER

Jessica thought sex with Corian was wonderful, just one of the many great attributes she was looking for in a husband. But on their wedding night, Corian introduces her to what he really expects of a wife: submission in all ways, including to his half-brother, Cain.

A NIGHT TO REMEMBER

"I can't believe this!" Jessica fumed, her long legs striding rapidly across the floor as she paced the room, wineglass in one hand. "It's supposed to be my wedding night! I'm supposed to be on a beach, in a bikini, looking at a sunset! Instead I'm in a fucking crap hotel, drinking a wine that has no body!"

I do appreciate your body, new wife of mine, Corian thought to himself. *The sight of your lovely ass jiggling in those too short cutoff jeans is the best thing I've seen all night. I just wish your mouth were as pleasant.* "Sweetheart, I already said I'd make it up to you. I can't do anything about a Nor'easter that covers three states—"

"We're not even in the honeymoon suite!" Jessica raged, whirling and jutting her bottom lip out at her husband, her dark blue eyes flashing. "We're in a room with twin beds, Corian. TWIN BEDS ON MY BRIDAL NIGHT!"

If only I was in an adjoining room, with a door that locked from my side. Corian closed his eyes and rubbed his temples, wincing at the beginning headache that was already threatening to turn into a migraine. "Look, this isn't how I wanted our first night as man and wife to be, either. I told you we'd push the beds together, it's not like we have to have sex on the bed anyway."

35

"I have waited years for my perfect bridal night, and I'm going to have it!" Jessica screeched.

Corian opened his mouth to retort, when there was a knock at the door. Curious—and eager for a distraction for Jessica—Corian, got up and answered it. "Cain!"

The tall, broad shouldered man smiled a grin of perfect white teeth, his honey-colored eyes mirthful. "I'm glad you're happy to see me. I was worried I might be interrupting."

"Not likely," Corian muttered under his breath, pointedly glancing over at his wife. "She's been bitching non-stop ever since our flight out to Maui was cancelled. With the surprise blizzard, everyone was scrambling for rooms."

"That is one of the reasons I'm here," Cain said with a knowing smile. "I already had a reservation at this hotel, because I planned to stay the night after your reception. I booked the honeymoon suite, as it's got an attached Jacuzzi in a separate room."

"And what, you're offering your room?" Corian replied with a chuckle. "I know you, brother, you're not altruistic. What's the angle?"

"Let's say I've noticed your wife's got a pretty sharp tongue," Cain said with anticipatory delight. "I think you should both start your marriage off right: a Jacuzzi, champagne, little chocolates, and a night to remember."

"I think I know what you have in mind," Corian said slowly. "I'm game, but I need to make sure that Jessica is cool with it."

"Why don't I ask her?" Cain strolled into the room, towards Jessica. "Oh Jess?"

"Cain!" she said excitedly, coming over to him and giving him a big hug. "I swear you and Corian were fraternal twins separated at birth. You're spitting images of one another, except you have dark hair and light brown eyes, and Corian's got the blond hair and dark eyes."

"Half-brothers," Corian corrected. "I told you, my father was married twice."

Jessica grinned. "I know. I just like to tease." She hugged Cain. "Are you staying here tonight?"

"That's why I'm here, to extend an invitation to come up to my room and join me," Cain purred. He cupped her jaw, then let his hand fall, tracing a line down between her breasts. "That is, if you're in the mood to play."

Jessica's eyes got wide, as she looked from Cain to Corian.

"You said you wanted a perfect night," Corian offered. "Cain's got the honeymoon suite, he's got champagne, and we can order in some food." He smiled sexily. "And my brother's got a few other talents too, which you might find enticing."

Jessica blinked, again looking from Corian back to Cain. "Are you both serious?" she said finally. "This isn't some kind of weird loyalty test, is it?"

"No," Cain assured her. "I'm not looking to break up what you just made official today, my dear. Remember how I told you I was in business? I am, but I have a side hobby: bondage games. It's a very lucrative field ... not that I usually charge."

Jessica's mouth dropped open.

"He's just being modest; Cain is an expert," Corian explained. "I didn't want to admit it to you, Jess, but I have consulted with him before."

"You told him about our sex life?" Jessica blurted out, her tone fast becoming accusatory.

"No, he came to me to ask for different options to titillate you with," Cain corrected. "I don't charge for my services, Jessica. I only take on encounters that interest me. You, my dear," he said, caressing one breast with the back of his hand, "you and my brother together interest me."

"When were you going to tell me about this?" Jessica said, her eyes narrowing as she rounded on Corian.

"I'm telling you now," Corian stated bluntly, his own eyes narrowing. "I think this will be good for us. Grab your things, we are leaving with Cain."

"I'm not going."

"Yes, you will." Cain bent down, hoisting a surprised Jessica over his shoulder.

"Put me down!"

"I see you can't wait until we get to my room," Cain said jovially. Holding her legs with one hand, he reached up with the other and smacked her on the ass.

"What in the hell do you think you're doing?" she cried.

"Corian, if you'd be so kind to use my handkerchief?"

"I'm not going anywhere! What are you—?" Jessica's strident words were cut off as her husband fastened a gag around her mouth. She reached to remove it, but Corian had already grabbed a set of handcuffs from Cain, and he stopped her, fastening her wrists into the metal rings.

"Mppphh!"

"There's a set of leg leathers in my jacket pocket," Cain said, using both of his hands to grip the now wriggling Jessica. "If you'd be so kind."

"My pleasure," Corian said, buckling them on.

"Thank you, I've been bruised enough," Cain laughed. He headed off down the hall. "We'll wait for you, top floor, room 405."

Corian breathed a satisfied sigh, watching his brother walk away with his bride over his shoulder. Then he hurried inside to gather their luggage.

"How's that champagne?" Cain asked.

"Delicious," Corian answered happily, munching a chocolate covered strawberry. "But the peaceful ambiance is best of all."

"Mmmph!" Jessica said from the bed where she lay still trussed, glaring daggers at them.

"Your lady is right, we have made her wait long enough," Cain said eagerly, setting aside his wineglass. "Corian, if you would please undress, we will begin." He stood, then began to disrobe. Corian followed suit, stripping off all his clothes.

Jessica promptly went silent, her eyes staring at their well-built, muscular bodies.

"Yes, we are very similar in almost all ways," Cain said, sitting on the bed and taking off her leg restraints. His golden eyes almost glowed in the dim lighting. "The key differences are our eyes, hair … and temperaments."

Corian dimmed the lights, then came over to the bed, sitting on the other side of Jessica.

"You are a lovely woman, Jessica," Cain continued, touching her shoulder gently. "But you must learn to control your tongue. No man enjoys a harpy as his life partner, much less in his bed. Corian wants very much to please you, to make your life together wonderful. You need to please him the same way."

"Mppmmph!! Mprrf!"

"Your tirade earlier is unacceptable behavior," Cain went on, ignoring her. "Because you don't know how to behave, it's Corian's duty as a husband to help you, Jessica. He needs to make you behave."

"Fuurk! Nrrph! Nrrph!"

"Corian, take her across your lap. Pull down her shorts, and administer a good five hard spanks, please."

Jessica writhed and shook, but Corian positioned her, stripping off her shorts to reveal a blue bridal thong with the embroidered slogan, "I Do!" "I guess you consent, Sweetheart." He spanked her five times in succession, her ass cheeks vibrating with the impact of his hand.

"Very good. Jessica, are you ready to submit?"

"Yuubrredtd! Nrrph!"

"I'll take that as a negative response. Another five spanks, Corian, please. Harder this time."

Corian slammed his hand down hard onto Jessica's ass, the force of the blow making her body jerk. Corian spanked her once more, and she began sniffling.

"Halt, please. Jessica, are you ready to behave?"

Jessica's back quivered, then she nodded her head once.

"Corian, remove the gag please."

Corian untied the handkerchief, then removed it.

"I can't believe you spanked me," Jessica said indignantly. "On my wedding night, no less!"

"You needed a little discipline," Corian said gently. "You're always yelling at me about this or that. Most of the time it's something that has nothing to do with me."

"I'm venting!" Jessica retorted, sulking. "I'm allowed to vent to my husband."

"But not at him," Cain corrected. "Marriage is about creating a safe haven for yourself and your spouse, where you are both cherished. A calm in the storm of life, if you prefer something more poetic."

"I do want that for Corian and me," Jessica said in a small voice.

"Good," Cain said approvingly. "Now attend to what I say. You need to learn restraint and control, Jessica. These are two of the tenements of bondage play for a submissive. Corian is a dominant, as I am. He hasn't shown you that side of himself much, for his own reasons. But that ends tonight. You need to understand you will be spanked from now on, when you need a reminder of how to behave. Corian is good-natured; I know he will not abuse this privilege and administer punishment only when absolutely necessary."

"Do I get to spank him?" Jessica challenged, some of her fire returning.

"What bedroom rules you decide on are entirely up to you," Cain murmured gently. "I'm just here to get you on the right path to happiness. You have both pledged your love to one another for the rest of your lives. Relationships change, and people change. What matters is that you work together to satisfy both of your needs as they evolve."

As much as Jessica hadn't wanted to be carried gagged to Cain's room, what he said was intriguing. She reached for a strawberry, and munched it, positive that they'd try to spank her again. When they just watched her eat the decadent fruit, she reached for another, thinking about what Cain had stated.

"Usually, I like to meet with a couple before the actual encounter, so I can find out what they truly desire," Cain purred, running just the tips of his fingers down one of Jessica's smooth legs. "Secret fantasies held silent for years often are hard to disclose. I need time to finesse the lovers and coax their forbidden dreams from reluctant lips. But we've no time for that tonight. I need you to be honest with me, Jessica, knowing that whatever you say, I'll not judge. My goal in being here is to give you both a night to remember, and to hopefully inspire future nights. But enough of being long winded." He paused, then smiled wickedly. "Tell me, brother, what are your fantasies?"

"I'm pretty much open to anything," Corian stammered, flushing scarlet. "You know that. But I was waiting for marriage to explore bondage and toys. Jessica and I have had sex before, of course, but … um … not anything too exotic."

"Stop stammering like a schoolgirl caught with her panties down," Cain said curtly. "I know your tastes. Don't be afraid to indulge them. This woman loves you, and wants to please you, just as you love and want to please her. But you have to tell her what you want, just as she needs to tell you what she wants. Communication is key here…and trust."

"I like oral sex, but I haven't really enjoyed the missionary position," Jessica said blatantly, lying on her stomach as she reached for another strawberry. "Doggie style is fun, but it also doesn't make me come."

"What makes you come easiest? What feels the best? Oral?" Cain asked.

"If I'm very stimulated, everything Corian does feels good," Jessica replied. "But I come easiest by oral sex, or if I'm on top."

"And what stimulates you?" Cain purred, pulling out a riding crop from beneath the bed pillow. He ran it up one of Jessica's legs, and rested in on her butt cheek.

"A lover who takes charge," Jessica admitted, blushing furiously. "I ... I sometimes push Corian hard, when I know we're going to have sex later on. With what I say, I mean. He's rougher with me that way when we have sex, more forceful."

"You always said you liked me being gentle?" Corian interrupted, upset.

"I know, but —"

"No, Corian," Cain said, turning and whacking his brother lightly on the chest with the riding crop. "This night is not for any judgments of any kind. Jessica is allowed to ask for what she desires. Jessica, please go on. You were saying a man acting as a dominant alpha stimulates you."

"Yes," Jessica said, flushing deeper. "I like it when Corian tries something new. Even if I don't especially love the act, I love that he's not afraid to show me his lust in a new way."

"Because seeing him lustful and excited is a great aphrodisiac, is it not? You feed on his lust, and it ignites your own."

Jessica nodded.

"Tell the truth ... do you like what happened so far tonight?"

Jessica grinned widely, looking at the sheets. "Yes. I can't believe you carried me up here. I've read about things like that ... but I never thought it could happen to me."

"A great deal more is going to happen to you tonight, my dear," Cain said seductively. "Now I must ask for your permission, both of you, to touch you."

"Of course," Corian answered.

"Yes," Jessica said. "But you've already touched me, Cain."

"The ways I'm going to touch you aren't ways you've been touched

41

before," Cain purred, running his crop up her leg. But this time, instead of resting the tip on her ass, he tilted his wrist, the tip sliding up between her thighs at an angle. With a deft movement, he smacked her pussy.

"Oh!"

Cain pulled the whip back at lightning speed, as Jessica jerked, her legs kicking. Corian chuckled, then moved around Cain, pulling Jessica onto his lap.

"Now Corian ... what are your fantasies?"

"I would like to double team my lovely new wife with you," Corian replied. "I've always had the fantasy, but never trusted any of my male friends enough to try it. But I trust you, brother."

"Expected," Cain said with a devilish smile. "Your tastes run similar to my own. But what else?"

"I'd like to shower with you both, maybe play in the water a little. And ... some more discipline. Jessica says she really wants me to take charge. I want to." Corian ran his hands down Jessica's back. "I really want to. I've been more gentle than I guess she likes because I'm afraid of hurting her."

"Understood," Cain said. He lifted Jessica's chin with the tip of the crop. "From now on, if you say 'red' that means you want him to stop, Jessica. Anything else you say; stop, no, please don't, etc., will be disregarded. Do you both understand?"

"Yes."

"Yes."

"Very good." Cain nodded, then stood up, pacing back and forth, looking at the couple, as if deciding something. Jessica shivered slightly, watching him walk, imagining all manner of things he might be thinking.

"Jessica, please take off your clothes. Then lay back on the sheets and raise your arms above your head."

Jessica took a long shuddering breath, slipped off her clothes, then scooted backward, lying down, her head on the pillows. She put her hands above the pillows, nervously gripping the headboard.

"Corian, go into my pleasure bag there on the chair, and get my silken ties. Use them."

Corian rose and got the cream-colored silk, wrapped them twice around his wife's wrists, then secured them to the headboard.

"Now her legs."

Jessica struggled a bit as Corian attempted to tie up her legs. "Behave," he said sternly.

She giggled but submitted and lay still as he secured her spread legs.

"Very nice," Cain purred. "Now Corian, get the blindfold."

Jessica took another shuddering breath as Cain took the blindfold from Corian, and carefully slipped it over her eyes.

Cain used the crop to lightly pat Jessica's nipples, so that they stood at proud attention. Corian leaned in, licking the left nub, as Jessica let out a groan of pleasure. Cain leaned in from the right and licked the other taut nipple, then both men began to suckle, their hands roaming up and down Jessica's soft, flushed skin. Jessica's mouth went slack, her breaths coming faster, wordless cries at first barely audible, then gaining in volume.

"What a lovely breast," Cain murmured softly, cupping the warm flesh. He pinched the nipple lightly, then twisted.

"Oh!"

"Yes, they are perfect," Corian murmured, his ministrations with Jessica's left breast mimicking his brother.

"Ah!"

Cain rubbed his hand lightly over and over Jessica's breast, the nipple tightening to the point it was almost painful, tugging at it with his lips, then his fingers, as his brother mirrored his movements. Jessica groaned and moaned, writhing.

"There. She's ready."

Ready for what? Jessica thought, then there was a clink of metal, and a sudden pressure constricted her left nipple. "Ow!" The right nipple followed. "Ow! Hey!"

"Shh," Cain purred in her ear. "We're just beginning."

Jessica took a breath to protest, but it turned into a cry of pleasure when she felt a warm tongue gently tongue her clit, then reach up inside her, probing.

"That feels good, doesn't it?" Cain purred in her ear. "Corian had lessons from the best, my beauty."

"Oh! Ah! Yes …"

Cain cupped her breasts again and squeezed gently. "You are absolutely beautiful, Jess. Give voice to your passion. Don't hold back."

Jessica began to moan, as Corian intensified his efforts, her orgasm approaching. But as she neared, he stopped, and withdrew.

"What ... OW!"

The shock of the soft clamp closing on her engorged clitoris was enough to prompt a yell.

"Breathe!" Cain commanded, smacking one clamped nipple lightly with the crop. Jessica let out her breath in a whoosh.

"You are gorgeous," Corian said gutturally, as he moved up Jessica's body, kissing and caressing. "Please, baby, would you let me slide between your lips."

"Just a tease, Jessica," Cain cautioned. "Corian can't be spending himself so early on."

"Yes," Jessica said, licking her lips provocatively.

Corian carefully straddled her on his knees, then brought his throbbing penis to her lips. Jessica stuck out her tongue and licked as if tasting an ice cream cone, then leaned her head forward, sliding her mouth over the head of his prick.

"Ahhh!" Corian made as if to thrust deeply into Jessica, but Cain flogged him hard across his ass with the crop, breaking the control of his lust, and changing his groan to a yelp.

"No. It's her turn to tease. You will hold still and take it like a man. Like an alpha."

Corian gritted his teeth, then balanced on his knees. Jessica resumed tonguing the head of his penis, alternately sucking and licking, often sliding her mouth down his cock as if to take it all in, only to stop and withdraw.

"I can't hold it," Corian panted. "I'm going to come."

Thwack! went the crop. "Enough, Jessica," Cain dictated. "Corian, unbind her. Then lay down, and help her to get astride you, still blindfolded."

Carefully, the couple moved into position, Corian beneath, and Jessica on top of him, her long blonde hair over her naked shoulders, her clamped nipples red and engorged with blood.

"Now tell her to move, brother," Cain purred. "Give her a little tug on the chain."

"You heard him, my love," Corian murmured. "Move." He tugged gently on the chain, making Jessica cry out. Careful of her swollen clit still held captive by the clamp, she slid back and forth across his engorged dick, lubricating the already slick flesh with her juices. Corian moaned, then shifted beneath her, grasping her hips and sliding inside her wet womanhood with a possessive cry.

"Gently now," Cain said harshly, tapping Corian on his chest with the crop. "Fill her easily, as deep as you can. Slow and sure."

"Oh my God, you feel so good, baby," Corian moaned, his face contorted with the effort of restraint. "You're so beautiful."

"Say what you want," Cain purred in Jessica's ear. "Tell him what you need."

"I want to come," she gasped out. "Please."

"Stop," Cain commanded.

Deftly he removed the clitoris clamp, as the couple was motionless.

"Resume, Jessica." Cain reached out with his hand and spanked her gently on the ass.

"Uh!" Jessica moaned, as she began rocking.

"Corian feels good, doesn't he?" Cain murmured, as he took up position behind her, spreading lube on his condom-encased cock.

"Yes."

"Stop," Cain instructed, as he reached up to cup Jessica's breasts. She let out a cry when he touched the nipples. Carefully, he disengaged the clamps, making her scream as each ultra-sensitive nub was released.

Jessica had time to draw one shuddering breath, then felt Cain's prick nudging at her sphincter. She relaxed, then felt him push his way inside. She let out a small sound when the feeling went on and on.

"You're so big," she breathed.

"I am," he answered silkily in her ear. "But my brother has taught you well, my beauty, you accept me fully. Now let me join the fun." Carefully, Cain began to thrust, the motion of his body pushing Corian deeper inside Jess, until she could feel their pricks were inside her to the root. She groaned, then gave herself up to the sensations flooding her as both men thrust, desperate for release.

Corian reached orgasm first, his movements frantic, as Jessica felt the first stirrings.

Too soon it was over, Corian spasming as he shot his load, his cry of climax satisfying.

"Now for us," Cain purred. He plied Jess's super sensitive clit with one hand, his thick cock sliding in and out of her ass. She came screaming, his guttural cries seconds behind her. As he finished, he withdrew, then went into the bathroom. "Come in, when you are ready," he called as he left.

"Wow," Jessica said, when she could draw breath. "I don't know what to say but wow."

"I hope you liked that as much as I did," Corian said with a grin.

"I didn't know things could happen like that to real people," Jessica said with a happy sigh, as she slipped off the blindfold. "Yes, I liked it very much. But what could we possible do that's more than what we just did?"

"I'm not sure, but let's find out," Corian said, offering her his hand. Jessica took it, and the both of them went into the bathroom.

Cain was there, already scrubbed fresh, checking the temperature of the water. "Please, see to yourselves," he said, as he stepped into the tub. "Then come in."

Jessica and Corian cleaned up, then stepped into the tub, luxuriating in the hot water. All three splashed a bit, and enjoyed the jets massaging their muscles.

"So, are there penis clamps?" Jessica said pointedly, examining her breasts. "I think I'm going to be bruised."

"There are several comparable toys," Cain answered, producing a ring. "True penis clamps are not for beginners; they are something to lead up to with multiple sessions and careful practice, something we can explore at a later date if you both have, let's say, a yearning. Next, we'll use a cockring. Corian, if you'll slip out of the water and sit on the edge of the tub? Jess, I may need your sweet mouth, as the hot water will have taken a toll on my brother."

Jessica moved through the water to Corian, then slipped between his parted legs. She began stroking his flaccid penis with her hands, then began tonguing the tip as it started to fill with blood. Soon, the prick was fully engorged, purple and hard.

Cain handed her the ring. "Put this on him and slide it down to the very base."

"Ow!" Corian said, as Jessica slipped it on. "Damn."

"Fair's fair," Jessica quipped. "Where's that blindfold?"

"I have another right here," Cain said, handing it to her. "But it's for you, my dear. Remember, you are the submissive. Corian is the dominant. Now submit."

Jessica shot him a smirk. "Are you going to make me?"

"No," Cain purred. "Corian is. Corian?"

Corian pushed off the edge into the Jacuzzi, then grabbed ahold of Jessica. He brought her to the edge of the tub and put the blindfold on, just as Cain reappeared from the other room with the silken ties.

"Hold her arms out in front of her."

Cain looped the strands around her wrists, then tied them fast to the spout. He turned on the Jacuzzi, then carefully applied a clamp to his shaft, then slipped on another condom. "I'll begin, brother. I'll need you to step in to finish."

"Ready and able." Corian sat on the edge of the tub again, just to the side of where Jessica was tied, so he could view her and Cain.

"Spread your legs," Cain purred. "I want to pleasure us both, my beauty."

Jessica shivered, but did as asked, expecting the hard thrust of a penis. Instead she felt Cain grasping her hips, then moving her closer to the jets, easing up one of her legs so that her vagina was near the underwater jet. Then she felt Cain's hand reaching down, circling her nub before slipping inside her vagina. She jerked, but he held her fast. "Just as ready as I knew you would be," he whispered in her ear.

He parted her swollen lips with his fingers, then she felt the head of his cock nudging against her, seeking entrance. As he began to push inside, Jessica let out a cry from the pressure of his body.

"Yes, a clamp makes a man thicker," Cain whispered, as he pushed in persistently. "And you're going to stretch for me, my beauty."

Jessica let out a gasp, then a cry as she felt Cain run into something inside her. "Just your cervix," he said, grasping her hips. "No barrier to me." He pushed in further, making Jessica yelp from the odd sensation.

"There," he said approvingly. He began to move his cock in and out the slightest bit, nudging and nudging inside her, as she felt his fingers part her folds, exposing her clit to the thunder of the jet. The **water** teased her like an insistent tongue, caressing her clit and bringing her the first stirrings of an orgasm. They came together, Cain pushing deep inside her, holding her hips hard against his as he strained.

He withdrew, motioning to Corian to take his place. Corian slipped inside, and began moving, also thrusting deep, though he didn't cause any pain. Again, Jessica came, bringing Corian with her. As he ebbed, Cain was there again to take up position, slipping into Jessica, stretching her again to her limits.

This is amazing! I don't want it to stop!

Corian took over again from Cain when he came, then one last time, Cain replaced his brother, stretching her channel. As they both came, Jessica went limp, her eyes fluttering. Cain caught her, then helped her out of the tub into Corian's waiting arms.

"I didn't want to stop," she said breathlessly. "But I feel dizzy."

"A little overindulging," Cain said tiredly, with a smile. "Get into bed. Corian will bring your nightgown. I will be right in."

Jessica made it into bed with Corian, fighting to stay awake as he helped slip the nightgown over her head. Nestled together, the sated couple fell asleep.

Cain came in a few moments later. As his eyes found the sleeping pair, he let out a happy sigh, smiling as he flicked off the bedside light, and slipped into bed beside them.

THE END

BEST OF FIVE

Looking for real-life inspiration for her tales of erotica, Mistress Ava challenges her courtesan co-worker, Crixus, to a duel of seduction.

BEST OF FIVE

Ava lay on her back, watching the shadows move on the ceiling, her white breasts bared above the pushed down cups of the bustier. Lazily, she stretched out one stocking leg over the other, moving her hips slightly as she tried to relax.

"That was heaven," Mike said, removing the condom and placing it into the trashcan. He flopped back on the bed, his muscled chest still heaving. "You were heaven, Ava."

"Thanks," Ava replied, looking over with an easy smile.

"I think I ripped your outfit," Mike said apologetically. "I'll buy you a new one."

"It's just unhooked, not ripped, I think," Ava said, shrugging.

"No, I ripped it."

"It wouldn't be the first time you destroyed my lingerie in your passion," Ava teased. "I'm sure it won't be the last."

"Probably not," Mike admitted, kissing her hand, then her cheek. "Just let me know if you want a replacement." He paused. "I'm sorry, but I've got to go. If I don't finish that presentation, my boss will kill me."

"No problem," Ava said, nodding. "Have a good night and call me next week."

"You're the perfect woman," Mike said lovingly, kissing her hand again, then her lips. "I'll see you again soon, Ava."

She smiled until he'd left, then laid back down in the bed, making a face. She was every man's dream, and most of her nights were full. But she had never felt lonelier or more unfulfilled. *Go figure.*

A va eased into her bath, letting the hot water run out of the tap through her fingers, the delicious warmth soothing her aches of the workday. With a decadent sigh, she lay back in the water, considering her earlier discussion with a male friend. *Why is writing about seduction and sex so much harder than performing it?*

Ava chuckled to herself with a smile that was almost a grimace. *Because you can't use your body, Ava, only your words.*

A woman's POV was easy; Ava had first-hand experience. But some of her male POV's didn't sound as real, or so her first rejection letters had said. Intrigued, she'd asked a close friend for his perspective. His response had been a revelation, not because it contained a wealth of hidden knowledge, but because it was the last thing she expected to hear. "They want to buy a clue," he'd said simply, taking a bite of pizza. "They want to know what turns a woman on."

Ava had laughed, then given him a look of disbelief. "What? My readers are likely adult men, some probably veterans of more action than a Jason Stratham movie," she joked. "Why wouldn't they already have a very good idea of what to do?"

"Because men are told from day one to be gentle and treat women delicately, to be the flowers and poetry guy. Then we get older and find out what women really want is the exact opposite."

Ava laughed, trying and barely succeeding in not choking on her mouthful of pizza. "True, women as a rule don't ask for gentler, they always ask for rougher. But an adult would already know that. That's something you discover when you're a young adult."

"Not all men discover it. Women talk to other women and give details. Men just say the deed was done, no details."

"Nothing else? You don't give any details?"

"No, not necessary."

"Details are necessary," Ava amended, still laughing. "Women love to talk about details. Why don't men? How could you not want to imagine the entire scene?"

"Because it's the same process for everyone, so we don't need details."

But sex is not the same, really. The orgasm, sure, but the experience can be utterly changed with different partners. I can't understand not wanting details. "So why read erotica written by a woman if you don't need details? What's sexy about a woman's fantasies?"

"Because they want to know what a woman finds sexy. What women want."

"But this is just a story, it's not based on the particular author's desires. The level of description and kinds of sex—bondage, domination, sex toys, ménage, etc.—is dictated by the publisher who puts out a call for specific stories."

"When you think about why you wanted to write your first story," he said deliberately. "What scenario did you imagine? Something that got you hot, or something you'd fantasized about, right?"

Ava felt herself blushing. "All people are different, though. What one finds sexy could repulse another person."

He shrugged.

"Half the fun of sex is discovering what the person you're with really likes, and their reaction to what you do."

"I agree," he said with a smile.

"Doesn't everyone get experience with trial and error? I did. Forget reading a book, it's much more fun to figure out firsthand."

"That's because it's real," he said. "Even if it's not real, you're approaching it as real. And yes, honest is best. People know when they read honesty, and when it's fake."

"Everyone's been there, heard their partner say in confusion, 'why are you doing that?'" Ava commented. "And apologized lightly, trying to make it seem if your blunder was intelligently made."

He laughed, "Yeah, we've all been there."

"Thanks for this," she said, scribbling some notes.

"Just remember that a man will buy anything a woman writes as long as it has sex in detail," he said, closing the box. "You're a window into the female mind, showing them that it doesn't have to be kid gloves, either domination or romance. It can be something in between."

"Thanks," she said again with a smile. "I'll have to dedicate a story to you."

"Just name a well-endowed hero after me, and we'll call it square," he said with a laugh.

What I need is some time with a man who'll meet me word for word, give me some feedback on what men want. I need a window into the male mind. But how do I get that?

Feeling guilty, Ava sidled up to the desk, then looked at her watch again. Her appointment had been for an hour ago. Why wasn't she being led to a room?

"We're ready for you," a man in a tuxedo said politely. "This way, Mrs. Carrington."

Sin said this place was reputable, and worth the high price tag ... and that I'd find what I was looking for. I hope she's right.

Ava followed Tux Man into what looked like a hotel room, except the bed was clearly a bondage bed, and so was the nearby chair. *Holy shit, even the table was equipped with some restraints!*

"Crixus will be in shortly. There is a robe that you may change into in the attached bathroom, but I recommend discussing your desires up front before putting on any elaborate costumes. We want to give you your best fantasy." Tux Man left, shutting the door behind him.

Ava sat on the bed to wait.

A man entered the room, bare-chested to the waist, his thick short dark hair glossy. His chest was shaven except for a small patch over his breast area, the dark skin gleaming with some type of oil. *Just as if he'd walked off the cover of a cheap romance novel.* The effect was ruined though, because his attention wasn't on Ava, but on a handful of papers he was perusing.

"More orders," he said winking at her. "I'm a popular guy."

Is that supposed to impress me? All it does is make me wonder if he has any diseases. This was a bad idea. "You're Crixus? So how does this work?"

"Anything you want," he said, posing and putting his hands above his head, flexing his biceps a bit to make them bulge.

Ava resisted the urge to laugh. "Anything?"

"You can unleash any fantasy you want," Crixus said. "I'm yours for the night."

"And what if I want to use one of those dildos on the wall on you, Crixus?"

To his credit, the man didn't blink an eye, just offered an easy smile. "Sink in deep inside my flesh, my mistress. Your pleasure is my only goal tonight."

Ava stood and offered her hand. "Thank you, but that's not what I need, Crixus. I appreciate your time."

Crixus gaped at Ava as she walked past him out the door. She began down the hallway only to catch a glimpse of a man being led with a leather studded collar and leash on his knees by a woman dressed as a topless cheerleader. The sight was so surprising that she stopped for a moment to watch them go into an adjoining room. Chuckling, she turned to leave, and ran straight into Crixus, who grabbed hold of her.

"You're mine for tonight," he said huskily. "You're not getting away so easily." He moved backward into the room she'd vacated and sat her down on the bed.

"But am I getting off, is the question," she quipped, as he sat down beside her.

Crixus blinked at her, then roared with laughter, lying back on the bed. "You're something." He favored her with a dazzling smile. "It's nice for a change for me not to know what's going to happen."

I know the feeling! Ava reciprocated the laughter, then favored him with one of her sexy glances she reserved for her customers. "Tell me what I have to do for you to let me go, kind sir."

"Why don't you take a shower, then come out and sit with me?" Crixus offered. "Then we can talk about what you'd like."

"No," Ava said. "What I want is simple: a game, if you want to call it that. I want you to use not just your body, but your words to seduce me. I'll use my words and my body to seduce you. Best out of three wins."

"Agreed," Crixus said with a glint in his eye. "Go on and get wet, Princess. We'll play when you emerge."

Ava nodded and left for the bathroom. Standing in the spray, she let the hot water caress her bare skin for many minutes, luxuriating in the feel of the water running over her. Once clean, she emerged, leisurely rubbing some of the lotions offered on an elaborate tray onto her skin. After twisting her hair up into a bun, she left for the room. But when she got there, Crixus wasn't there.

"What the fuck?" she swore under her breath. She shook her head, then shrugged her shoulders. *Well, he did say he was a popular guy. I'll give him ten minutes.*

Ava only lasted seven before she fell into a deep sleep.

A va was awakened by the sensuous brush of lips on hers. She opened her eyes to find Crixus above her, a thrill coursing through her at the sheer size of his naked upper torso leaning over her.

"Good dreams?" he asked meaningfully.

"Was I moaning?" she teased.

"A tad," he answered, then to her shock, he slipped his hands between her thighs. She shivered as his fingers rubbed a circle beneath her damp thatch, then slid deeper, penetrating her. "They must have been good dreams. You're more than ready now, Princess."

Ava disentangled herself from him, then stood near the bed. She fluffed her hair, while carefully easing down the top of her robe to bare her shoulders. She smiled, sliding a finger down her chest, moving apart the robe to bare most of her breasts. "Are you going to talk about how you're going to satisfy me, or actually satisfy me?" she said sexily, as she dropped her bathrobe to stand naked before him. In a deliberate motion, she unclasped her twist of hair, the long damp locks spilling down over her naked shoulders.

Crixus took hold of her waist and pulled her close, his lips seeking her breast, hungrily fastening his lips onto her nipple. She gave a sharp intake of breath, her nub tightening under the deft ministrations of his tongue. Crixus sat down, pulling her astride him. He took her hand in his, then put it on his swollen cock, the throbbing organ almost purple inside its condom. "See how hot I am for you?" he whispered. "I've been playing with myself the entire time you've been in there, imagining your hands washing every rack and crevice of your curves." He slid his hands up, cupping her breasts. "Imagining you touching yourself." His left hand slid down, again tightening on her thatch, grasping it possessively. "I imagined doing this. Did you imagine my hands on you?"

"Yes," she groaned. "In my dream."

He cupped harder, sliding two fingers inside to tease her. Then he began to slide them in and out of her. "Say it louder, Princess."

"Yes, I imagined you touching me," she breathed out with a shiver, letting her head fall back to face him, staring into his eyes with a look of pure lust. "I imagined your cock inside me, how you'd feel, the noises you'd make as you finally buried yourself all the way." She turned, carefully pulling away from his hand as her right hand reached down to wrap around his hard cock. "I thought about how hard I wanted to get you." She began to stroke him, Crixus shuddering, his eyes closed as she trailed kisses down his throat, her hand working him in steady strokes.

"You're almost hard enough," she said breathily. Carefully she used her other hand to cup his balls, squeezing gently.

Crixus grabbed her hand, stopping her movement, even as he pressed her down to the bed with his other hand. "Now, now," he chastised, moving her hands above her head to capture both under his large palm. "You're talking too much. I want to hear some moaning." He dipped his head again to her breast, tearing a ragged gasp from her throat. She writhed on the bed as he teased first one breast then the other. He looked up at her, a lock of his dark hair falling forward in an inviting curve toward his arrogant smile. "If you don't behave, I'm going to have to chain you up."

"No, you said you'd satisfy me," she demanded, her eyes sparkling with challenge. "I want you inside me now."

Crixus laughed, then gave a grudging nod. "So I did." He leaned in close, the tip of his penis brushing her thigh. She tensed in eagerness that became shock as she again felt his fingers stroking her clit.

"That's not inside me," she murmured.

"No, but this is," He growled.

She arched her back, the shock of his fingers delving deep into her wet channel as she let out a moan. "Don't worry, Princess." He kissed her throat, his hand squeezing gently as he rubbed her clit. "I'll fill you. But all in good time."

God, she wanted him inside her more with each passing moment. But she wasn't losing this bet, either. Try another tactic. "Don't you want to feel my body tight around you," she purred sexily. "I used my fingers on myself in the shower, but it wasn't enough, it wasn't your hardness, it was just my hands. I want you inside me, not some toy. Your hard cock pumping inside me, throbbing with your need to come. Make me come, Crixus."

He'd gone quiet, but he'd moved his body closer to her. She parted her legs, tilting up her pelvis to brush the tip of his cock. "Please," she whispered. "I'm begging you."

Crixus moved her suddenly beneath him, his hand grasping his penis to guide it in. She pushed up her hips, receiving the full length of his cock as he slid inside with a loud grunt. He began pistoning immediately, as she grasped his ass tightly, wanting him to lose himself and let go completely. Crixus came with another low grunt then pushed back a lock of his hair, a look of grudging respect on his face. "Okay, that one's yours. But we're doing the best of five instead now, Princess. Hang on for the ride."

She realized at that moment he was still hard within her.

"Tell me you want me deep within you."

"You're already in me," she said lightly. "And you've already filled me with your cum."

"Yes, you have all of me," he murmured, clutching her tight to him. "My cock is all for you, Princess, and I'm already ready again to spill my seed inside you. I can't wait to come in you again. Tell me you want me to come in you."

Odd as his words were, they were a complete turn on, her fingers already reaching out to pull his body deeper into hers. She felt the feeling building quickly, the orgasm easy, effortless as it engulfed her.

She gave a great shuddering breath, hiding her head in his chest, not wanting him to see her tears.

"Why are you crying, Princess?"

"Because I didn't ever think I'd feel like myself again," she said truthfully. "I haven't let myself go during sex in a long time. It's been so long that I was afraid to. I needed to feel like I was really wanted for me."

Crixus nodded, a shadow passing over his face. "You don't have to say what I can surmise. You're a professional. Your clients must find you very sexy."

Ava wiped at her eyes, regaining control as her breathing slowed. "But that's all for them; it's not for me. Thank you."

Crixus kissed her gently on the forehead. "Thank you. What you describe feeling ... I've been going through it, too. So we helped each other."

"So best of five, is it?" Ava said teasingly, as he moved off her and threw away the condom. "I'd say we were one for one, tied. Do you feel like adding some bondage into the mix?"

Crixus grinned, finishing his cleanup. "I thought you'd never ask. What did you have in mind?"

"What do you have?"

Crixus offered her his hand, and she took it. He led her to a chest at the foot of the bed. He opened the chest, exposing a foldout tier of nipple clamps of various models, some chained and some with weights. There were the expected crops, ticklers, blindfolds, gags, whips, but also a few things she'd never seen before. "That's not a clamp for a penis, is it?"

"A cockring and nipple clamps, for a man to wear," Crixus explained. "The other is a ball gag and nipple clamps, for use by either sex. All of these are already included in the price you paid tonight, and what we use will go home with you as a souvenir of the evening, unless you decline." He paused. "The idea is that a person couldn't possibly use everything in here on one visit."

Ava laughed. "I would think not." She pointed to a small contraption which had what looked like a metal cage attached to it. "What's that?"

"A chastity belt," Crixus said, making a face. "This one has an anal plug attached. I can't recommend that."

Ava roared with laughter, clutching the bed for support. "I suppose not. I wouldn't want stimulation at the same time I was unable to do anything about it."

"But isn't that the basis of bondage?" Crixus asked, his eyes again glinting. "To cause your partner to wait to satisfy themselves until they have permission?"

"You're right," Ava conceded, grabbing a paddle that had "SLUT" spelled out in pink on the black handle. She gave him a light slap on his bare ass.

"No, no, none of that," Crixus responded, taking it from her. He laid it on the bed, then led her over to the chair contraption, unfolding it and snapping it into place. The final product resembled a too-short leather padded massage table, with a smaller padded leather rest on either side. "This is a variation of a Berkley Horse, otherwise known as a chevalet." He began buckling her in, her upper back and torso splayed over padded leather with her breasts poking out and up. Her legs dangled to the sides until he took those as well, and buckled them into expandable leg rests, which folded out from under the main rest. "Its initial use was mainly for flogging, but this model can be used for all manner of delights." He produced a bar, which he affixed to her legs with cuffs. "This is a spreader bar, if you haven't had experience. It makes you unable to close your legs to me."

"And does this delight you?" Ava challenged. "Seeing me all tied up, unable to resist?"

"Yes," Crixus said. He knelt at her side, then took one pert nipple deep into his mouth. His hand found the other, squeezing hard. Ava let out a choked breath, then an irritated sigh when he got up and left her. Crixus came back with a blindfold that he quickly placed over her eyes.

"What are you doing?" Ava said in exasperation.

"You wanted my words," Crixus deep voice intoned right next to her ear, startling her. "You wanted less arousal by sight. I'm giving that to you."

Ava took a breath to make a smart reply, but instead let out a shriek as Crixus fastened a cloverleaf nipple clamp to her right breast. He attached a second to her left breast, producing a second yelp.

"Just gorgeous," Crixus murmured, running his hand over her bare throat, then possessively down between her breasts. He gave one of the nipple clamps a small tug, making Ava scream.

Ava fought for composure. "Tell me why you want me this way," she murmured.

"Because I love knowing I can do anything I want to you now, and you can't stop me," Crixus said lustfully. "I love that you're completely in my power." He moved his hand lower fondling her clit expertly, making her moan. "But most of all I love that you want this as much as I do, that doing this to you makes you as hot as it makes me."

"It doesn't," Ava protested.

"Don't lie," Crixus chided. He made circles over her clit, the already swollen flesh purpling under his ministrations. "I can feel how much you're enjoying yourself."

He was right. None of her customers had this kind of control during her sessions with them; she hadn't ever relinquished total control like this before. There was something so calming about not being able to resist him, or anything that he might do.

The shock of his mouth on her vagina brought Ava out of her musings with a sharp gasp of lust. Her lover kissed her a few times, his tongue delving deep into her aching channel.

"You taste sweet," Crixus whispered. "I love how you're so open to me, that you want my dick so much." Ava heard the snap of Crixus putting on another condom, then felt the head of his cock nudge against her clit, teasing her.

"Fill me up," she moaned. "I want your big thick cock inside me."

Crixus teased her a bit more, the big hot head rubbing against her clit, slipping inside as if he would enter, then withdrawing to tease again.

Ava could bear it no longer. "Fuck me!" she cried.

"Bad girl," Crixus said regretfully. He withdrew, then undid her leg restraints and began unbuckling her handcuffs.

What the hell?

Crixus repositioned Ava over the horse, buckling her in again so that her breasts were flat against the leather, and her feet touched the floor. The weight of her body on her swollen nipples made her scream again. Crixus refastened the spreader bar, patted her ass.

"What are you doing?" Ava demanded.

"Using one of the tools you picked out," Crixus answered. The next sensation was the slap of the SLUT paddle onto her bare ass.

"Stop that!" Ava yelled.

"Say you're a bad girl," Crixus replied.

"I'm a bad girl," Ava said at once. "Now take these off."

"No. Admit it and mean it. You're a bad girl."

I have to take control, somehow. "I am a bad girl," Ava said almost tearfully. Her tone warbled between a throaty whisper and a meek girlish tone. "I can't help it, Crixus. I want you inside me throbbing. I ... I know it's bad. I know I'm a bad, bad girl. But you feel so good when you slide that hard cock of yours into me."

Crixus had stopped talking.

Press on. "This wantonness … it makes me feel dirty. I'm so needy, I can't help asking for it." She paused for effect, dropping her voice lower. "I can't help it, Crixus. I need to be filled. I'm begging for it. Please …"

She felt Crixus parting her buttocks, then easing in a small anal plug. "There," he said smugly. "You're filled."

"That doesn't satisfy either of us," Ava managed almost regretfully. "You need to come as much as I do. I'm warm, and wet and ready to let you do anything you want to me. Do you really want to waste any more time?"

"No," Crixus said in a guttural tone. "I want to hear you scream." Ava felt the press of his body against her buttocks, then the length of his cock sliding inside her. Crixus reached around, grasping her sensitive breasts and squeezing them.

Ava let out a screech, then began crying out as he hammered into her, both from the pleasure of his body in hers, and the pain of her clamped nipples. Crixus came with a shout, then collapsed on Ava, his weight pushing her breasts hard against the leather. The pain of the nipple clamps suddenly became sheer agony.

"Get the fuck off of me!" she yelled.

"Damn, but you do have a mouth on you," Crixus said, his tone good-natured. "Hold still." He loosened the restraints on her hands, then undid the clamps. The shock of the pressure releasing made Ava scream twice more.

She rubbed her swollen nipples, trying to massage blood in and out of them.

"Are you really hurt?" Crixus asked gently.

"No," Ava admitted ruefully. She smiled. "And it's two to one in my favor."

"By the way, what are we playing for?" Crixus asked playfully. "You never told me."

"I will, I get to pick your brain for my books," Ava said, after thinking a moment. "That's why I'm here, actually. I want to make it as an erotic author, and I'm really good with the female point of view, but not the male point of view."

"Haven't heard that one before," Crixus said. "Here, let me help." He moved closer, gently massaging her breasts with the flat of his hands. The sensation wasn't erotic, yet it really did help their soreness.

"Thanks," Ava said, giving him a kiss on the cheek.

"Why don't you just ask your clients for what they are feeling when you're together?"

"I thought about that, but it seemed unprofessional," Ava replied.

"How long have you been doing this type of work?"

"The writing? A few months, with nothing published. The sex, about a year now."

"What got you started, if you don't mind me asking?"

"My husband passed away. He had a lucrative job, but it kept him always on the road. I was never lonely somehow even with him gone all the time. But after ... I just felt very alone." She made a face. "We were never savers, though we should have been. As you know, sex for pay is very lucrative, especially if you're willing to give clients a specific fantasy."

Crixus nodded. "And you also never have to go without."

It was Ava's turn to nod. "Yes, but it wasn't like I thought it would be. My clients desire me, but there's no passion to the sex, no love."

Crixus frowned. "It's a danger of the trade, your partners falling in love with you."

"Does it happen to you a lot?"

"No, because I'm careful now not to let encounters be more than a sexual fantasy. I have regular clients that know where the lines are. I rarely accept new clients."

"Why did you come to me?"

"Sin called, said I should see you," Crixus said with a wide grin. "She's the one who helped me get started years ago."

"Small world. I also know Sin; she's given me guidance before in ... delicate matters."

"There's a high burnout in our chosen field of work," Crixus said grimly.

"Why don't you quit, then?"

"Why don't you?"

"I wasn't the one who said I didn't like it," Ava said, flashing a smile. "You didn't answer."

"I'm good at it," he said, shrugging. "And it's easy."

"It's not that easy, playing a part all the time." Ava shrugged. "The hardest part was getting used to sex with people I didn't love. I hadn't ever done that before. It weighed on me at first."

"So you're admitting now you don't really like it. If you feel guilty being here with me, you must feel guilty with your clients."

"No, I don't," she said. "With them, I'm Ava, not Torte. They don't even know my real name is Torte."

"So you don't feel immoral with them anymore."

"No, I don't," Ava said, musing. "It's all about the sex."

"No emotion?"

"Putting my body out there is one thing. Putting my heart out there is another."

"Well said," Crixus commented. He cupped her breasts gently, then kissed her throat softly.

Ava immediately tensed up. *I don't ever do kissing.* And yet she couldn't bring herself to tell Crixus to stop.

He kissed up her jaw, then nibbled at her lower lip. Crossing that hair's breadth, his lips met hers for a gentle kiss that quickly became deeper, stronger, until Crixus and Ava were devouring each other, their tongues licking and tasting, their hands roaming each other's skin.

Crixus disentangled himself abruptly, and moved to the side of the bed, slipping on another condom. "When you began having sex for pay, you couldn't forget your memories of your husband," he said. "You brought the persona Ava in, to help you forget that. So of course you couldn't really get into the sex you had with your clients, or truly let go enough to really enjoy it. But tonight is not about him, or Ava, or you meeting a stranger's needs. Tonight it's just your needs, Torte." He kissed her. "And me fulfilling them."

Torte and Crixus kissed for a long time. When he moved to position her under him, she bit his throat lightly, then blocked him. He tried once more, but she evaded him with a wide smile.

"Come here right now."

"No."

"If I have to come and get you, you're going to get a spanking, Torte."

"Just try it."

Crixus wrestled with Torte on the bed as she flailed and kicked. He brought her across his lap, then smacked her ass hard with his hand. "Settle down!"

"Ouch!"

He spanked her again. "Are you going to hold still?"

"Nope!"

He slapped her ass harder, making her yelp. He slapped her five times more, her behind reddening with handprints, until she relented.

"Okay, okay! I'll hold still."

"Good," he whispered, pulling her astride him. "Because I really want to hear you scream my name." He grasped her hips, then thrust into her in long deep strokes. Torte matched him thrust for thrust, rubbing her clit against his lunging member.

Crixus paused, then slapped her right ass cheek again with his hand. "I said for you to hold still."

"And I said I would," Torte retorted, producing a crop in her right hand. Positioning it like she was riding a horse, she brought it down with a hard smack on his inner thigh. "Now gallop for me, stud."

Crixus gave her a wicked smile and began thrusting. Torte rode him, sighing in pleasure. Their climax was a long time coming, both participants covered with sweat, their bodies glistening, their breath coming fast. When they came, they came together, their cries mingled, clutching one another.

"Thank you," Torte said, as she eased down next to Crixus.

"Thank you," he replied. The words were easy, but his tone was different.

"What is it?" she asked lightly.

"Just that … I have an admission to make, too. I'm hoping to get out of the business in a year or so. I've been saving, and I would like to go back to school."

"I think that's a good plan. What do you want to do?"

"I'm not sure. I'd like to start my own business, but it's very risky. I work out a lot, so I'm thinking being a personal trainer might be the way to go, and then maybe eventually own my own gym someday."

"I think you'd be good at that," Torte quipped. "You're good at telling people what to do to achieve their goals."

Crixus laughed, then hugged her. "You're right."

Torte hugged him back, then leaned in for a kiss.

A buzzing sound filled the room, the noise insistent.

"What the hell is that?"

"Sorry, my alarm," Torte said, getting out of bed and finding her purse. "I can't believe it, it's after midnight."

"It's alright," Crixus said, propping himself up on one arm. "I'm yours until the end of the night."

Torte gave him a look. "I appreciate that," she said, coming back over to him. "But I know how I would feel in your shoes, because I've been there. Go home to bed and get some rest. You gave me my money's worth." She kissed him on the lips.

"You're sure? You won our bet, two to one. The last I count as a draw. Even if I won the next bout, I have to declare you the winner."

Ava nodded, dressing quickly.

"Don't you want your toys? As mementos—"

"No." She tossed him his pants, which he slipped on. She gathered up her purse, then headed to the door.

Crixus went after her and grabbed her arm. "Are you sure you're leaving ... it's not something I said?"

"Not at all." She leaned in and kissed him once more.

"Congratulations, in that this is the first time I feel ridiculous in my role as sexy alpha," Crixus said with a laugh, producing a ticket from his pants pocket. "This is a return voucher for 10% off your next appointment. I'm supposed to ask you if you want to set up your next appointment now."

Ava paused at the door, then turned back to face him. "Thank you. I feel that I should tell you that I won't be back. Not because I didn't enjoy the night, but because you made me understand myself. I've been hiding in plain sight. It's time I said goodbye to Ava." She blushed. "And time that I also picked out some new goals for myself based on what I really want out of life."

"Good to meet you, Torte," Crixus said. He took her hand and kissed it. "I'm Oz, as in Oscar. That's my real name."

"I thought as much. That's why I didn't say Crixus when I came." Torte smiled. "Good to meet you."

"Do you want to see me again?"

"Yes, I want to see you again," Torte said, throwing her arms around him. "I'd like to get to know the real you. Doing something we both want, inside the bedroom, or out of it. Are you interested?"

"I am. I can't date clients, though," Oz said softly. He took the ticket with her name and ripped it up. "You're not a client now," he said, kissing her hand again. "Are you free next Friday?"

"You really think this can work?" Torte said, snuggling into his arms.

"Yes," Oz said confidently, looking down into her eyes. "And we'll have a hell of a how we met story, to boot."

THE END

FOURPLAY

Mrs. Mauve Reynolds is a school secretary by day, but on weekends she gives private sessions in seduction as the professional dominatrix Vixen. When a chance encounter reveals her close friend Camilla is also a teacher of kink, the two women decide to unite for a night of shared pleasure, with a little help from dominatrix Sin.

FOURPLAY

I put down my Sunday paper, then checked again. *Still a few minutes after noon.* Carlos was late.

There was an insistent knock at the door.

With a relieved smile, I adjusted my dress. Carlos looked his usual clean cut and mild-mannered self today, his business suit impeccably tailored. He wasn't my most handsome customer, but he was one of the nicest. My business didn't always bring me into contact with the best men... "Hi there, lover."

"Hi," he said almost shyly, taking off his jacket and setting it on a chair. He took my envelope, placed the bills inside and put it on the table. "Where are we doing it? Right here?"

Such a relief for regular clients, to not have to check the money's all there. I shook my head, then led him to the living room. "Sit there."

He sat as ordered, watching me hungrily.

I went to my bag of tricks and treats, as I called it, and pulled out a cream-colored dildo. "Have you been good since I saw you last, lover?"

"That's almost as long as me," Carlos said quickly. "I—"

"No," I interrupted firmly. "You don't question me. Your questions have to wait. Now have you been good?"

"Yes."

"Then you deserve a reward." I deliberately lay back on the rug, parting my legs slightly to give him an eyeful of my dark pubic hair. My outfit was a short dress and heels, the kind a woman might wear in an office, sans underwear or nylons. *Carlos's favorite outfit in my wardrobe.* I often wondered that he came to me because he had a girl in his office that he liked from afar. *Forbidden fruit, the most tempting of all delicacies.*

Taking the dildo in one hand, I ran it up and down my thighs, letting the tip caress my soft skin as I counted to ten slowly. Pulling up my skirt over my hips, I groaned and moaned with closed eyes, imagining a dream lover teasing me with his hard erection. Times with my clients always went better when I was in the mood.

"Please," Carlos begged. "Please, let me do that. I want to be inside you—"

"No," I moaned firmly. "You have to wait. And no touching yourself."

A few seconds went by, as I played with the dildo, inserting it slightly into my vagina, feeling myself relax as arousal took hold of me with rough hands, my clit swelling with my own need to be filled.

"Please," Carlos said again, his desperate yearning for me obvious in his tone. "Please, I need to touch you, Vixen."

I slowly worked the dildo in and out of myself, focusing on his desire for me, my excitement mounting as I imagined his need to possess me. "Tell me again that you deserve me."

"I've been good," Carlos blustered. "I deserve you, I need you—"

"Come here."

He staggered to me, unzipping his pants, his swollen penis already protruding out of the waistband. Carlos might not be my most handsome client, but he was the most well-endowed. I felt an extra thrill run through my loins as he bared his penis, then slipped on a condom.

I pushed him back to the rug and straddled him. He grabbed hold of my hips and thrust up immediately, sliding deep, but not all the way inside.

"Good boy." I breathed, loving the feel of his hard and eager body within me, his urges so barely kept in check. "Now fuck me like you mean it."

We rocked, him clutching at me, sliding his hands over my body, his hands caressing lightly through the silky material of my dress. "You're so beautiful," he groaned. "I can't wait to make you come."

I twisted and turned on him, enjoying his cock, yet careful not to actually come. *Hold it, and count to ten.* Reaching ten, I rocked harder, then began screaming, faking an orgasm. Carlos let me "come" then I dismounted.

"You faked it," he said accusingly, putting his penis away still gloved. "I'm leaving."

"That's because you won't give me what I really want," I pouted prettily, batting my eyes at him. "You know what I need. Give in to me."

"I can't," he protested, anguished.

"You can," I purred, kneeling before him. "Let me see your cock."

Breathing hard in his excitement, Carlos took out his penis. The stiff organ was more engorged than ever, a clear sign he was just where I wanted him. "Strip that off."

"I can't. I have to go back to work. I'm going to get yelled at already for taking a long lunch—"

"Strip it off. Now."

Carlos pulled off the condom. His penis glistened, the small vein near the proud head visibly throbbing.

"Clean yourself."

He did as I asked, using his silk pocket-handkerchief.

"Come here and offer yourself to me."

I grasped his legs, sliding my hands up his outer thighs, then took his proffered penis in my mouth, the length sliding deep. "Oh yes, please," he groaned. "My wife never lets me do that. That feels so good…"

I closed my eyes, not in pleasure, but in guilt. Pushing the emotion away, I sucked him as he groaned and moaned. Grabbing his balls in my hand, I squeezed them in rhythm, making him cry out. As I felt his first shakes of pre-orgasm, I slipped him from my throat, then kissed the quivering tip of his now wet dick.

"I want you to come," he growled, his tone aggressive. "I want it to be real. No bullshit!"

As if anything about this scene was real. I looked up into his eyes, then smiled sultrily. "Put another on."

He slipped another condom on, almost panting in his wanton desire.

"Lay on your back. You know what I like."

"I do, baby," he said lovingly, as I mounted him again. He slid deep this time, so deep it hurt. I told myself to ignore the discomfort and kept moving, knowing that the pressure would ease in seconds, to be replaced by sheer bliss.

"I want you to feel good," he whispered. "Tell me, baby."

"Slow down. Long strokes," I groaned, letting my upper body loosen up to move freely with his thrusts, my head falling forward to let my long hair whisper across his face. "I want you as deep inside me as you can get, deeper than any lover I've ever had. Possess me utterly! Make me yours!"

Carlos began to stroke thoroughly, grunting every time he slid home, his thick root sliding across my swollen clit. The barest hint of orgasm quickly became a raging fire, burning away everything but the need to come. I ground into him, needing that hot flash of pleasure to engulf me, to lose myself to my orgasm. *Remember to scream.*

The orgasm hit in a long liquid rush. I yelled my head off, giving voice to all my relief and joy as my tension left me, leaving me shaking gently. Carlos came under me a few seconds afterwards, clutching my ass hard as he shot his load. I contracted my muscles, tightening around him to heighten his orgasm. He jerked hard, then relaxed, breathing in long gasps.

I dismounted immediately to lie beside him on my back. Reaching to the nearby table, I passed him the tissues, and we both cleaned ourselves up.

He took my hand when it was over. "You were wonderful, Vixen, as you always are."

"Thank you," I said politely.

"I'd like to lay here with you," he said in longing, looking up at the ceiling. "It's the one place I don't have to be anyone but myself."

I said nothing. *This is his fantasy, and he's paying well for it. Let him enjoy it.*

He took my hand. "Do you enjoy our times together?"

I squeezed his palm. "Of course. I wouldn't keep seeing you as a client if I didn't—"

"I mean me," he interrupted. "Do you like me?"

Uh oh. Dangerous territory. I neither wanted to lose a client in these hard, economic times, or gain a lover in real life, no matter that I didn't currently have one. "Yes, I like you, Carlos. I really enjoy our sessions. And I hope I gave you your money's worth today."

"As always," he said with a leer, getting to his feet. I followed him, straightening my dress.

We walked to the door. "Have a good afternoon, Carlos."

He kissed my cheek. "You, too. I do have a company to run."

He turned to leave, then turned back. "Look, I'm sure you get this from a lot of your clients, hell, maybe all of them. But if the time ever came when you wanted more, I—"

I shook my head, still smiling. Then I kissed his cheek. "You have a good life, Carlos. Enjoy it. I'm happy to share these stolen moments with you."

He fidgeted, uneasy.

I know what you're waiting for. I grasped the lapels of his jacket, then pulled him close to whisper in his ear, "Until your cock's inside me again, be good, baby."

Carlos smiled in pleasure, flushing slightly, then got in his car and left.

I went back inside, picked up the envelope, counting out my three hundred dollars and trying to maintain the aftereffects of my excellent orgasm. Carlos might be back, or he might not. This happened sometime with clients, that they started believing the fantasy was reality. It was usually the good ones who were considerate, too. But it was a pitfall of the trade.

Either way, I wasn't going to break my rule of dating clients. What happened during my working hours didn't spill over to my real life. *Ever.*

My cell phone chirped with a new text. I picked it up out of my purse, checking the number. *Bryan, one of my regulars, saying he had given my number to a friend who "Badly needed a good time."*

"Exactly what I asked you not to do, ever," I said aloud, annoyed. "And of course, exactly what you did." I texted back '*does he understand the rules?*' meaning cost, what I did and didn't allow, and discretion.

Bryan replied immediately. *Yes, he's a good guy. You'll like him, promise. He'll call tonight, he says he wants you to see him ASAP, that he'd pay extra.*

I shrugged, then clicked off the phone. I guess we'll see.

"**H**ave a good summer, Mrs. Reynolds!"

I waved and watched the last student leave, then began tidying up my office, excited by the prospect of two months of time to reflect ... and make future plans. *Tom's been gone now for almost a year. It's time to decide if I should start dating again. And I need to make a decision; keep being a school secretary, or just be a professional dom.*

I'd blundered into the sex game when my husband Tom was still part of the picture; he'd been a dominant and I'd been his submissive, trained in the five years we were together in most every sex toy and scenario there was. I'd gone along with it, because I knew he needed it to be satisfied. When he'd asked to bring other men to our bed, I'd began to balk, stopping his visions of threesomes at letting them watch he and I play our games. *But that had only whetted his appetite.* After I'd found him with both a man and a woman one Friday afternoon when I'd arrived home early from work, I'd called it quits.

But Tom's male friends ... they remembered what they'd seen. Several had called me, and come around, trying to talk me into bed. I'd tossed them out on their asses. But Todd ... he'd just knocked on my door one day, and propositioned me, saying he'd pay $100 to just have me dress up in my lace bustier and garters and caress then spank him for thirty minutes, with no sex included. After a few times, he'd asked for sex, too, and told me to name my price. I liked him, and his weight-lifting, ultra-toned chest, so I'd agreed. In time, he'd asked if he could suggest others to me that he knew. I'd been hesitant, but he'd been nice enough to work with, so I'd agreed. Most of his friends had been great, like Carlos. Two hadn't, but I no longer saw them. *Pitfalls of the trade...*

I knew that sooner or later, what I'd been doing might well get back to the school authorities and then I'd lose my job. So I had to make a choice this summer: fully embrace my dominatrix persona Vixen and quit my job or take the safe route and go back to being just Mauve. I'd known this from the beginning, but the truth was that I liked the excitement of my sexual exploits. Having men drooling over me made me feel very sexy, especially after how Tom had made me feel. *Can I really let that go?*

My best friend Camilla Fields breezed in the door, all smiles, breaking my reminiscing. "I hope you're ready to celebrate our last day by getting a drink at Shenanigans," she teased. "You've been avoiding me since last fall."

"I have not," I replied, forcing the testy note from my words. "I've just been busy." *Busy with my new part-time job, fucking men for money.* "But so have you! Is it three or four times now you've cancelled on me for dinner?"

Camilla blushed, embarrassed. "I'm sorry about that, Rey. I've been distant the last few months, I know. That's why I wanted to make sure to catch you before you left. I meant it about that drink. Are you ready to go?"

I hesitated, her use of my nickname making me want to say yes. Nothing waited at home for me except my answering machine. *And a possible new client. But I really didn't feel like working tonight, even for double rates.* "Sure, just let me put away a few things. Say a half-hour?"

Camilla nodded. "I'll meet you there."

"Hi."

I looked up with a smile, expecting to see Camilla. Instead, a man I didn't know was looking at me expectantly. "Hello."

"I happened to be here with my friend, and he pointed you out," the man said confidently, gesturing to a far table where a familiar male was waving happily. "Bryan."

Of all the bars in this town ... sigh. "I'm glad to meet you?"

"Um, Caesar."

Not your real name. "Glad to meet you, Caesar. What can I do for you?"

"I was hoping to set up a session," the man said nervously. "Like you have with Bryan. But I'd want a different scenario."

"Such as?" I asked pleasantly. "Speak freely."

The man flushed.

I spied Camilla coming toward the table, and inwardly groaned. "If you'd like, we can have a session with what Bryan usually has, then go from there. Has he told you prices?"

The man nodded, as Camilla came strolling up, then sat down. "Hi. Who's your friend?"

I prepared myself for mortification, a flush already creeping up my throat. Instead I got the shock of my life as the man turned to Camilla. "Raven!"

Camilla's face was reddening, but her expression was proud as she smiled. "Hello, Leo."

Leo a.k.a. Caesar, flushed as well, and the three of us burst out laughing. "Raven, you've been holding out on me," he teased. "I thought you only worked alone."

"She's just a friend," Camilla a.k.a. Raven answered. "What are you doing here?"

"A friend of mine told me about this woman he sees named Vixen," Leo said. "I told him about you, Raven. Bryan wanted me to meet Vixen, see if she would see me, too. I was planning on calling you tonight, in fact."

To compare me to my friend. Wow, this had to be about the most awkward moment imaginable. I forced a smile. "I'm glad to meet you. As Bryan's already likely told you, I'm Vixen. If you want to see me, you should make an appointment to discuss what you're looking for in an experience. The first time, please come with the person who recommended you …"

"A foursome!" he exclaimed. "That would be awesome. Count us in!" Leo hurried back to his table.

"What the hell did you just get me into?" Camilla asked heatedly.

"I didn't get you into anything, Raven," I said, sarcastically emphasizing her trade name. "I had no idea you were doing this, too. I didn't mention you at all; Caesar, the man you call Leo, is some friend of one of my regulars. I don't want to meet him without having someone vouch for him, even if you do know him. And you heard me, I said nothing about a foursome!"

"Leo's not anything but a regular top," she said dismissively. "But he's going to expect us both to be there." As if cued, her phone beeped once. She raised her eyebrows and showed it to me: a text from Leo, asking for an appointment to see both of us with Bryan for a foursome in a week's time.

I shook my head. "Let him know it's three times the price, and he'll back off."

"I doubt that," Camilla said ruefully. "He's wanted his own private orgy for a while now. The addition of another man wasn't the problem. I just didn't know if I felt comfortable with another woman."

I cast her an appraising look. "Taking our friendship to a new level?"

To her credit, she didn't back down an inch. "I like sex, I always have. Being with men I don't know that well is a kind of thrill for me, Mauve, especially as it's a lot of money for very little time, and most of what men want is pretty predictable, as you already know." Her tone softened. "But I've never been with a woman. I'd feel more comfortable if it were you with me, for my first time."

I let myself truly consider her words. "We'd have to put a limit on what was included. I also don't have any experience with women myself. We'd need someone to help us."

Camilla nodded, then clinked her glass with mine. "I have a friend we can see. Sin's the one who initially helped me get my first clients. Let me set up a meeting with her next week to get some pointers."

That next week, I was a bundle of nerves as I dressed to go over to Camilla's home, thinking about scenario after scenario, not sure I wanted to go through with it, and yet curious how much different sex would be with not only having multiple partners at once, but also including a longtime friend of the same sex.

Sin. A woman with a name like that should be a master of bedroom games. *I guess I'm going to find out.*

I sipped my wine, trying not to drink it too fast as we waited for Sin to arrive.

"Relax," Camilla said for the second time. "Sin's great, she's very matter of fact."

The doorbell rang shrilly. Startled, I put down my wine before I dropped it, then rose from the chair and followed Camilla to the door.

"Hi, thanks so much for coming, Sin," Camilla said, as a tall platinum-tressed woman strode into her home. "We really could use your help. This is my friend Vixen."

"I won't get into the dangers of having two men at once," Sin said haughtily, casting an appraising glance my way before she focused back on Camilla. "I know that you are a professional, Raven, and will check out these men before any clothes come off. But there's more to an interlude than just safety. Do you have a list of what you're willing to do with them, and each other?"

I flushed, as Camille answered, "Vixen is willing to let me take the lead. My plan was to pair off at first, let the men get off at least once, so they're more relaxed, then to have them watch us get off, then possibly do a true foursome, with all four of us having sex at once."

"Do you know how difficult that is, not just to make sure that everyone enjoys the act, but that no one injures someone else?" Sin remarked sarcastically. "Impossible, for someone with no experience, such as yourself."

I opened my mouth, scathing remark ready, but Camille beat me to it. "Everyone has to learn somehow, if they want to try this, and we do," she said heatedly. "No, Vixen doesn't have experience, but I know the female anatomy well-enough that I can bring her to orgasm, and that's if the two guys don't decide they want to participate and not watch us."

"Eighty percent of women have to have clitoral stimulation," Sin stated. "Only a small minority is multi-orgasmic. Vixen, are you good enough to fake it and have them not know it, if you are expected to come but can't?"

"I know my own body," I argued. "I can figure out a way to come, if somehow I'm not stimulated enough to climax."

"But that is exactly what I'm saying," Sin said in exasperation. "There's not room for making something like this up as you go along. You have to be in control of not only each other, but also both men. You have to direct the action, period."

"We can do this. We're ready," Camille persisted.

"You're not or you wouldn't need to announce it," Sin said with a snort. She turned to me abruptly, her long platinum hair like a shimmering curtain. "Vixen, are you comfortable being with a woman, being touched by one? Can you climax with Raven?"

"I'm open to the idea," I said firmly. "I said I was. We're doing this."

"Hmm," Sin said, then gave a reluctant sigh. "Alright, There's a way this can work, if the guys in question both are tops, but not excessively dominant. And if you," she poked me with the tip of her stiletto, "can play a submissive for this scenario."

A thrill went through me, equal parts uneasiness and eagerness. "I've only ever been a dominant. Men come to me that are submissive."

"Bryan's a submissive?" Camilla asked, incredulous.

"That's how you've gotten along so far on your own, maintaining total control," Sin remarked, her sapphire eyes glittering thoughtfully. "But you've had a few run-ins with dominant males now and again, didn't you? Bruised more than your ego, I'd bet."

"I can control Bryan, if Raven can handle Leo," I shot back.

"I have taught Raven the rules of the game, she knows not to bite off more than she can swallow whole," Sin said, her lips in a sultry smile. "But you, Vixen, I'm not so sure. You should know if you get two men into a bedroom, they will egg one another on to do things they might never consider doing on their own. What have you done before, besides oral, anal, and regular sex?"

This is not the time to admit never doing anal. "Most of the men I see want sex, with a little bit of talking naughty, and some light domination, like waiting for permission to touch me or themselves. I've done some roleplaying, also."

"The tip of the prick, so to speak," Sin said, then laughed. "There's much more that consenting adults do with each other, especially when you have multiple males or multiple females. You are going to have both on your night in question." She paused. "Let's sit down, and script out this fantasy." She strode to the dining room table, and artfully kicked out a chair, sitting down gracefully. "How much are you asking in terms of price? What is the time limit?"

"Three times the going rate," I stammered, my head swimming with possible scenarios. "We thought three hours, tops."

"At three hours straight, you're all going to be exhausted," Sin supplied, taking a pen and paper from an equally flustered Camilla. "And sore. I recommend two hours and ask for five times the regular rate." She looked at each of us in turn. "Each."

"That's fifteen hundred dollars each," Camilla murmured.

"You are giving them something they can't buy elsewhere," Sin stated. "You are worth that amount, girls. Accept also that they will brag about this, and you may be asked to do this again, at minimum these two men may very well ask for this again. It's seldom that a sexual experience is really enjoyed, then abandoned never to be tried again."

"You're right," I managed with my suddenly dry throat. "About all of it. We're in over our heads, Sin. Will you direct us?"

Sin offered a smile, this one kinder. "I'll give you ideas, and you can take it from there. Anyone at your party will be expected to join in, and I'm not available now. Don't worry, you'll do fine." She pulled out a chair near her. "Now come and sit down. We have a lot to talk about."

C amilla looked at me, something new in her gaze as she watched me walk toward her down the long hallway in my secretary outfit, unsteady in my five-inch strappy sandals.

"How do I look?" I asked.

"Good enough to eat," she said with intended double meaning, sending another thrill down my spine. I bit my lip lightly, suddenly nervous. "We're going to have a good time, and make a lot of money," she whispered, embracing me.

"I know. It's just butterflies."

"Trust me." She nibbled my ear lightly. "I won't let you down."

We separated, as Leo and Bryan came into the room. "Girls, you look lovely," Bryan murmured, handing Camilla the money. She counted it quickly, then took it into the other room. The men's attention shifted to me.

"How does this work?" Bryan asked, circling me. "Can we just have you together?"

"No," Camilla said curtly, returning to the room with a clacking of heels. "First we talk. You've got two hours, and we want to make them count. Tell us what you had in mind."

Bryan looked at Leo, who stared back at him. "We thought we'd fuck you both separately, then double team one of you."

"Granted," Camilla said, giving them bedroom eyes with a side dish of ultra-sexy smile. "But you want more than just a quick screw, correct? We want to give you your complete fantasy."

"I wanted to try spanking," Leo piped up. "Um ... as in spanking one of you. And I want some oral sex."

"Blindfolds," Bryan said. "and restraints." He grinned. "On me. I'm a submissive."

"And I want to watch you two together," Leo said suddenly. "Just a little, before we start. Like an appetizer, y'know?"

Camilla nodded. "We can do all of that. Did you take the Viagra we recommended using for tonight?"

Both men nodded, Leo blushing faintly.

"Bryan is the submissive, you two are the dominants, and I'm the ringmaster." She gave another seductive smile. "But that doesn't mean I won't join in with full enthusiasm when its time." Her face became stern. "You will refer to me as Mistress, and to her as Vixen. You will ask me if you want something and request the same from her. Be explicit in your requests. We will voice various suggestions from time to time; you may take them or not, it's your choice. The safe word is red. Use it if at any time you need to stop for any reason. All parties are to stop if any person says that, no exceptions."

Both men were staring with their mouths dropped open, lust pouring off them.

"Do you agree? Say yes or no."

"Yes," both men said, then they shot an excited look at one another.

"Please take off your clothes," Camilla said to them, handing them each a pill. She indicated a small leather bundle. "And put those leathers on, if you like."

Both men began taking off their clothes. Camilla turned to me, her sexy smile becoming reassuring. "We'd better get moving too. Grab some of that arousal gel and apply it, then hand it to me."

She and I applied the clear liquid gently to our clits, the slight cool feeling quickly turning to a warm pleasurable tingling. Camilla stroked herself gently, then opened her eyes, staring at Leo. "You like to watch me play with myself?"

Leo approached, his cock already standing proudly from the small leather ball support, straining against its condom sheath. "Yes. But I want a better view, Mistress."

She splayed her legs, then rubbed her finger back and forth across her swelling clit, feeling the warmth spread as her body responded. "Do you want to touch me?"

"Yes." Leo came eagerly forward, hand already reaching.

"No, not your finger," Camilla said teasingly. "Your cock."

Leo took his stiff penis in his hand, hurrying to assume position. With a grateful grunt, he slid the head inside, then tried to push deeper.

"No!" The crop descended, striking Leo squarely on his nipple, eliciting a yelp of surprise from him. "You're not allowed inside yet. Just the very head of you, Leo."

The man groaned reluctantly, then withdrew his cock, leaving just the tip inside Camilla. "Please."

"Tell me you want to sheathe your cock in me."

"I want it, and you do, too," he pleaded. "You're so wet."

"Yes, but first you must attend to Bryan," Camilla reminded, she pointed with the crop to me, as I finished putting restraints and a blindfold on a naked Bryan. He was spread-eagled on the bed, face up. "Then you may have your reward."

"What must I do, Mistress?"

"Vixen will flog his cock and punish him. In turn you must punish her, if she doesn't play fair to him. But you have also been naughty, Leo. Your punishment for now is to watch ... and not touch yourself."

Bryan's penis was solid as rock, the lengthy shaft standing proudly at attention. I smacked the tip of it sharply with my riding crop again and again, until he begged me to stop.

"But it feels good, doesn't it?" I whispered to him, as I cupped his balls in my hand and squeezed. "You like me slapping your cock, don't you?"

"Yes," he gasped, "But I can't stand it. Please stroke me! Please."

Again I flicked the tip of his cock, Bryan arching his back in response, semen leaking from the tip of his prick. "But you look so good tied up there, my sweet. So easy to tease. And you haven't pleased me yet."

"Come here, and I'll put my tongue to good use," he promised, licking his lips.

I smacked his thigh hard with my crop, leaving a red mark. "No. You're mine to torment."

"Punish her," Camilla said coldly to Leo. "But you may not touch yourself ... or ask her to touch you."

Leo exhaled loudly, and I worried for a moment he wouldn't do as she'd told him. But he came to me and grabbed the crop from my hand. "No more. He's earned a taste of you."

"But what if I want to taste you?" I said coyly, putting my arms around his neck. I licked my lips suggestively and smiled.

I enjoyed the fight I could see on Leo's face between wanting to plunge his cock into my mouth and obeying Camilla. "No," he said gruffly. "Give him a taste of you."

Carefully, I sashayed to the bed, then sat astride Bryan, his mouth just inches from my vagina. "Stretch out your tongue, lover."

Eagerly, Bryan licked out, catching just the tip of my clit. He strained up, trying to enter, but I just laughed and got up off him.

"Punish her!" Camilla said. "Spank her."

Leo was already moving. He grabbed me and hauled me over Brian's prone form, struggling feebly. He administered several light whacks to my bottom with his hand.

"Stop!" I shouted, quivering. "I'll behave."

"Good," Leo said. "Now do what he likes you to do. Or I'll spank you again a lot harder."

I bit my lip and nodded, but inside I was relieved. *He's unsure as I am about where the boundaries are ... or what Bryan's special desires might be.* Carefully, I sat on Bryan's face, this time letting his tongue delve deep inside me. I cried out, enjoying his licking and nibbling until I could feel my climax was close. Then I carefully bent down, closed my eyes, and swallowed Bryan's cock. His jaw went slack for a moment, then he delved deeper as if he'd eat me, as he began filling my throat in regular strokes.

"Come here, Leo," Camilla demanded. "The challenge is the usual one: I'll swallow your seed if you can make me come in under a minute. Begin."

Female moans filled the air a moment later, then rapid panting. Camilla cried out in climax under thirty seconds. Her cries brought me to climax, shuddering happily if soundlessly.

Male groans began, the leather of Leo's thongs creaking as Camilla sucked him off. Bryan came with a series of moans and oaths, Leo following him.

"Short break," Camilla said to them, as I undid Bryan's straps. "Five minutes." She took my hand and led me to the bathroom.

After she closed the door, both of us broke into wide grins, amazed at our performance. "Wow," I said, giving her an appreciative look. You weren't kidding, Camilla. You did have complete control out there."

"Sin was adamant I had to," she replied. "But what next? I'm sure I can top what we did, but we still have an hour to go."

"They said they wanted to do oral and spanking. Maybe some light domination?"

She nodded. "Yes, we'll get you into the blindfold and restraints. But are you comfortable? I can have them tie you up and spank you, but that's a lot on you for both of them. So I'm going to go down on the other one while he watches his friend have you. Do you want to stick to our original clients for this, because they likely won't want to wear a condom?"

I nodded.

"Okay. Let's go."

We sauntered back out. But the guys were already at work, with Bryan back in the restraints, and Leo blindfolded. "Do you have another one of those?" Bryan asked.

Camilla handed me a blindfold, and I put it on Bryan.

"I thought I should be punished," Bryan said. "I came without permission."

"And I touched Vixen without permission," Leo added. "I need to be punished."

Camilla and I looked at one another in surprise, then grinned. "Yes, you're right," she said haughtily. "And I know just what to do."

We put condoms on both of the men, whose Viagra-induced pricks were still unflagging. Then we began stroking their cocks, until they were panting and begging.

Camilla handed me a crop, then nodded. Together we smacked the tip of their erect cocks, making them howl.

"Silence!" she thundered. "You do not have permission to come, either of you! You are going to please us and behave. Say yes you understand."

"Yes, we understand."

We smacked their penises again, this time eliciting shouts. "Yes, Mistresses!"

"Yes Mistresses!"

I straddled Bryan, and she straddled Leo, letting our juices lubricate their members as we rubbed gently against them. With planned precision, we tilted our pelvises, letting just the head of the cocks inside.

Immediately, both men strained hard, thrusting up to enter. The duel crops came slashing down, hitting their chests.

"You will not move. You will stay still. You will not come! Is that understood?"

"Yes, Mistresses!"

With a sigh of satisfaction, I began to tease Bryan in the way I knew he liked, sliding just a bit onto his cock, then almost letting him withdraw fully, until his soft insistent whisper of, "Please, Mistress!" made me let him slide home once again. But my own need to come soon overrode my desire to tease, and I ground against him, loving the feel of his thick cock inside me. I could feel him under me, fighting his own desire to come, fidgeting as he tried to fight it.

I rode him hard and fast, letting the orgasm wash over me, the slow moan erupting unbidden from my throat. I dismounted, then took his cock in my hand, and ripped the condom off. I worked it in my hand, hard and fast, a towel ready in my other hand. Bryan tensed with a shout, then shot his load, the semen spattering onto the towel.

As I cleaned up and unbound Bryan, I noticed a sated Camilla dismounting. But Leo hadn't come.

"Very good, very good," Camilla said to him. "But you want to come badly, don't you?"

"Yes, Mistress!"

"Very badly? Say it!"

"I want to come very badly, Mistress."

"I want to watch you take my friend fully," Camilla whispered, running the crop gently down Leo's chest, conjuring an anticipatory shudder. "Now obey." The crop whispered through the air, striking Leo's chest once more, leaving a red mark. "Or suffer." She removed his blindfold. "Now take her."

I had already been on my back on the bed beside the couple, gently fingering myself as I watched the interplay. I readied myself as Leo came to me, then mounted me. I felt his hot shaft slide home, as he took hold of my thighs. I tilted my hips to better receive him. Leo pressed forward, sliding fully inside with a grunt of possession.

"Now fuck her. Make her submit to your will."

I grasped Leo's ass, pushing him deeper with each steady thrust. Leo sped up, his movements rough and jerky with denied need. Then he groaned, rolling with me onto his back. Possessively he grasped my hips and thrust up, making me take all of him, then paused.

There was a whisper of skin on skin as other hands suddenly grasped my hips.

"Let him in," Camilla commanded. "He needs to be inside you, Vixen. Tell her now, Bryan, and she will obey."

"Let me in," Bryan whispered coarsely. "I need to be inside you." I felt the touch of his hard cock against my sphincter, then the touch of his hand as he applied lube.

"Do as he says," Leo said throatily. "Submit."

I held still as Bryan eased himself inside my tightness. In my nervousness, I shifted, pushing out his member.

"Relax," he breathed into my ear, the words half comfort, half command. "You are mine, and I'll have you now. Submit."

I bowed my head lightly, then let my muscles relax. The slow steady press of his hot organ renewed its assault, this time sliding inside partway.

"There," Bryan stated, as he stroked my hip. "You're a good girl. But I'm not going to settle for less than all of you." His hand slid forward and down, splaying itself tight over my lower belly. With a clench of his powerful bicep, he pushed me back against him, driving the full length of his cock inside me. Trapping my lower body with his right hand, he used the left to capture my upper body, taking firm hold of my right breast, squeezing possessively as he kissed the back of my neck. I let out a gasp. *I'm so full.*

"Yes," he groaned in satiation, beginning short quick thrusts. "You're mine, Vixen. You're going to take everything I have to give you. Say it."

"I'm going to take everything you have to give me," I breathed.

"Tell us you want us to fuck you."

"I want you to fuck me."

Bryan and Leo began to move gently in tandem. I felt the beginning of orgasm, but it was different, indelicate and rough. The feeling built in my ass, then pure pleasure burning white hot as the climax took hold of me, my mouth slackening. "Yes please! Oh God! Yes!"

"Take it all," he commanded, thrusting deep and fast. "Scream for me."

I let out a guttural roar, not caring if it was sexy or not. The feeling was too powerful, too necessary, and I wanted it too much to let it be anything but what it was. I finished coming, only aware then that Bryan had also come, his body finishing its last jerks.

Bryan withdrew, and Leo began thrusting madly, spending himself in a few seconds with loud shouts.

After, both men removed the condoms and we lay recovering.

"That was wonderful," I said languidly. *I feel as if all the bones in my body have loosened somehow. I've never felt so relaxed.*

"Anal orgasms are like that," Bryan said nonchalantly. "I'm not sure why, except that having one seems to relax not just the same muscles that regular orgasm does, but every muscle in the entire body."

"I always wondered why you enjoyed that," Leo said to him tentatively. "But seeing her pleasure, I understand why." He paused. "I might like to try that sometime, just to see what it feels like."

"There's no judgment here, only the pursuit of pleasure," Camilla said. She turned and got on all fours, looking back over her shoulder with a sexy smile. "Come and play, Leo. That is, if Bryan would be so kind as to roll over and let me mount up?"

Bryan scrambled onto his back, hurriedly strapping on another condom. Camilla mounted him, settling onto his cock with a sigh. "Come here, Vixen," she commanded. You're part of this too."

Uneasy, I went closer, waiting for a command.

"Sit on his face, with your weight on your knees, and face me."

Carefully, I eased onto Bryan, letting out a cry of surprise as I felt his tongue lick up into me. He gripped my ass, pushing me down onto his mouth, which began licking and nibbling my clit. I swayed, then eased my breasts down on his chest.

"Kiss me," Camilla said.

Carefully, I leaned forward and kissed her, first tentatively, then more hungrily as I felt her hands slide into my hair, bringing my lips more fully down to hers.

She drew back for a moment. "Leo, anytime."

Leo gave a great shuddering breath, lifting his hand away from his cock, already purple inside its condom. He climbed behind Camilla, then carefully grasped her hips, and pushed past her sphincter, filling her with a loud possessive grunt. He began to pump almost immediately, his movement insistent, filing her with each thrust. His climax was rough, but he didn't withdraw.

"Kiss her more," he groaned. "I want to watch."

Camilla kissed me again as if she would eat me, her tongue entangling with mine. Leo was watching us, kissing Camilla's back and fondling her breasts. The sensations I was feeling were strange and wonderful, Bryan's mouth eating at me as I kissed her. Watching myself as Leo spent himself in her as I kissed her, an evocative turn on if ever there was one.

"Vixen, dismount, so that Bryan can finish," Camilla commanded. "Kiss him and taste yourself on his lips."

Shivering, I carefully dismounted, as Bryan began to move, and began kissing him, laying across his chest and rubbing my breasts on his chest as our tongues entangled and explored. He sped up quickly, his groan soft against my lips as he pumped his last.

"Damn," Bryan said weakly, as Camilla dismounted. "I'm not sure I can move."

"No problem. Vixen and I will tend to you both."

She and I went to the bathroom and came back with wet washcloths, cleaning up the guys and us. Then we lay together, breathing hard.

"That was amazing," Leo said. "Can we do this again?"

Bryan nodded. "Please?"

Camilla and I looked at one another, then smiled together.

THE END

SWEET HOT BUNS

A trip to the local store for baking supplies turns racy, when John the dominant invites himself to the freshly single Karen's home for a taste of some hot, sweet buns.

SWEET HOT BUNS

amn it, why did I wear the sequin underwear today, of all days? Karen adjusted her faded jeans, grimacing at the scratchy feeling of the sequins against her upper thighs. *Whomever designed this at Victoria's Secret should be fired.*

You know why, you were trying to impress John. Great job there, he didn't even notice, he only looked at the books you were returning, to make sure they were all there. Karen dejectedly picked up a bag of flour, then grabbed some sugar. A slight burning sensation slipped across the back of her neck. With an irritated sigh, she put the sugar in her cart, then slipped off her sweatshirt. Carefully, she reached up to the black lacy band around the back of her neck, and flipped over the clasp, so it wasn't rubbing against her neck. She lifted it slightly, slid her fingers under the two bra straps, straightening them so they lay flat again against her neck and bosom. *Ahh...*

"Ahem!"

Startled, Karen whipped around to see an old couple staring at her, the man's eyes wide, the woman's disapproving. With a forced smile, Karen hurried out of their way and down the aisle. She stopped near a clothes rack, rubbing her eyes.

Of all days to wear the black lace backless bondage bra, I had to pick today, when I'm running a lot of errands. Good move again, Karen. She angrily consulted her list, then headed to the checkout line.

All of the normal checkout lines were two deep, the customer's carts filled to overflowing. With a sigh, Karen moved to the self-checkout lines, and began going through her items. She'd only got to the second item when the machine began to beep incessantly, the computer screen flashing. In desperation, Karen looked around, but there was only one attendant, and he was already busy helping another woman and her two crying toddlers to weigh what looked like a several pounds of produce.

Karen closed her eyes. This is the worst day. *My boyfriend's dumped me for a toothpick "mean girl," the price of all my groceries went up again, I'm wearing underwear that's both chafing and ineffective, and I've got a defective self-checkout machine. No more, please.*

"Hi there. Sorry you had to wait."

Karen opened her eyes to see that the attendant was tapping various keys on her screen. He cleared the error, then began scanning her items. Karen let him and began bagging groceries.

"Todd, what are you doing?"

The attendant and Karen turned. A man in a shirt and tie with a stern expression was coming towards them.

"I told you before not to bag groceries in self-checkout."

"Sorry. I forgot."

"Please get back to your post, there's another problem at Checkout two."

Todd hurried away. Karen bit her lip, ignored the manager, and went back to bagging her groceries, hurrying as fast as she could. Suddenly, to her absolute horror, the snap clasp of the bondage lace bra gave way, her breasts threatening to spill out.

Oh My GOD! Karen folded her arms quickly across her chest, leaning over the self-scanner, flushing crimson.

Before she had time for full-fledged-panic, she felt two hands grasp the lace straps, yank upwards, then a quick snap. Breathing hard, Karen turned to stare at the manager, who looked away.

"Thanks," she stammered. *Hey, he's really cute. Thick hair ... and a wonderful ass.*

"You might want to secure that with duct tape out in public," he replied.

He was implying the top was too small. Thoroughly embarrassed, Karen grabbed her purse and ran out of the store. She made it to her car and was fumbling with her car keys when the manager caught up to her.

"Hey, wait a minute, miss. You forgot your groceries."

"They aren't mine, I didn't pay for them." She got into her car and tried to close the door.

"Please stop. I think you're beautiful."

Of all the things he could have said ... I wasn't expecting that. Karen stopped trying to close the door and looked up at the man. *Average height. Warm brown eyes, with a hint of blue. Cute dimples when he smiles.* "Do you make it a habit of following women to their cars?"

"Only the ones I help with bra malfunctions," he replied, laughing. "I was happy to help, by the way. If I hadn't been on the clock, I would have been honored to use my hands while you refastened the strap yourself."

No one had ever said things like this to Karen. *I thought this kind of offer to hook up with a guy this hot only happened to popular girls?* "I'll bet you would. But who says I want your hands on my breasts?"

"I was hoping you would," the man said with a grin. "I'm John, by the way."

"I'm Karen."

"I've got to get back to the store," John said apologetically. "Please come back in, if you would. I have your order waiting for you."

Screw it. I always dreamed of flirting with a stranger. Let's see what happens when I call his bluff. "I can't go back in there, John. I've got to go take off my underwear, which is sequined and chafing my ass. But tell you what, you bring my order to my place tonight, and you can touch more than my breasts. I'll let you ride the whole carousel."

John's mouth fell open, to Karen's absolute delight, but he recovered quickly. "You're on. But you were going to bake something, from your ingredients. Are you sure it can wait?"

"I was making cinnamon buns. But don't worry, you can help me later tonight."

"You're on. When and where?"

Karen hastily scribbled her cell number on a piece of paper. "Text me about six tonight, and I'll send you the address."

That afternoon, after removing the offending underwear, Karen got more and more nervous about her daring behavior as she waited for six to come. Cleaning house in preparation for John's visit, she kept thinking *so what if I don't know him? I haven't ever done anything like this, and I want to. Besides, I know where he works, and people saw us together, he can't be a serial killer or anything. And he isn't going to rape me, because I'm up for anything he wants to try, even if it's something kinky.*

K aren spooned out one of the fresh buns, the soft outer layer tearing a bit, the filling steaming slightly The scent of warm cinnamon suffused the air. She grabbed a ladle and drizzled icing over the top, then handed it to him. "Give it a try."

"That is so erotic," he sighed.

Taken aback but pleased, Karen smiled and flushed. "So how is it?"

"This is orgasmic," he said, eating the bun in big spoonfuls, and scraping the plate.

"Want another?"

"Later," he said, grabbing Karen by her belt loops. "I want to see the rest of that black lace bra. I'm so glad you're still wearing it for me."

Carefully, Karen pulled off her flour stained shirt to reveal a deep V-neck bra made entirely of black lace, except for the straps that crisscrossed her ample cleavage.

John slid two fingers inside the center straps, caressing the curve of her breast with the ends of his fingers. "Very pretty." He slid his fingers in further, sliding them back and forth over her nipple. Instantly the tip hardened, the bud showing through the lace. John moved his hand back, then slid in into her bra, cupping her breast fully in his hand as he kissed her, his mouth opening hungrily on hers. Karen clung to him, submitting to his intrusion, welcoming his tongue as he tasted her.

"I like it," John murmured. "But I need to feel your breast in my mouth. Right now."

The stove beeped.

"Just let me put this next batch in—"

"No." John turned off the stove. Taking her by the nipple, he led her into the bedroom, even as she protested.

"I need to finish baking—"

"No. You said you'd be done at eight. I'm a patient man, but a deal's a deal."

"You're being unreasonable."

"And you're being insubordinate. You know what that means." John unbuttoned her jeans, slid them down to bare her curvaceous ass, and pulled her roughly across his lap. He brought his hand down hard across the soft skin of her left cheek.

"Ouch! Hey! You said you wanted buns!"

"And I do." John cupped her reddened cheek possessively, then rubbed it, his hand sliding down between her legs to cup her thatch. With a swift manipulation of his fingers, he penetrated her then stroked her, her body jerking over his as she twisted side to side. "Shh. I know you're not ready. I can help with that. Please stand up and take off your clothes."

Karen stood, but made no effort to disrobe.

"Please take off your clothes. Put on the velvet top I brought with me."

"I'm embarrassed."

"Disobedience deserves punishment. Please, do as I ask."

Karen paused a moment longer, then grabbed the red velvet top, sliding it over her head. Then she grabbed the bra, unhooking it and pulling it off with relief. She took off the rest of her clothes, then went to stand beside the bed, nervous but eager.

John came up behind her, his hands sliding up her body, his left hand again caressing her breast, circling the nipple so it budded tightly against his palm. He dipped his head, sucking and tonguing the sweet flesh, as Karen cried out repeatedly. Then he turned his attention to her right breast, until that was as taut as its twin.

"I love this velvet, you know why?" he murmured in her ear. "Because I love reaching in and touching you, the way you move when I touch you intimately. You're different like this, you're free. None of the hesitancy you show when you're clothed, none of the shame."

Karen rubbed back against him with her ass, feeling the hard prong of his shaft.

John let out a groan. "I love the feel of velvet against my cock, of it shifting back and forth. It makes me think of your body, how good you'll feel when I slide in."

Karen pushed back against him, hoping he would enter her. But John only sighed, then took her across his knee again.

"No, wait!"

With a resounding slap, his hand came down again on her bare ass.

"Stop!"

"You waited to obey me," John whispered. "You know better. That means a spanking, Karen." Thwack!

"I'm embarrassed!"

"You have nothing to be embarrassed of." Thwack!

"Stop! Stop!" Karen writhed, protesting, but the spanking continued. She finally relaxed and went limp, weeping softly.

John stopped, then hugged her. "Tell me why you didn't obey me."

"Because I don't think I look good."

"What do you mean?"

"I'm … I'm big."

John kissed her lips lightly. "Nonsense. Your figure is lush and full and beautiful. I love your curves, I love looking at them." He patted her bottom. "Please, stand in front of me."

Karen did as he asked, wiping away tears.

"You're beautiful," John whispered as he slowly ran his hands over her body. "Every part of you is beautiful. Please, say it, Karen. Believe it."

"I'm beautiful."

John pulled the neckline of the red top down to bare her breasts, then pulled a golden string with two loops out of his pocket. "Hold still, my lovely one."

"What are those?"

"Nipple loops." He affixed one loop around each nipple, then pulled the string at its center towards him. The loops tightened on her nipples almost painfully.

Karen cried out. "Ah!"

"Yes, that's just perfect," he murmured, his mouth dipping again to taste her nipple. Then he moved back, giving a light jerk on the string. "Come."

"Ah!"

Carefully, John led Karen to the bed. "Get on your knees."

She did as he asked, then sat down.

"No." He jerked the string. "On your knees."

Karen exhaled quickly, then knelt.

John quickly disrobed and put on a condom. Karen thought he would take her from behind, but instead he knelt in front of her, kissing her neck. Abruptly, he pushed his body close to hers, his chest smacking the nipple rings, sending a fresh torturous tingling through her body down to her groin.

"Oh!"

"Oh yes." John lay back slowly, pulling Karen astride him. Again, she thought he would enter her. But instead he pulled her up farther, onto his chest. "Spread your legs"

Karen did as he asked, tentatively. Aggressively, John forced her legs apart, then pulled her groin onto his face. He began licking and sucking at her clit.

Karen went limp, moaning as she thrust lightly onto his face. But a sharp tug on the string brought her up immediately, her back arching. "AHHH!"

"Mount me, Sweet Buns, you're certainly ready for my shaft now."

Breathing hard, Karen scooted backwards, then pushed onto his burgeoning erection, settling it within her with an eager sigh.

Thwack! John slapped her ass, making the flesh jiggle deliciously. "Now work for your orgasm."

Karen began moving, her desire to come undeniable. Yet as she came close to cresting the wave, a jerk on the string broke her rhythm, leaving her gasping. Her nipples were now aching with blood, bright red and swollen. She stopped moving, uncertain.

Thwack! "I said work for your orgasm!"

Again, Karen began moving. This time the orgasm was closer, and she almost was there when John again jerked the string, breaking her concentration.

"Please," she whimpered.

Thwack! "Move that lovely ass," John commanded.

Again Karen began rocking, John's hard cock slipping and sliding inside her, teasing her swollen clit. This time the orgasm was so close she could taste it when the jerk of the nipple string broke her climax. With a ragged whimper, she stopped, tears leaking from her eyes.

"Shh, shh," John said softly. "God, You're so beautiful, Karen."

"I'm not," she sniffled.

Thwack! "Say it!"

"I'm beautiful," she managed, swallowing hard.

"You are stunning," John crooned, gently cupping her swollen tender breasts. "Magnificent." He rubbed the nipples, making her scream when his fingers touched their now ultra-sensitive tips. Carefully, he loosened the loops, then began to massage her breasts with his hands as he thrust up gently in rhythm.

Karen had only a few moments before the orgasm hit, one so strong she found herself screaming at the top of her lungs. She'd no sooner finished then John lifted her off him, and pulled her onto her knees, quickly taking up position behind her. He spread her legs and slipped his cock inside. Grasping a breast in each hand, he began pumping hard, squeezing her still sensitive nipples so hard she cried out. He came with a guttural roar, then hugged her tight.

Wow. Karen lay panting, trying to get her mind around what had just happened.

"I loved being with you," John whispered gently.

"I loved it too," she replied. "I have to tell you ... I've never done anything like this before. Not even remotely like this."

John chuckled. "Neither have I."

Karen turned to him and made a face. "You seemed to know all the right things to say. This can't be your first time."

"I've been with one other girl," John said hesitantly, his surety gone. "She taught me some bondage stuff. But she wanted to dominate me. It's hard to find a submissive."

"Is that what I am, a submissive?"

"My submissive," John said affectionately. "Please tell me that this wasn't just something to make your boyfriend jealous."

"I don't have a boyfriend."

"Then who was the lace bra and sequins for?" John said, his tone almost a growl.

"My ex, who left me for a thinner popular girl," Karen said bitterly, running her hands through her tangled hair. "He got the rest of his things today."

"Good," John said, hugging her. "Because I want you all to myself, Karen."

"We just met, nipple rings non-withstanding," Karen quipped. "You don't know me enough to want me all to yourself."

"I know you're beautiful, sexy, funny, adventuresome, intelligent, and can bake amazingly," he said, kissing her cheek. "You're someone I want to know, and spend time with, in and out of bed." He gave her another passionate kiss. "So are you free this weekend?"

Karen batted her eyes at him. "Yes ... master."

THE END

THE TAMING OF THE SUBMISSIVE

When recent widow Desiree refuses to take alpha vampire Devlin's no for an answer, he enlists his descendent Cain to teach the aggressive female a few lessons in manners. But Cain needs a lesson as well in behavior, and Desiree is just the woman to educate him ... with a little help from Devlin.

THE TAMING OF THE SUBMISSIVE

"You're going to enjoy this. Sign here."

Desiree looked up into the sapphire eyes of the platinum-tressed blonde woman, and smiled, even as she thought to herself, *I'm not so sure.*

The contract was one page, and basically said that she was participating of her own free will, that she would not share identities or talk about went on behind closed doors. She printed her name on the signature line deliberately, then handed it to the woman. The woman took it without looking at it and put it in a file, then showed them into a room down the hall. "Please have a seat anywhere you like. Someone will join you shortly. Enjoy," she said, leaving the room with a sharp clack of her stiletto heels.

"Are you sure you want to do this?" her husband Robert asked for the fifth time, nervously eyeing the king-size bed heaped with pillows, the overstuffed loveseat, and two sofas.

Desiree looked over at him, sighing inwardly. That he didn't want her to do this was obvious. But she wanted to know a little bit about how sex would be with other men. Her husband was loving and good, but he wanted to have sex in the same way every time and wasn't into experimentation. Desiree hadn't been when they married, but the older she had gotten the more she wondered what else there was. Reading a few erotica books her husband had gotten her for a present had sparked a desire to discover information for herself … firsthand. Then she had seen an ad about this company, Sexual Joy, online. It had been the only one within driving distance, so she'd shown the ad to her husband. Who had reluctantly agreed to come with her today to a consult.

A short man with dark hair walked into the room in a bathrobe. He was well groomed, smiling, and friendly. But there was also something smarmy about him that put Desiree off immediately. "You're just as beautiful as your name, Desiree," he said teasingly. He offered his hand to her. "I'm Colt."

What kind of a name was Colt? This man sure hadn't been born to it, unless his mother had given it to him for his awkwardness as a child. "Good to meet you."

Another man walked in, from his looks Colt's younger brother. "This is Dagger," Colt said. The new man also was wearing a bathrobe.

Desiree was suddenly uneasy. If she were reading an erotic story—or anywhere but physically here—she'd be laughing at these two obvious wanna-bes. But they were obviously going to be her partners today.

"I'm going to touch your leg," Colt said gently. "We don't want to rush you, Desiree. We'll progress as you tell us it's okay." He reached out and lightly touched her knee through her jeans. Desiree didn't jump.

"Good," Colt said, giving her a caress before taking his hand back. "Now if you'll remove your top, we'll begin."

"And what if I don't want to?" Desiree challenged, her normal fiery nature rising up. "Are you going to make me?"

Colt visibly moved back as if cowed. "Of course not," he murmured. "This isn't bondage. We're all willing participants here." He turned to her husband. "Sir, you're welcome to remove your clothes, or stay dressed, depending on how involved you want to me." He smiled. "Voyeurs are completely respected here, if you prefer only to watch."

Her husband shifted in his chair, then stood up. "I'll wait outside," he said stiffly, then walked out.

Colt stood up. "I'll be right back," he said, following her husband out. Desiree watched him go, torn, wanting to tell Robert that he didn't have to leave. But if only this slight touching bothered him, what would he feel like when she was naked?

Another man entered—another lookalike with dark hair who announced his name was Cloak. *Cloak and Dagger? Where was Bullet for Colt, then?* Desiree had to stifle her immediate urge to laugh. Without any more talking, both men disrobed. Neither was visibly aroused, though Dagger began playing with himself as he looked at her. Desiree looked away, and began to undress, her uncertainty growing. She took off her top and her bra, then sat there, feeling cold in her nakedness and not at all sexy. *Was this really what she had come here for? This didn't feel like a fantasy. It felt sordid and tawdry. What if they were recording this? There had been nothing in the contract about that.*

"You don't have to hide," Dagger said nicely. "You're voluptuous, Beautiful."

Automatically, Desiree went to answer, "No, I'm fat." But her words died on her lips as she beheld his tiny penis, barely the width of her pinky finger. She hadn't known penises existed that were that small.

Colt came back in, then shut the door. He also disrobed, and then sat down in front of her. His penis was erect, as were the other two other shafts in the room now.

Too many penises at once, Desiree thought, *even with that teeny one. This is just too much.*

"Now," Colt said nicely. "Why don't you—"

"No," Desiree said, gathering her bra. She put it on, then pulled her top over her head. "I'm going now."

"Wait," Colt sputtered. "You can't—"

"I can," Desiree said loftily. "This isn't what I had in mind. Sorry to all of you and thank you for your time. This just isn't for me." She walked out.

"I'm sorry I left," her husband apologized, as they walked to their car. "But I couldn't watch them touch you."

"I didn't want them to touch me," she replied, grabbing his hand in hers. "I had a fantasy and thought this was what I wanted. But it wasn't." She smirked. "I know it's kind of mean, but there was no way they were going to be able to give me what I wanted, no matter what they said or did."

"Good," her husband said. "Because I might be willing to make a stop on our way home." He winked at her. "That is, if you want to."

Desiree looked over at him with bedroom eyes. Hope mixed with lust rose up within her chest. *Please let this not be fantasy. Let this be real.* "Change your mind?"

He nodded. "I talked a bit to that woman who signed us in, and she had some good advice. If you want this, I want you to be happy," he said. "Let's go."

Desiree folded the last of Tom's shirts and put it in the box for the Salvation Army. *How had ten years passed so fast?* Joyfully for the most part. *And sexual in the extreme.*

That long ago stop at the adult bookstore had broadened Desiree's horizons in all kinds of pleasurable ways. With the assistance of the woman called only "Sin", Tom had discovered how to be a top to Desiree's bottom. Sin had also helped Desiree too, in introducing her to the fun of costumes and toys. Tom and Desiree had attended what Sin referred to as "couples training," learning some of the ins and outs of adult toys, bondage games, and role-playing. She'd enjoyed all of the bedroom fun, and it had brought she and Tom close in ways they hadn't expected. *Then had come the sudden heart attack.*

There was a knock at the door.

Must be more flowers. The wake isn't until Saturday. Desiree hurried to the front door and opened it. Strangely, there was a man on the stoop, standing there in the rapidly deepening twilight, one she knew very well. "Devlin!"

"Enchante, Desiree," Devlin said, giving her a slight bow. He offered her a dozen white roses. "I've come to pay my respects, if you'd be so kind as to invite me in."

"Of course," Desiree said, opening the door. "You are always welcome here."

The tall, blond, handsome man strode in, heading for the kitchen. She followed him, unsure of his motivation. He had grabbed a kitchen knife in one hand and was rummaging around under the sink with the other.

"If you're looking for a vase, I keep them in the cupboard here," she said, moving to the left of the refrigerator, and bringing one out to hand to him.

"My mistake," he replied. "Please, allow me to put them in some water for you."

Desiree handed Devlin the flowers, and he carefully trimmed the stems under water, then arranged them in a vase. "There you are, my dear."

"Thank you for coming," Desiree said, taking them, and putting them on the kitchen table. "I'm afraid I have nothing to offer you."

"It is I who have something to offer you," Devlin said, baring one sharp fang in a faint smile.

"Always teasing," Desiree bantered back with a flirtatious smile. "As if I haven't known you were a vampire for these last ten years."

"Yes, I hadn't planned to have you walk in on one of my feedings during your wedding. But your bridesmaid was too attractive to resist," Devlin said, not at all embarrassed.

"Maid of Honor, you mean, though I'm guessing she wasn't by dawn. Caprise enjoyed the night and you did as well. It was a surprise, but not a bad one."

"Very true," Devlin said, looking at his hands as he steepled them. "But I'm not here to tease, my dear." His honey-colored eyes flicked up to stare into hers. "I am here tonight to make you an offer."

Desiree's mouth fell open, because knowing Devlin, he could only mean one thing. "Tom just died, Devlin. My God, you're ballsy."

Devlin knitted his brow, then cast a baleful look down his nose at her. "For Tom's company, my dear, not your virtue. Treeline Services will fit nicely with my other companies, and I wanted to make an offer to step in to take over before clients get too worried that their current contracts won't be fulfilled. And before your two employees find other jobs with the competition."

"You're still ballsy," Desiree repeated. "I haven't made any decisions about Treeline yet."

"So I've been told," Devlin replied. "I take that as a compliment. In any case, you and Tom have been friends of mine for a decade, Tom for twice that. I want to help."

"You want to help yourself, you mean," Desiree said scathingly, her eyes narrowing. "I know what kind of man you are, Devlin, and the kind of things you're into. I—"

"Really?" Devlin said, standing in a fluid motion. "What kind of things am I into?" He was at her side in an instant, glaring at her.

"The kind who makes deals with the mafia, demons, and anyone else he needs to get business done," she replied, not backing down.

"Correct," Devlin said, baring his fangs in a wide smile. "As was your husband. Which is why we were acquaintances."

"How dare you!" Desiree cried. She took the vase of flowers and threw it at him. Devlin ducked, the glass vase shattering against the wall, showering them both with water, glass, and lush white rose petals.

There was a shifting of the blackness in the living room, and another man stepped into the light, his black hair shaggy, his tanned skin like leather. While neither the gun nor the knife he wore at his belt was in his hands, an unspeakable air of menace came off him like an invisible but deadly cloud. Desiree stopped still, her eyes wide.

Devlin took a large envelope from his jacket and left it on the table. He moved to the dark man's side. "Take a look at Treeline's books, Desiree. Then sign this contract and give me a call. But don't wait too long. I can't help you, once the authorities are involved. Adieu."

Devlin left, his silent man in tow.

Desiree wept, then began cleaning up the mess.

A week later, Desiree drove to Devlin's sprawling country estate, Hayden. She was stopped at the gates, the dark man himself standing in her way, other guards at his back.

"Let me in," she said.

The dark man grinned. "Sorry, you don't have clearance."

He sounds like he's lisping ... or hissing. Is he a vampire as well? "How do I get clearance?"

"Dev's got to give permission."

"Look, he was right, okay? I'm ready to sign over Treeline to him."

The dark man nodded once slightly, then looked at his guards. "Search her. Then escort her to Hayden."

D esiree walked around the perimeter of the decadent gold ballroom for the third time, her spike heels in her hand, fuming. *Tom, why didn't you tell me? And Dev, why are you such an asshole?*

"My apologies," Devlin said, coming in and closing the doors behind him. "My night hours are usually full from dusk to dawn. But Lash tells me you are here ready to sign."

"I found more than five hundred thousand dollars in proceeds that I have no record of making," Desiree admitted. "The money is in several accounts under Treeline's name, including CDs. Those come due in a few weeks."

"Tom planned the money for a retirement fund, from what he shared with me," Devlin mused. "Which can be arranged with a series of transactions, once I assume control." He offered her a thick document with the back page turned over the front with several SIGN HERE stickers affixed. "Please skim this, but you'll see it's the same document I left at your home. Sign it, and I will take care of everything."

Desiree carefully skimmed each page, then satisfied, she signed it. She handed it back, with another envelope. "I signed the copy you brought me also."

"Very good," Devlin said. "As you can see, fifty percent of the proceeds from the company will continue to go to you, and fifty to me. But I will take care of all the decisions. You will sign whatever I need you to sign, when the occasion will arise. The first year, I may need you to come monthly to Hayden and meet with me, to transfer authority successfully. After that, I will need your presence here approximately four times a year, or quarterly. Is that understood?"

Damn, the man is dominating. "Agreed, so long as it's not illegal … which this has to be, right?"

Devlin sighed. "At risk to myself, I will share information with you. But it is not to leave this room. Is that understood?"

"Yes."

"Tom—and Treeline—went into business to cut commercial timber, but locally, there's not a lot of timber left here in New York to cut in big pieces, except on state land. Tom knew that. He bought land and he began planting fast growing trees, but also loaned himself out for cutting private lands, until he could build up enough land and timber of his own to support a family. He hadn't met you then." Devlin paused. "Because he was a small operation, he was approached by a group of people that wanted him to grow them some specific timber for regular harvest on their own land."

"Christmas trees?"

"Yew and hawthorn trees. Sometimes oak. Stake trees, grown on hidden lots that are protected from my non-human associates quite well."

"You've got to be kidding."

"I'm afraid the problem was a serious one," Devlin said darkly, frowning. "I was almost staked once. I do not want it to happen again. So once the vampire hunters' deal with Tom was made, I contacted him. And offered double what he was making growing the trees for them if he would let a few of my associates onto his jobsites as his crews to dose the trees that were set to one day be stakes."

"Dose them how? With what? To make them ineffective?"

"Ineffective against me," Devlin amended deliberately vaguely. "I have someone who arranged a spell of sorts. Magic is very real, in spite of what you might believe, Desiree."

"So … this isn't illegal," she said slowly.

"No. I'm paying you for a service that's completely legal. But it must be kept hidden, or the hunters will go elsewhere for their weapons. Once burned, so to speak, they might decide to grow their own wood trees, something that could prove deadly for me. That money you mentioned was Tom's kickback for keeping my secret."

"I'm … I'm sorry," Desiree stammered.

"It was an honest mistake," Devlin said with a gesture of understanding. "Just don't question me again."

"I have a better idea," Desiree said brazenly. "From now on, why don't you just pay the going rate for the timber you need to process in a yearly cash payment, off the books? Those few thousand dollars can be used as petty cash. There will be no need for any more elaborate schemes."

"Why would you give up the extra money?" Devlin questioned, his brows again knitted. "It's pure profit that I will ensure is hidden successfully, as part of our deal."

"Because I want something else," Desiree said.

"And what is that?"

"You."

Devlin's eyes widened, then he laughed richly, the melodious sound rippling through Desiree like a wave of seductive sensation. "Now it is you that must be joking."

"Not at all. If Tom was in bed with you on this deal, I'll guess he was sharing other secrets with you, too. I don't have my alpha male anymore, Devlin. I know your type well, even though I don't especially like you. It's obvious that you can give me something I've always wanted."

"And what is that?"

"A complete seduction. You're an alpha, Devlin. Don't deny it."

Devlin grinned widely, then bared his fangs and laughed again. "I will not deny it, my feisty little Spanish flower, I embrace it fully. But while turning you over my knee would give me no greater pleasure at this moment, I must regretfully decline."

"What?" Desiree sputtered.

"I'm otherwise engaged," Devlin said. "As in not available for dalliances. I also try not to mix business with pleasure, as it usually results in disaster, in my long experience. Otherwise I would take the deal in a heartbeat, my dear. I apologize, but I cannot."

Desiree walked out, her face flaming. As she was escorted back to her car, her one burning thought was that she would find a way to change Devlin's mind.

———

Over the course of the next six months, Desiree was summoned to Hayden each month to sign papers at Devlin's behest. When she came, she always did as she was bidden, signing whatever papers Devlin handed to her. But each time she also tried to provoke a response.

The first few months it was sexy clothes, from plunging necklines and spike heels to finally a leather dominatrix dress with panels that left her ass on display. But all Devlin said was "You tempt me to spank you, naughty Spanish flower. But you will not break my resolve."

The next few months it was suggestive touches coupled with Desiree's quick retreat with an evocative smile. But that also got no response, until in June, Desiree finally made an aggressive grab for Devlin's genitals. She connected briefly enough to have her eyes widen at the hefty prize he was packing, before he tossed her hand aside, his expression cold. "You are never to touch me unless I invite you." He began gathering the signed papers.

"Which you'll never do," Desiree said spitefully. "You've already said as much!"

"Actually, I am free now," Devlin said with a grin, evening the papers up with his hands. "You might say I've given up on my lady, for now."

Hope rose in Desiree.

Devlin's eyes narrowed cruelly. "I smell your hope. Cast it out, dear one. You've already proven yourself unworthy of my sexual attentions with your blatant and desperate attempts."

Fury filled Desiree, and she grabbed hold of Devlin's sport coat, ripping the thin shiny material clear down the seam. Unprepared for her sudden attack, he tried to fend her off, the papers scattering across the floor.

"Bastard!" she screeched, trying to claw his eyes.

Strong arms suddenly restrained her, and she was hauled off Devlin forcibly, and unceremoniously dumped on the floor. "I see why you called," a melodious voice said.

"Punish her, Cain," Devlin growled out. "Thoroughly. Desiree has been much too long without discipline."

"I'll have her back to being submissive," Cain said. "You have my word."

"Good." Devlin left without another word.

Embarrassed as she was, Devlin's exchange with the new man Cain had sent a shiver of excitement through her.

"Stand," Cain said sharply. It was not a request, but a command.

Desiree's first impulse was to sit still, to resist. But reluctantly she stood, her eyes still on the floor.

Cain took her hand. "Walk with me."

The couple walked out of the ballroom and into a long hallway, then into one of the rooms. The room was a peaceful green color, the bed linens and curtains matching, the furniture gleaming hardwood.

Desiree's lip trembled, as she went over to the headboard. "This is one of Tom's carved pieces," she whispered, running her hand over the smooth wood. She collapsed down on the bed, sobbing.

Cain sat down beside her and held her for a while, as she cried. When her tears ebbed, he brought her a wet warm green washcloth from the adjoining bathroom.

Desiree rubbed it lightly over her face. "God, I've been an idiot."

"Yes, to put it mildly," Cain agreed. "You taunted a person you should not have. Devlin is an alpha, but he's also a sadist, and he's going through … a rough period."

Desiree bit her lip.

"He does not fuck where he does business, to put it plainly," Cain went on. "Say now that you will make no more advances."

Desiree didn't answer.

"Say it," Cain hissed angrily.

"I won't make any more advances."

"Good. I will punish you, as I told him. As he remarked, you have been too long without discipline." Cain stood and took off his coat, laying it aside. "I am going to spank you now, Desiree. You are not served by my being permissive. I must show you definitively and with absolute surety the rules of what is permitted, and what is not. Lay across my knees. Now."

His dictated words, so much like Tom's had once been, prompted obedience. Desiree did as he said, lying across his knees. Her outfit of the evening was of all things, the dominatrix leather dress with holes in the back, letting her buttocks peep through.

"Very good choice," Cain said approvingly. "The better to make you see the error of your ways." The first crack of his hand slapping onto her ass cheeks brought a scream from her lips … and an inner sigh of utter relief.

"The punctuation you give each of my reminders will serve to remind you of the penalty for disobedience. I want to hear your cries. Begin."

Cain spanked Desiree until her cheeks were flaming red and sore, and her throat was hoarse from her screams. Within, she was exhausted, the tight spring coiled inside her for months finally unwound and free of tension. *Ahhhhhhh …*

"Stand up," Cain commanded.

Desiree hurried at once to stand, carefully easing her weight onto her feet, wincing as the edges of the holes in the dress chafed against her chapped buttocks.

"Here is my card with my number," Cain said, slipping a piece of paper into her hand. "You will call me as soon as you have recovered. Is that understood?"

"Yes."

"I will come to your home after obtaining the address from Devlin. If you do not call in seventy-two hours, I'll show up and discipline you then and there, in front of anyone else who might be there at the time. Is that understood?"

"Yes."

"If you are not at your home, I will enlist Devlin's man Lash to track you down, come to wherever you are—restaurant, movie, someone's party, another country—and remind you of who your new master is in public view. Is that understood?"

Desiree tried unsuccessfully to keep the eagerness out of her reply. "Yes."

"Very good," Cain said approvingly. He walked her to the front door of Hayden, then kissed her chastely on the lips. "I look forward to seeing you again. Travel safe."

Desiree carefully collected her purse and coat, then made her way to her car. The drive home was a painful one, every movement of her legs causing agony in her chapped bottom. *And yet ... there's a release, too. It's as if all the stress of the last months and Tom's passing has finally been eased. I'm no longer alone, and I know what I need to do.*

Desiree was waiting for Cain when he arrived in three days, just as he said he would. His face was thunderous as he all but ran up the path, but when she opened the door clad in her proper French maid's uniform, he nodded approvingly.

After she let him in and locked the door, she served him a glass of wine in a crystal glass on a silver platter.

Once he had sipped, he nodded to her. "I see you're in a reasonable mood, Desiree. Please, sit with me, and let's discuss how best to serve your needs."

Desiree sat in the large overstuffed chair across from Cain. "I'm not sure what to say, Cain. I guess I got used to Tom—my late husband—taking charge of me. At first, I wasn't sure that I liked it, because I'd always been pretty dominating myself in bed. He'd just sort of gone along with me, when we started. But over time he got more into it, until he really liked punishing me. And I discovered that I liked being punished. When he died ... I just didn't know what to do. I'd lost not only my lover, but my master, too. I know that sounds stupid, but—"

"No, it doesn't," Cain interrupted. "There's a freedom in utter surrender. You're relinquishing all right to choose, all right to decide on what will happen. Utter trust is given and accepted. You loved your husband, and so the role of submissive was acceptable, especially as he likely encouraged you to act up in preparation for his discipline as a way to ask for it without asking. That is what you were doing with Devlin. He is not in a position to answer you. But I am ... and I will."

A shiver of anticipation went through Desiree. "I take it you have a lot of experience. Are you acquainted with Sin? She is the one who helped Tom and I get started."

Cain nodded. "Sin's a dear friend of mine. I thought you might know her also, when you thought to dress up in that outfit, complete with good wine."

Desiree flushed happily. She forced her mind back to practicality. "Would we be exclusive? You're very handsome Cain, and forceful. I don't expect you're currently without a partner."

Cain set his glass down with a sigh. "I am, now. I wasn't before. I would have come a month ago when Devlin asked me, but for that. But Vic ... she's taken up with one of my other friends, which happens all too often."

Desiree's hopes deflated like a week-old leftover party balloon. "Are you intimate with your friends? I'm looking for one master to serve, Cain."

"I would not share you," Cain said affectionately, patting her hand. "It's very rare to find a submissive that's been trained well, Desiree, especially one that knows the dance between dom and sub. If after a few sessions you want to be exclusive, I will happily give you that promise."

One hurdle down. "And are you safe to be intimate with? You mentioned that Devlin was a sadist."

"I am not a sadist," Cain replied. "A true submissive is never safer than in the hands of a true dominant, because both know where the power of the dance truly lies. But I'll not ask you to believe that, Desiree.

In terms of physically: I will use protection, until there comes a time—or not—that you ask me not to because we make other arrangements. I don't usually use handcuffs, and the knots we'll use will be ones you can untie easily, if you have the will to." He kissed her hand gently. "It's my job to make sure that you won't have the will, my dear."

"Our safe word is red. You agree that you will stop with no hesitation?"

"Yes. I liken the power over another person as to being given a gun. Terrible power to destroy or harm, irreparably, if misused. A true dominant understands the enormous responsibility he has to his submissive and is utterly careful not to shatter what is by necessity a gift."

"So you will not expect me to take everything you think of and automatically like it?"

"No, of course not." Cain chuckled. "A skilled dominant can read their lover's fantasy, know how far to go, and what to play, just like a violin string. And what lines not to cross."

"You're saying you can read my fantasy? Tell me what I want."

"You want me to seduce you here, tonight. Which I will do. You are trained well as a submissive, but you've got enough will and passion to initiate play, which is very unusual. I'm so glad that Devlin called me. It's my regret I didn't come sooner to take you in hand."

"Perhaps I should punish you," Desiree quipped.

"No more wine for you," Cain pronounced harshly. "Come here and sit on my lap."

Desiree went to him and sat on his knee.

Cain reached up under her many layered lace skirts and slid his fingers between her legs. But her legs were firmly closed.

"Open your legs. Now."

Desiree trembled slightly, then opened her legs. She drew in a quivering breath as Cain touched her intimately, his fingers gently exploring her wet thatch of hair, and the soft swollen lips of her womanhood.

Cain kissed her throat, then hurriedly unbuckled his belt, freeing his cock. The lengthy organ was already swollen and thick, the tip leaking semen.

"Sit beside me for a moment, as I ready myself to take you," Cain instructed. "And slip down your top to expose your breasts."

Desiree smiled faintly, her eyes still downcast. Carefully she moved the lace bodice of her outfit down under her breasts, the material lifting the soft globes so that they stood out, her nipples already tight with lust.

Cain rolled a condom down on his cock, then beckoned to Desiree. She slipped astride him, careful not to let him enter her.

"Hold still," he growled. He carefully entered her with the tip of his immense throbbing cock, then stopped, pulling her close, his mouth licking and sucking at her breasts, kissing, and fondling them. The sensations after so long being unfilled filled her with yearning, and she bore down, eager to feel Cain fully sheathed inside her.

The slap of his hand onto her ass brought her back to reality with a cry.

"Not yet," Cain murmured, tonguing her left nipple. "I want to really enjoy you, before I take you for my own."

"Please," Desiree whimpered. "I've got to have you inside me. I need to feel whole again. The only way I can do that is to please you fully, my master." Her tone changed from submissive to hesitant desire. "You're so thick. I have been good, and done my best to serve you, my master. Please. Please fill me."

Cain slapped her ass lightly. "God, you temptress," he groaned. "Very well. But take me slowly this first time. You will be silent, until I give you permission. Is that understood?"

"Yes, my master."

Desiree eased down on Cain's shaft, his immense size stopping her from quick acceptance. Working steadily, she slid him deeper into her channel, until she abruptly felt him run out of room.

"My favorite part," Cain said gutturally, grasping her hips. "Hold still." He pushed her hips down on his, her body accepting his last few inches with a single grunt. Desiree shuddered slightly at the intense pressure but didn't cry out.

"Very good," Cain said, kissing her deeply on the lips. He began to move slightly, just enough to stimulate her clit as he filled her totally.

Desiree's body was responding at full throttle, her desire to climax a physical need within her clawing at the edges of her reason as she fought to stay silent. With sheer will, she restrained her ardor, her only tell a slight trembling, and the way her lips parted to release each shuddering breath.

"Now you are mine," Cain said possessively, his slight thrusts becoming more rapid. "Call my name, when you come."

Desiree tried to hold off as she'd been taught, but she needed it too much. She came screaming Cain's name over and over, as she clutched him close.

"Desiree! Desiree!" he groaned, jerking suddenly beneath her. He finished, then carefully lay back on the bed, still within her.

"Should I attend to you?" Desiree asked, when they had recovered enough to speak. "I am fit to continue, my master."

"Come," Cain said, offering his hand. "We'll attend to one another. You also need pampering, my dear."

The couple showered together, taking turns in the heat of the spray. Then Desiree helped to towel Cain off.

"You are exceptional," Cain whispered, taking Desiree's hand, and kissing it. "I ask permission to see you twice a week, on whatever days you'll permit."

"Gladly given, my master. I haven't asked, but where do you live? If you couldn't get here on short notice, it must be several states away."

"I travel for business," Cain said. "So I'm often away from home during the week. But where I live can be anywhere. I know Devlin would love me living closer. I'm sorry again for the circumstances that brought us together, even as I'm so happy to have discovered you, Desiree. I can't ask you to leave your home." He smiled and kissed her cheek. "I will begin looking for suitable houses tomorrow, and bring to you any that I find enticing, for your consent. Though I will ask you to wear that dress I discovered you in very soon for me. And perhaps get others of a similar style in both white and red."

"I'm happy to move closer to you as we get closer," she answered, biting at her lip. "As long as its south. If I'm to wear dresses that constantly bare my ass, I need a warmer climate."

"Then it will be so," Cain said, hugging her. "Because I'm never letting you go."

As Cain slept that night holding her close, Desiree lay contented in his arms. But in that peace, thoughts troubled her, unbidden. *Is this moving too fast? While I don't like Devlin, Tom trusted him, and he's done everything he said he would for Treeline and me. He obviously knows Cain well, and wouldn't set me up with someone that would jeopardize the company or our arrangement. Cain seems to be perfect for me, and everything he said was exactly what I was looking for in a partner ... and in a man. I guess I'll go along for now and see where it goes.*

Cain and Desiree's relationship progressed as if it had been perfectly written for them. Cain did move closer within the next month to a suburb an hour north of New York City. The house was a lovely two-story home with three bedrooms set on a few acres. In the following months, Desiree began spending more and more time there, as Cain loved finding her waiting for him on his return from his frequent travelling. But she balked at giving up the freedom of her own home to become the mistress of his without more assurance that their relationship was permanent ... or exclusive.

Cain was everything Desiree wanted in a master. Their times outside of the bedroom were equally satisfying, as they shared a love of fine dining, old epic novels, classic movies, and time at the gym. The only thing that bothered Desiree were Cain's frequent absences. Her response to his weekly requests for her to move in with him was, "What am I supposed to do when you're not here?" His replies, different versions of permission to do whatever made her happy, were met with shakes of her head.

Things came to a head one Friday evening, when Desiree arrived for a weekend with Cain only to find he wasn't there. Fuming, she called him.

"I'm sorry, sweetheart," he apologized. "It was my fault, for not leaving earlier for the airport. I missed my flight. But that turned out to be a good thing, because the client called. He's pissed, I'm going to need to stay an extra day ..."

Desiree stayed silent, seething as she glanced over at the heavy bags of groceries she'd just carried in. *So much for my elaborate welcome home dinner.*

"I know you're upset, and I promise I'll make it up to you tomorrow night. Please, just relax and do something that makes you happy—"

"I will," Desiree said lightly. "Be safe. Goodbye."

She was still standing there a moment later, thinking about all the possible scenarios to punish him, when the doorbell rang.

Desiree answered, to find an attractive couple waiting, the male some relative to Cain's by his close resemblance. "Hi, I'm Jessica and this is Corian," the woman said with a smile.

"Corian," the blond man said, offering his hand. "Cain's half-brother. You must be Desiree. Cain's told me a lot about you." He grinned. "I was sure that Cain wouldn't ever settle down. I'm really glad you tamed his wild spirit."

Have I? "It's great to meet you," Desiree said, holding open the door. "Please come in. I'm sorry, but Cain's held up on business. He won't be home tonight."

"We were just in town for the night and wanted to stop by and see the new place," Jessica added. "I'm sorry we didn't call ahead. Cain's usually out of town more than he's in town, so we thought it was a stretch anyone would be home. I'm very glad to have met you though, Desiree."

"Please come and join me for dinner," Desiree offered. "I was just about to get started. I'd love to hear all the naughty stories you know about Cain."

Jessica, Corian, and Desiree had a great time, the three sharing the cooking and enjoying their efforts with a bottle of wine, as Corian made good on Desiree's wish to hear about his brother's exploits. Finally though, Desiree turned the subject to Jessica. "How did you meet?"

"We met in college," she replied, clasping Corian's hand. "We've been married about a year now. Cain was Corian's best man."

"That celebration must have been something to see," Desiree joked, remembering Devlin's behavior at her wedding long ago. "I'm sure Cain was right in the midst of the rowdiness. Did my bad boy seduce your maid of honor?"

Jessica bit her lip, flushing bright crimson. Corian looked at the floor uncomfortably.

Desiree kept her face neutral with effort. *Cain slept with his brother's bride on their wedding night ... and somehow Corian was okay with it. She's too embarrassed and he's too ill at ease for it to be anything else. Holy shit.*

"We should be going," Corian said, taking Jessica's arm, and pulling her up. "Thank you so much for the great dinner."

The couple left hurriedly amidst a few more murmured thank you's. Desiree murmured goodbyes, then closed the door, leaning on it heavily. *If Cain could dare to bed his brother's wife on their wedding night ... he could dare to do anything. How much longer will it be until he asks one of his friends into our bed? Who is to say he wouldn't have asked tonight, if he'd have been home when Corian and Jessica pulled up?*

As upset as Desiree was, she made herself focus. *Stop having hysterics and think this through. If Cain hasn't changed and he does want another man or couple to join us ... am I okay with that? Tom and I never had anyone else in our bed while we were married, but not by my choice. I did want to try more than one man back then. Cain and I aren't married now, in fact, he hasn't ever said we'd be exclusive, either. He keeps telling me to do whatever makes me happy, that I have his permission. Did Tom tell him of what happened long ago at Joyful Sex? Is this Cain's way of telling me without stating it that he's okay with another man joining us?*

I can't say for sure. But his actions leave a clear path to one possibility that I do desire ... Devlin.

I know his character, that he's close friends with Cain ... and that he's apparently not spoken for or wasn't a few months ago. I just have to be woman enough to ask ... and submissive enough to ask him in a way he won't refuse.

Desiree picked up the phone, took a deep breath, and began dialing. When it was answered, she gave her name and asked for Devlin.

"Enchante, Desiree," he said pleasantly a few moments later. "And how is life with Cain?"

"Very good. I am calling on his request."

"I see," Devlin stated in a tone that said he did not. "And what does he require?"

"He requires nothing. He asked me to extend an invitation to you to join us at a date of your choosing for ..." Desiree thought frantically. "... a formal apology."

"There is no need for that," Devlin said smoothly, though a different tone—*interest?*—was in his words. "I understand from him that you are well in hand now, and that both of you are happy. That makes me very happy."

Entice him. "Yes, we are happy. But I transgressed where I should not. I need to make amends for my offense. Cain also wishes to demonstrate my submissiveness to you, sir." She paused. "For that I must ask as he bids me, if you are available to come, and currently unattached."

Desiree held her breath, knowing Devlin had gotten her extra emphasis on the word "come." There was silence. Desiree fought her urge to fill it and waited.

"What is allowed," Devlin asked in a voice of devilish yearning and dark need. "I am currently unattached, though that situation will not be for much longer; likely within the next week. But I cannot commit without knowing if you will do everything I require of you, Desiree. And that Cain will allow it."

Desiree fidgeted, already excited at the prospect of finally bedding Devlin. *Careful, keep this real, or he will know!* "I cannot speak for my master," Desiree said in a submissive voice, though she was unable to keep her own desire completely concealed. "It is for him to say what is allowed. But be assured I will do everything he allows to the fullest extent, with no hesitation, sir."

"Ahh. You have been well tamed. Tell him then I shall be there tomorrow at dusk. I'm looking forward to seeing the new house. Adieu."

Desiree hung up the phone with trembling fingers. *Tomorrow night it is.*

C ain called on Saturday afternoon from the airport, as Desiree was spot-cleaning the house to prepare for Devlin's arrival. "Don't hang up. I'm sorry again I'm late, sweetheart. I'll be home for a late dinner," Cain said lovingly. "I've really missed you. I've got a surprise for you, Desiree."

I've got a surprise for you, too. "Corian and Jessica came by last night and had dinner with me," Desiree said. "They were very nice, and we had a good time. The stories they told me were very ... captivating." She paused, savoring the moment. "Devlin's also coming by tonight."

"I'm glad you met my half-brother and his wife," Cain said slowly. "Did Devlin say why he was coming over?"

"To see the new house. And to get a formal apology from me," Desiree said carefully. "You gave him your word to tame me, remember? He said to tell you he would arrive at dusk."

"Damn it," Cain swore.

"You never swear," Desiree said, an uneasy feeling spreading through her. "What's wrong?"

"Listen, Devlin is a man of his word," Cain said quickly. "I'm going to get off the phone and go to the customer service here, check again that there's not an earlier connecting flight to get me home before dark. If he arrives before me, just make him comfortable, and ask him to abide by his own laws."

"His own laws?"

"Vampire Law," Cain said quickly, as if naming something official. "Tell him you've given me an oath, and I take it seriously. Do not elaborate. Is that understood?"

What does that mean? "Yes."

"I'll see you soon. Remember what I said."

Desiree put down the phone, her nervousness growing. *What have I done?*

A t dusk, the doorbell rang. Desiree answered it promptly, wearing an authentic peasant style dress in white and red cotton. Devlin was standing there on the stoop, dressed in an expensive red silk suit. A big broad-shouldered man with reddish-skin stood at his shoulder.

"Come back at midnight," Devlin said, as he entered.

The man nodded and vanished. Desiree gaped for a few moments, then shut the door.

"This is a very welcoming home," Devlin said, as he strode into the living room, where a fake fire added cozy ambiance to the deep browns and greens. "I commend your choice of color. I've become quite fond of green these last few months."

"Thank you," Desiree answered. "We chose green in a lot of our rooms, as a reminder to the night we met."

"Please give me a tour," Devlin said, his honey-colored eyes gleaming in the dim light. "Begin here. End in the bedroom."

Desiree took him around the house, showing him all the rooms in the house, until they reached the master bedroom, which was done in blues and greens. "This is beautiful. But this is not Cain's bed," Devlin remarked, touching the carved wood.

"We put our former beds into the guest rooms," Desiree explained.

"Cain and I decided on a bed for us to share together, as a symbol of our commitment."

"That doesn't sound very submissive of you," Devlin said curiously, turning to gaze at her.

"I am submissive in all ways that my master requires," Desiree answered, bowing slightly. "But that is while in bed, not out of it."

"The latter statement is not entirely accurate, but I understand your intended meaning," Devlin replied with a smirk, moving closer. "And where is Cain?"

"Delayed at the airport," Desiree said, casting down her eyes. "He will be here as soon as he can. He instructed me to tell you to abide by your own laws."

"Really," Devlin said with a large grin, baring his fangs. "What laws would those be?"

"Vampire Law," Desiree said quickly. "He said to tell you that I have given him an oath, and that he takes it seriously."

"I see." Devlin laughed, the rich sound both stimulating and somehow frightening. "Anything else?"

"To make you comfortable."

"Ahh," Devlin purred, "just what I was hoping to hear." He moved closer. "Get on your knees."

With a tremor of real fear, Desiree got on her knees, her eyes cast down.

"Apologize."

"I am sorry that I touched you as I did, Devlin, and called you names. I should have taken your refusal for your answer. Cain has shown me the error of my ways and made me promise never to make advances to you again. Please forgive my transgressions."

"Apology accepted."

Desiree waited a full minute, then carefully looked up. Devlin was looking down at her with a faint smile, his hand extended. Flushing, Desiree took it and stood.

Devlin pulled her close, his face inches from her, as if he would kiss her. "You say you are tamed, that you are willing to do all I ask with no hesitation. Is this so?"

"If my master allows it," Desiree said meekly.

"Your master is not here," Devlin said with delicious glee. "He has invited a creature of appetite into your home and left you at the mercy of the ravening wolf before you. Will you run, or will you stand and fight?"

I know this game; Cain and I have played it. "I will do neither," Desiree said. "I will satisfy his desires, take the power and lust he offers, and submit to his fangs and phallus, whichever he offers."

"Yes, you will," Devlin said. Making a fist in her black hair, he pulled her close, burying his teeth in the side of her neck.

Desiree flinched, then clutched at Devlin, pleasure suffusing her and her nervousness vanishing to be replaced with desire. He held her close, drinking her blood in long pulls as she clung to him. Then carefully, he withdrew his fangs and eased her limp body down on the bed. Carefully, he picked her up in his arms, and carried her into one of the guest rooms, laying her down on her own bed.

"It is not polite to take you in your master's bed," Devlin said with a smile, as he unzipped his pants, letting his large, rigid member spring forth. "But your bed will be sufficient. Get on your knees, my dear."

Woozy from blood loss, Desiree tried to get unsteadily to her knees, and failed. Devlin lifted her up onto all fours, threw up her long skirts, and brought her back against him in a rough motion, sheathing himself in her wet channel with a grunt. Desiree let out a cry but didn't struggle.

With one hand keeping her hips captive, Devlin's other hand reached around her and ripped open her bodice, letting her breasts spill free. His hand grabbed one, then the other, rubbing and squeezing. Desiree moved her head to scream, but her open mouth was covered by Devlin's, as he began to thrust.

Desiree gave herself up to the sensations, her gentle moans smothered by Devlin's insistent kisses. He broke the kiss, throwing his head back to shout as he came, Desiree's cries loud as he hammered into her.

Carefully, Devlin withdrew, then moved onto his back, watching her. Desiree carefully moved, wincing slightly at her soreness, and went into the bathroom, cleaning herself hurriedly. Then she emerged with a warm wet washcloth, which she proceeded to wipe down Devlin, cleaning the semen off his still hard cock and balls nestled in his pubic thatch of thick golden hair. "Are you ready to resume?" she asked, as she took the soiled cloth into the bathroom.

"Yes," Devlin said gently, when she emerged. "Take off your torn clothing, and get into bed, my dear."

Desiree pulled the ripped dress over her head, and then pushed it aside with a toe. She climbed into bed naked, her expression shy.

"Thank you," Devlin said kindly, taking her in his arms. He began to kiss her throat gently, eliciting soft groans of pleasure. "I have long wanted to do that. So it's fair I give you what you have long desired: a total seduction."

Devlin's kisses became more possessive, as he turned her slightly to face away from him, then brought his body against hers to spoon her. He slipped a hand under her, again cupping first one breast then the other, circling her hard nipples with his fingers, then squeezing them. With his other hand, he reached down between her legs, expertly finding her clit. "Spread your legs. Now."

Desiree leaned back against Devlin, spreading her legs wide, her trimmed pubic hair a small postage stamp atop her shaven pussy.

"I heartily approve," Devlin whispered circling her thatch once with his long fingers. "Now touch yourself as I fill you."

Desiree did as he asked, the thickness of his cock sliding inside her again both welcome and unnerving, as she'd never done this position before with a partner. Moments passed as she touched herself, the juices of her excitement and lust flowing more and more swiftly as her need to come intensified. But Devlin did not move or give her permission to move or come. Finally, the frustration mounting, Desiree shifted slightly, changing her movements. Her orgasm built in a few strokes, threatening.

"I'm going to come," she panted. "Please, give permission."

"No," Devlin said smugly, withdrawing from her, and moving to the edge of the bed to sit. "You have misbehaved by speaking out of turn. I assume you, like other women of this age, have seen that popular recent sexplay movie? That is nothing compared to what I have in mind. Hand me my belt from my pants. Now."

Desiree drew a long shuddering breath, fear again flooding her senses. She took the thick, tooled leather from Devlin's discarded pants, then handed it to him.

"Now bend over my knees."

Fear got the better of Desiree, and her rigid control broke. She fell to her knees. "Please, master. I'm sorry."

"It is too late for that," Devlin chided. He beckoned to her with his free hand. "Come here. Now."

Heart pounding, Desiree went to him, and lay over his lap, with her buttocks exposed.

Devlin brought the belt down with a whistle, the tip cracking into Desiree's buttocks. She let out a yelp reflexively, though the pain was slight.

"Be silent," Devlin growled. "Or I will cease to be gentle with you."

Again the belt whistled down, smacking hard onto Desiree's defenseless ass. This time the leather did hurt. Desiree let out a gasp.

Twice more the belt connected with a snap, the pain becoming more intense. Tears leaked from Desiree's eyes, but she kept silent, the only sight of her discomfort great hitching breaths as she fought for control.

"Very good," Devlin said quietly. But instead of approval, his tone held fierce anger. "But this is not enough punishment for the likes of you."

Desiree shuddered.

"Stand," Devlin intoned. "And face me."

Her tears now a steady stream, Desiree did as he asked, getting unsteadily to her feet, her frightened eyes blinking rapidly as she looked at Devlin.

"Your performance was perfect save for one thing," Devlin said with a sneer. "That Cain and I have been friends for a long time now. I know him very well. Too well for you to trick me, girl. He did not invite me here; you did. It seems he has not tamed you as I asked him to; you have only become more impetuous."

Desire opened her mouth to beg for mercy, then shut it, biting her lip hard so she tasted blood. *I can't stop him or sway him. I must submit.*

"Face the wall."

Desiree took a deep breath and faced the wall. She felt the press of Devlin's naked body against hers, then the touch of his lips to her ear. "I smell your fear, my dear. It is intoxicating, just as your screams will be."

Desiree leaned up against the wall for strength, terror making her legs weak.

"Say you are sorry for lying to me." Devlin stepped back, then brought the belt down onto Desiree's ass. She let out a screech as the metal buckle connected with her already throbbing rear.

"Say it!"

"I'm sorry for lying to you! I'm sorry!"

"You made advances and disobeyed your master. Admit it!"

The belt came down again, making Desiree howl. "I was wrong," she cried loudly. "I disobeyed my master."

"You dishonored him and I with your behavior, but most of all, you dishonored yourself as a submissive," Devlin hissed. "And for that you deserve to be punished. Say it!"

"I deserve to be punished! I deserve to be punished!"

Devlin brought the belt down once more, then Desiree collapsed to the floor, sobbing.

"Desiree," Devlin said coolly. "Come here. Now."

"I can't walk," she managed through her tears.

"Then crawl. Now."

With difficulty, Desiree turned and got to her feet, staggering to Devlin. He caught her, then eased her down to the bed, turning her on her stomach. Gently, he moved lower, his lips gently kissing her throbbing buttocks. As the pain eased slightly, Desiree took a deep shuddering breath.

Devlin again pulled her close to him, again making a fist in her hair. "I will say but once this final time: submit to me."

"Yes, master," Desiree whispered.

Devlin lay down on his back, then motioned to her to mount him. Carefully, she settled astride him, drawing a hitching breath as the bottom of her chafed buttocks touched his thighs.

"Come," Devlin ordered, as he began to move under her in long slow strokes. "Give voice to your passions."

Desiree moaned, then gave herself up to the sensation of Devlin's body beneath hers, his erection stroking her channel, the root of his rubbing on her clitoris. He watched her as she swayed above him, his honey eyes now a burning molten gold, his lips slightly parted, baring his fangs each time he slid deep inside her again.

Her orgasm, so long thwarted, returned with a vengeance. As she came, Devlin pushed her down onto his cock, driving into her repeatedly, wresting every last whimper and quiver from her aching body.

Desiree collapsed onto Devlin, lightheaded. When she could move, she raised her head, then kissed his lips lightly in thanks.

Devlin grabbed hold of her, his arms wrapping around her head in an all-consuming kiss as he rolled onto her, pushing her down into the bed, his hard shaft sliding in deeper as he began to thrust again.

Desiree arched her back at the sudden pain from her abused buttocks, her lips parting as Devlin licked and fed at her mouth. With a sudden guttural snarl he came, his roar loud and long as he spent himself.

Devlin looked down at Desiree with a sated smile, then kissed her again, his tongue slipping into her mouth to tangle with hers. After the long lingering kiss, he moved back, then rolled onto his back beside her.

Wow. He was everything I hoped he would be ... and more. "Should I attend to you, master?" Desiree asked.

"Yes," Devlin said, his tone now kind. "And to your own needs, as well."

Desiree again cleaned Devlin's sexual organs, then saw to her own. As she took the soiled washcloths back to the bathroom, she took a moment to check her throbbing buttocks in the mirror. *My ass is red and welted. I'm going to be sore for days, but he didn't break the skin.*

As she walked back out to Devlin, she saw he was sitting up in bed, putting on his shirt.

"Are we finished?" she asked.

"Yes," Devlin said, stretching slightly. "Cain will be home soon, my dear. You should prepare for him. While he'll be greatly relieved to find you undamaged, he will likely mete out some punishment of his own for your well-crafted deception."

True. "Thank you for not, um, damaging me."

Devlin stopped dressing and turned to her. "Make no mistake, I will not tolerate you lying to me ever again. That is why I used the belt on you: so you would remember."

"I'm not likely to forget," Desiree answered, wincing. "I was sure you drew blood. But I'm unmarked."

"Were it not for Cain's feelings for you, I would have left you bloody and not healed you," Devlin replied evenly. "Vampire saliva has healing properties, as you now know." He stepped closer. "You are to tell him that, when he arrives. His pretense of an oath was a nice try, but it's not what stayed my hand. Neither one of you are vampires, so Vampire Law does not apply. And even if you were ... everything we did here tonight is allowed."

"I'm not sure what to say," Desiree murmured. "I said what he asked me to. That is the truth. Perhaps the law is vague and can be interpreted differently?"

"Unlikely," Devlin laughed, as he pulled on his pants. "As I am the one who wrote it close to two centuries ago, Desiree. I know what I meant in the words. There is no grey area."

I had no idea he was so old. Or in such a position of power. "Thank you," Desiree said, as Devlin put on his suit coat. She handed him his belt. "What you did wasn't what I imagined. It was more. I will remember, and not invoke your anger again."

Devlin slipped his belt through the loops. "I have seldom been pursued so thoroughly for so long, especially after repeatedly refusing," he remarked with a measure of respect. "You were also more than I imagined. Your fear, your offer of a blood kiss, your tears ... all of it was perfectly executed. I commend you, my dear."

"Thank you."

Devlin walked out. Grabbing a bathrobe, Desiree followed him to the door. She was thinking what to say in farewell when there was the sound of a key in the lock, and Cain burst through the door, his expression both anxious and angry.

"Your home is lovely," Devlin said cordially. "Your lady is as well. Be assured she made me very comfortable."

Cain stared at him, then looked over at Desiree searchingly.

"I have addressed her lies," Devlin went on. "She is unscarred, though she will remember how to behave from now on when dealing with me. But I suggest you also step up your game, after she's had at least a few days to heal." He took Desiree's hand, and kissed it chastely. "Thank you my dear, and goodnight." He opened the door and walked out, just as the clock began to toll midnight.

Cain kicked the door shut, then turned to Desiree. "You did this? You invited him here to our house to screw him?"

"You have invited me to live with you every week," Desiree replied coolly. "But you have never told me you and I were exclusive. You slept with your brother's bride—and probably him—on their wedding night, Cain. How many other people have you slept with on all of these trips you're always gone on?"

"I haven't been seeing anyone else since we met!" he thundered.

"You never said anything about being exclusive."

"I knew you wanted that, you said so on our first session, that it was a condition of being with you."

"But what do you want?" she challenged. "You've never said."

"It's my responsibility to know what you want and make it real for you. I told you that then too!"

"So what is real and what's not?" she challenged. "Devlin says you care about me. Is it true?"

Cain produced a velvet box. "This is real ... and the reason I was so late getting home. It wasn't ready on time."

Desiree froze, her thoughts racing and conflicted. "We never talked about marriage."

"I know you were married before ... and that a solid commitment was what you wanted and needed from me, eventually. Yes, it hasn't been that long, but I'm a man who knows what I want, and I want you." He looked away. "Or at least I did before tonight."

Desiree's breath caught in her throat. "Do you not want me now?"

"You lied to me and to Devlin so you could what? Make me jealous?"

"The truth is ... I wanted a certain fantasy many years ago, but my husband wouldn't allow it," Desiree said slowly. "I wanted to be with two men. I went so far as to go to a place called Joyful Sex —"

"I know it. It's out of business—"

"I'm not surprised, it was smarmy," she interjected back. "I backed out at the last minute. I couldn't give power over myself to men who I knew were incapable of dominating me. My husband and I, we got into kink by ourselves. But after I learned about you having multiple partners, especially with your friends ... I wanted to know if it was something I could do."

"So why pick Devlin?"

"Because I don't know any of your other friends that you share partners with," Desiree replied. "Even if I did ... I didn't know if I could be intimate with a stranger. With Devlin, I knew I could go through with it, because I've known him for years. And maybe one of the reasons I chose him was because I knew that he wasn't the type of man that would let me back out at the last minute, even if I wanted to."

"So you and he went through with it. I don't have to ask if you liked it, you obviously did."

"I hope this isn't the same kind of judgmental conversation your brother had with his wife the morning after you left after bedding her," Desiree said pointedly. "But I'll guess he's had a similar conversation with her in the months they've been married, if not several."

Cain's mouth fell open.

"No, you never thought of that, did you? Have you seen them since? I'd guess not."

Cain dropped his luggage and sat down heavily on the couch. "No, I never thought of that. I enjoyed the night, and they did, too. I didn't do it to make him jealous, or to take her away from him. I just did it because I knew that they both needed a hand figuring out what was possible in the bedroom, and I had the experience to help."

"You didn't think of the long-term consequences to their relationship... or their egos."

Cain was silent.

"Devlin said he would be attached to some lady and unavailable in a few days," Desiree said more kindly. "You keep telling me to do whatever makes me happy, that I had your permission. I saw a chance and I took it. Neither Devlin nor I did this to make you jealous, and I'll guess the reasons he went through with it were the same ones you just stated for cuckolding your brother. I know now that if you do ask someone else to our bed ... I can do it." Desiree bit lightly at her lip, grateful again it was healed. "But that said ... I'd rather not include any others, if it's all the same to you."

"I don't want anyone but you," Cain said, rising and giving her a hug. The embrace lasted, the hug becoming tighter. "I'm sorry that I wasn't more explicit about my feelings, or what I wanted. I've always been about the experience. Most of my adult sex was me training someone to be my submissive, and part of that training involved other men for experience. You're different: I don't want to train you, I want to spend my life with you." He paused. "Having had Devlin, do you want more men to join us?"

Desiree shook her head. "He gave me what I needed, cleared my head."

"You're sure?"

"I loved what he did to me," Desiree said honestly. "It was intense ... but a little too intense."

"I'm asking because Devlin has long been after me to share an experience with him with a woman," Cain said hesitantly. "I visit him every few years, and I've always refused. If you'd be willing, I'll tell him that I'm ready now for that, if he agrees that you'll be the woman."

"I thought you didn't want to share me?" Desiree questioned.

"Look in the mirror," Cain said, turning her towards the large oval glass to his right. "You're almost glowing, Desiree. Devlin was, too. That's why I know he won't refuse my offer, whatever he might have said to you tonight. I meant what I said when I told you I wanted to make you happy."

"But I want to make you happy, too," Desiree said slowly, turning to hug Cain. "You are my master in the bedroom … and you're my partner outside it. If this is something you want to do with he and I, I'll do it gladly, but—"

"Yes."

"Then it's settled," Desiree said with a smile. "Now do you still want to marry me?"

"Very much," Cain said. "Go fetch the box, and I'll propose properly."

Desiree gave him a flirtatious look as if she would say no, then went and got the box, opening it to reveal a large diamond solitaire. She slipped it on her ring finger, then turned to Cain. "I accept."

"Haven't you been punished enough for one night?" Cain said darkly, his expression stern.

"Not by my rightful master," Desiree teased.

Cain narrowed his eyes, then took her hand, silently leading Desiree upstairs, still smiling eagerly with downcast eyes.

THE END

IDENTITIES

Beleaguered erotica author Tracy is trying to balance both her ailing father's and her newly adult daughter's needs, leaving little time for herself. When fellow erotica author Robert begins drawing her into real "research" for her sex tales, Tracy discovers a new side of herself, even as she wonders if Robert's interest in her is more than professional. Complicating matters is Tracy's neighbor Matt, a solid and sexy shoulder to lean on who is more than eager to join Tracy in a little personal experimentation with her newly acquired knowledge. On the road to discovery, Tracy must not only choose which man she wants in her bed, but also the woman she wants to become.

IDENTITIES

Tracy sat smiling, watching the clock while trying to appear as though she couldn't be happier. That wasn't true, of course. What had possessed her to think that a Thursday afternoon would be a good time for a book signing? Not one person had come by in the last three hours. To top it off, the sky outside the windows had darkened with the threat of rain, which meant that the lawn at home wasn't going to get mowed today, either.

It couldn't be helped, though. This was the only time she could get away to sign.

Frustrated thoughts raced through Tracy's head. Why had she let her publisher talk her into doing those spanking stories? Until that foray into erotica, Tracy Chapman had been known as a "sweet romance" author, with nothing harder than some French kissing. All she'd wanted to share were some tales of romance with the world, to prove that women over twenty could have a romantic life even if they had children at home, or an elderly parent. Her novels *Happiness in Time* and *If You Only Would* had garnered some fair reviews, but nothing stellar. But ever since *Hot Stuff* had gone public, Tracy had been tagged "as one of those" authors.

Once the book was out, it had outsold her sweet romances two to one. Now fans of *Hot Stuff*—and her publisher—were clamoring for a sequel. How was she going to think up new tales? Her protagonist hadn't been fiction; Tracy had based the woman on herself. But she'd never done any of the naughty things she'd written about. How long could she fake it before her sexy scenes sounded as fake to her readers as she knew they really were?

To complicate matters, her heroine's troubled life of drudgery wasn't all fabricated. Tracy's father had recently moved in with her. Dad was mid-level dementia but holding his own so far. He could take care of himself for now, but that was going to change soon, if his doctors were right. In addition, Tracy's daughter had also moved back in with her, filling up the other small guest bedroom.

Katrina had been let go from her job last month, and her lifestyle of living on the edge of her means had quickly caused her to lose her apartment. While Tracy appreciated the help with her father, she was feeling overwhelmed lately. Some of that was the never-ending work from the moment she opened her eyes to the moment she lay down to sleep. But more of it was trying to decide who she was. It was laughable really; shouldn't a mature woman know who she was, and what she wanted? Yet more and more, Tracy wasn't sure what she wanted out of life.

A year ago, she'd been employed at Label Ltd., a large company with good benefits and a pension big enough to live on if she was careful. Retirement was looming on the far horizon, a beautiful promised land of no more waking in the dark each morning, and maybe time to finally get in shape and do some of the things she never seemed to have time for. Then had come the economic downturn, the shadow signaling all of Tracy's carefully lined up dominos to topple crazily, her promised land falling far beyond her reach.

She'd been laid off with no pension and only a year of benefits. She went to several job fairs, and submitted many applications, and got not one nibble. Thank God her house was paid for, and her husband Shane had left her a great IRA close to a decade before. But there was only one option, now that the promised land was gone: find a job. Finding part time work at Taste of Taylor had been a godsend.

The cozy bakery and coffee shop was a soothing place to work on weekdays. Weekends were crazy, but Tracy never worked there aside from the occasional fill-in when someone was sick. It wasn't long before she felt like part of the team. In her hours there during the slow afternoons, she'd begun penning some of the romantic dreams and fantasies she'd always hoped for and never lived. She hadn't planned on submitting them—Lord, or even having anyone else read them—but with Katrina's encouragement, she'd found the nerve to contact several publishers. Now close to a year later, Tracy had two books published.

Well, two books and the erotica. Those last had been her daughter's idea. After Katrina had settled in to the guest bedroom, she'd taken an interest in Tracy's "hobby"—so much so that she'd pressed her mom to try a genre that she'd never have considered herself.

"Everyone is writing it and making money hand over fist," her daughter had said. "You need to try this."

Tracy had agreed hesitantly. But the next day, staring at her scribble pad trying to make some start, she'd decided that this was not going to work. Tracy had never been spanked in her life for titillation ... and had never missed having that experience. How did one go about writing stories like these, when they had no personal experience with the acts being described? Books on writing always said to seek out an expert, someone with experience, if you didn't have any firsthand knowledge of something you wanted to write about. But this wasn't information on police procedure, or how to correctly lace up an early 1800's bustier. This was S-E-X, moreover what most people would call bondage. Who could she possibly ask for advice, even if she somehow found the nerve?

Use the Internet, her publisher had urged. Tracy's daughter had a more succinct and aloof answer. "Just Google it, Mom!"

Later that night, Tracy had made some discreet searches online. The Internet had been a help, but only to a point of gathering BDSM lingo and getting a look at some "toys." Finally, with the help of a fiction book of Katrina's, Tracy had successfully "faked" two stories about BDSM. She'd worried when she sent them to the publisher they would be rejected, but to her astonishment, they were both accepted.

And "Hot Stuff" was born ...

Tracy was jolted out of her reverie as rain began pouring down outside Taste of Taylor. There was a rumble of thunder. In seconds, the previously empty coffee shop was inundated by people trying to avoid the storm outside, each one letting a gust of air into the shop as they eagerly entered. Tracy threw her hands across her bookmarks and laminated reviews as they shifted and flapped, threatening to spill off her small table and onto the floor. Even as she secured the closest promo items, the bookmarks for "Hot Stuff" fell of the table and onto the floor.

"I've got it," a handsome older man assured, bending beside her table. He scooped the bookmarks off the floor and gave them to her. "Sorry, I mean I've got them."

He's cute, reminds me a little of Wesley from The Princess Bride. Tracy took the bookmarks, her hand touching the man's fingers. The brief contact was electric. "Thanks," she said shyly.

"Hot Stuff," the man remarked, looking over her table as he brushed back some platinum locks that had come loose from his ponytail. "How hot is hot?"

Tracy blushed. "Pretty hot." She gestured to one of her laminated reviews.

The man cracked a grin as he picked up the review. He looked over at her, raising his dark eyebrows. "So you're one of *those* authors."

Tracy blinked, staring at him. "Yes," she managed finally, straightening her bearing with effort. "I am."

"Glad to hear it," the man replied, putting down the review and offering his hand. "Because I am, too. It's good to meet a fellow literary pornist. I'm Robert Stranger."

Is he my age? I think so but I can't tell for sure. Tracy rose from her seat, taking his hand in hers. "Glad to meet you, Robert. I'm Tracy."

"So I see," Robert replied smoothly, looking her up and down once boldly before smiling again at her.

Yes, he really just did that. Secretly flattered, Tracy narrowed her eyes in response. "Really? And what do you see, Mr. Stranger? Which I might add is an apt name."

"A woman I want to get to know better," Robert replied easily. "Will you have dinner with me, Miss Tracy." His smile widened. "Or is it Mrs.?"

"Neither," Tracy answered smoothly, holding his brazen gaze evenly. "It's just Tracy." She let her lips form just the hint of a smile. "I'm sure you want to be just Robert, unless you want me to call you Stranger."

Robert held her gaze for a few moments, then laughed. "That depends on if you don't talk to strangers, I suppose." He watched her again, amused. "But I have to conclude you're not a good little girl, if you write books like Hot Stuff."

Damn it, he'd talked her into a corner, with her choices to look like a prude or a slut. Tracy looked down at the table, searching for an answer, then seized a copy of *Hot Stuff* with sudden inspiration. "Why don't you read it and tell me?" she said in a teasing tone, handing him the copy. "Good—" She deliberately lowered her voice, putting heat into each word. "—or bad."

Robert chuckled again, delighted. "So I will then, Tracy." He reached down to the table and grabbed one of her business cards. "Expect an email soon."

He pushed out the door, disappearing into the crowds that again were massing on the sidewalk outside. Tracy went to the window, heat slowly filling her cheeks as she thought about what she had done.

Why did I do that? I don't know him at all, and he could have been lying through his teeth about everything he said.

The storm was clearing, though the rain was still sprinkling down steadily.

Well, maybe I'll get a good review out of it at least ...

Tracy's iPhone buzzed on the table. She hurried, then unlocked it, looking at the text from her daughter.

Come home ASAP. Granddad.

Stifling a sigh of realization that the next few hours would be arguments about forcing her father to take his medication, Tracy began packing up her books and other items carefully in the plastic tote she had brought them in. She couldn't afford to have any get ruined. This signing was already into the negative numbers. There was nothing more to do today but get back to the drudgery of her real life.

Tracy rubbed at her eyes, then looked over at the clock. 11:17pm. She looked back at the mostly filled page, wondering what to do next. *This would be a hell of a lot easier if I knew anything about what I was describing.*

Tracy's heroine, Rebekka with two K's, was in the throes of self-discovery with several of the sexual toys she had recently been gifted by a mysterious stranger. But other than showing the obvious reactions of physical dimensions and capacity, Tracy had no idea what to write down.

Rule one in written sexcapades: don't introduce a sexual toy or aid that you don't plan to use in a later erotic scene. Her publisher had said that just created reader disappointment. Tracy grimaced, then shook her head and laughed. *Time again for an easy orgasm for Rebekka …*

Her phone vibrated on her desk. Startled, she reached for it, checking her email. There was a new message from robertstranger@robertstranger.com:

What's your number, Tracy? I want to call you to discuss

Tracy blinked, her mind trying to process what was happening. *Discuss what? Hot Stuff? Had he left off the end of the email accidently? Or purposely?*

Instead of opening the email—in case Robert could tell when emails were picked up somehow—Tracy looked up his website first. Before this went any further, she wanted to know for certain who this guy was. She looked at the main page, then flipped through the secondary pages, the graphics making her flush as she read.

It had been in Robert's tone when he introduced himself that he expected her to have heard of him. Now Tracy knew why. He had written over sixty novellas and books, the most noteworthy an erotic series about a young pagan woman, Kiyra, raised by natives in a third world country who later became not only a savvy rich and powerful madam, but also traveled the world, having exploit after exploit with men—and women—of various cultures. The latest book series number was high into the teens, and many review sites were listed on the website pages, raving about the various books and their "sexually imaginative" content.

So Robert really was an erotica author, too, like he'd said. And if people were raving about his work—specifically how hot it was—then it had to mean he knew what he was talking about—or had found a way to fake it. Either way, a conversation with Robert about her book could only help her work.

Tracy hit reply, then emailed her phone number to Robert. To her surprise, instead of texting her as she expected, her phone actually rang.

She fumbled with it, then put it to her ear. "Hi, Robert."

"Tracy," he said, his words like a caress. "And how are you this fine evening?"

"Trying to write yet another orgasm scene," she replied, putting her smile into her tone. "I have to find yet another brand new way to say climax."

"Cumulation," Robert said in a low tone, making Tracy shift in her chair, even as she clutched the phone. "Try that one. It works for me."

"Does it?" Tracy replied, putting meaning into the words.

"Yes," Robert said, his tone suddenly light. "But I didn't call you to put words in your mouth, my talented author. I called you to tell you that I had a look at *Hot Stuff*."

Tracy waited, scared to make a sound, wanting him so much to say it was good and fearing he was going to tell her he knew it was all a big fake. But as the seconds fell off the clock like tiny frozen minutes, she finally could wait no longer. "And?"

"It's good," he said, his tone still light. "It's a good first effort. But I think you could go a lot farther."

Had he even read it? Something made Tracy think he had skimmed one story, and not gone beyond that. "Really," she retorted icily. "And what would you recommend as a first step, Robert?"

"Research," Robert said, as if he were describing a trip to the library. "I suggest you go to your nearest adult outlet and have a look around. Maybe check out a strip club or two."

"Is that what you do?" Tracy replied a little harshly. "I've seen your website, Robert. I hardly think all those 'imaginative' books came just from a collection of toys and videos you amassed."

Robert chuckled. "No, you're right. I didn't want to fake my stories with just props." He paused. "So I didn't." He chuckled again. "But I hardly felt right in encouraging you to take my route, Tracy."

He was ... God, she wasn't experienced enough to know the right word for what he was. Ladies' man didn't seem to cover it, especially if he was telling the truth and men were also in his sexual repertoire.

"Are you still there?" Robert continued. "I didn't mean to shock you."

Yes, you did. The very thought annoyed her, that he was toying with her for some reason she couldn't fathom. "Thank you for your advice, and I'm glad you liked the book," Tracy said in her most effusive voice. "I'll see about doing that soon. But I've got to go now, Robert."

"Of course," he said cordially. "Goodnight."

Tracy echoed his sentiment, then hung up the phone. She stared at it a long while, before she resumed writing.

A few days later, Tracy entered her local Adult outlet, her hand firmly on her purse strap, her eyes scanning the aisles for any deviants.

She hadn't known what to expect, having never been in such a place before. Somehow, she'd expected seediness, and filth, people lounging in corners and dark rooms where men masturbated to porn or live, scantily clad gyrating women. Instead, the store was super bright with megawatt lighting, the aisles clean and all items marked clearly with prices. The biggest shock in real life was the outrageous prices on some of the items.

Tracy took her time, wandering the aisles, wondering if she should take pictures or just buy some items. In spite of her initial worry, some of them looked kind of fun, like the furry handcuffs. And there were several leather outfits that looked like a LOT of fun …

"What are you doing here?"

Tracy turned in surprise and horror to see her daughter, Katrina, staring at her, a crop in her hand.

"Research," Tracy said quickly, pleased at her quick thinking before she remembered she was telling the truth. "You?" she asked, making pointed eyes at the riding crop her daughter had hold of.

Katrina colored, but didn't put down the crop. "Picking up a bachelorette present for a friend." She shifted, and the other item she was holding, a small bag of outrageously priced penis-shaped pasta, slipped out of her hands and landed on the floor with a crinkling of plastic.

Tracy laughed, and Katrina followed, bending and picking up the bag. "Slippery little buggers."

They parted ways quickly, as Katrina headed to the counter, paid for the crop and pasta, then left. Tracy went back to the crops, then decided that was a little too outrageous. There was no way she was going to use it on herself, and she had no partner, so what was the point? She turned instead and headed to the dildos, grabbing the least scary one, then added another one that promised it would feel "like real." Rolling her eyes, she headed to the counter to make her purchase.

That night, Tracy worked, yawning, trying to decide if she should go to bed or fight to keep writing. She was on a roll with the plot, even if the sex scenes were absent. She could always fill them in later …

Her phone rang. Tracy looked over, then her eyes widened, not sure if she should be thrilled or scared. It was Robert.

Before she could think, she picked up. "Hi."

"Hello, Racy Tracy," Robert said back. Unlike how he had sounded when they had last talked, his tone was suffused with desire.

Tracy felt a charge go through her. "Isn't it kind of late?"

"For a social call, yes," Robert agreed. "But I had something else in mind, if you're game."

Was this really happening? Tracy pinched her lower left arm and winced. She shifted in her chair, trying to keep from trembling. "What?"

"Let's call it another kind of research," Robert replied evasively. "Can you imagine a villa, rustic, some of the paint peeling. A courtyard beneath, and a balcony overlooking fields of dark swaying grasses and low trees."

Tracy nodded, then felt dumb. "Yes," she replied. "I've seen pictures of Spain."

"Imagine you are there on the balcony, looking out, the wind ruffling through that short fiery hair of yours. A simple halter top, a long silk skirt blowing in the gusts of wind. Can you see it?"

Tracy nodded. *Spain would be so beautiful.* "Yes."

"Good." Robert's voice deepened. "Can you see me there, waiting in the shadows, watching you?"

Tracy's breath caught in her throat. "No," she said, letting out a shaking breath. "I thought I was alone."

"Never," Robert whispered. "I have watched you, walking the fields, loving the light on your hair and the tenderness in your gaze. So long, Tracy, have I watched. I have wanted you since that first moment."

Tracy's heart was racing. *How was it possible to be this excited, just hearing his voice?* "Why?" she managed.

"Because you were meant for me," he whispered in silken tones. "We were meant for each other."

Tracy found her voice, the sheer wanting in it making her flush as she said, "Then why are you in the shadows? Come to me."

"No," Robert said. "I will not cross the distance. You must come to me, my shepherdess."

"What would you do if I did?"

"I would take you in my arms. But instead of holding you, I would kiss you with every bit of the fire that I have been holding back since that moment I first saw you, my mouth ravaging yours until you were swooning in my arms. Only then, when you could no longer resist me, your eyes wide and filed with desire, your breath uneven eager panting, would I slowly undress you, slipping each fold of cloth from your flushed skin as I kissed every inch of you. My lips would tease your breasts, loving the feeling of your nipples stiffening under my tongue. You would cry out as I cupped them, rubbing the hard nubs, squeezing and possessing—"

Tracy gripped the phone in a death lock, trying to quiet her breathing. She was floating awash in sensations his words were creating inside her. *How could someone get her this hot without laying a single fingertip on her? This was crazy! And she had never been so turned on in all her life.*

Robert was still going on. "—I would lay you down, unable to wait another moment, my body already throbbing with need of yours. And when I entered you slightly, you would feel a little fear, that I was so large—"

Tracy snapped out of her fog of sexual desire, her slack expression curving into a grin. He expected her to go along, maybe was trying to give her what he thought she wanted to hear.

"—But I would be gentle, stroking you with my hands. And little by little I would push inside—"

But I am not just a participant here, Robert ... I'm your equal. "No," Tracy said throatily. "You would not enter slowly. Because when you lay me down, I would guide your hand to my thatch to touch me."

There was a few seconds' pause, then Robert said back, "And what would I discover?"

"That I was a river for you," Tracy murmured hungrily. "That I was ready for your cock, that all I wanted was to have you inside me."

Robert's next words were full of eager lust. "Then I would give a soft push, and slip inside completely, my moan of gratitude loud in your ears."

"I let out an eager cry, and clasp you to me," Tracy said, cradling the phone as she desperately reached for her new dildo, ripping it out of the paper box. "And you would slide into the hilt easily, my glove of a body around you, as if I were made for you."

"You were made for me," he said possessively. "And tonight, I am taking what is mine, Tracy."

God, he had said her name. "Please," Tracy said. "Take me, Robert. I'm yours."

There was a pause. "Touch yourself, my lover," he said. "Please, do it now."

Tracy took out her toy, inserting it easily. There was no need for lube. The full length slipped in easily and she imagined it was Robert, his penis hard within her. She began to stroke with it, shuddering. "I love how you feel," she groaned. "I don't want this to stop."

"It has to," he said gutturally. "I want to come too badly. But before I do I want to hear you come. I want to hear you say my name at your cumulation."

Tracy let out a cry, letting the phone fall from her grasp as she worked the toy faster, grinding it into her. The climax was near, she could feel it. The rush of his words was like a fire inside her, building like an inferno, consuming her utterly as it raced through her blood.

"Say my name," Robert said, his desire strong in the faint words.

"Only if you'll do the same," Tracy rasped out. "I want to hear my name when you come, Robert. Say it!"

Robert grunted, then groaned again. "Please, Tracy," he moaned. "Please I'm so close."

Tracy stroked faster with her toy, her other hand reaching down to rub her clit. The slippery engorged skin under her fingers began to tingle, then the gap closed, the tingle becoming a solid wave of rising pleasure as the orgasm washed over her. She dropped the phone and spasmed against the bed, screaming Robert's name, to God, an affirmation of pleasure and satisfaction. She lay gasping for each breath, then her ears registered silence. Her eyes sprung open, locking on the dropped phone.

Damn it, she was going to miss him coming!

Still shaking, Tracy grabbed for the dropped phone, praying she hadn't accidentally hung up, that she was in time. She heard Robert say her name faintly, then once again as the last stirrings of her own climax faded.

Then there was silence.

Shit, had he hung up? Was that it?

A second of utter fear engulfed her, then Tracy heard a loud groan, then a roar as Robert shouted her name, his cries almost like pain, like he was dying, and she had given him his last glimpse of paradise.

Pleased with her performance, Tracy lay back on the bed, covered in sweat, breathing hard. Robert was also breathing hard, from what she could hear. But he didn't speak as one minute became two, then three.

"I loved that," Tracy murmured. "I feel dumb, but I never knew it could be like that. That good I mean."

Robert drew a long breath, then let it out. "It's not," he said, satisfaction and happiness in his tone. "I am ... I have done this before, Tracy. And it's not like this, usually. Not this ... vivid."

Of course he had to have done this before. I wouldn't have known what to do or dared to make the first move if I had known. So why do I still feel a tinge of sadness at his admission? "It sounded like it was good for you, too," Tracy teased. "Very good."

"It was powerful," Robert said after a moment, as if he were afraid to admit it.

"For me, too," Tracy added quickly, not wanting him to feel as if she was asking him for more than what had just happened. *God, why were new relationships always so hard? And was this even a relationship at all?* "Which is why I need to know if we can do this again."

"I was hoping you would say that," Robert said, a wide smile in his tone. "Say tomorrow night?"

"Yes," Tracy said, looking guiltily at the clock. *Hell, it was two am! She had to take dad in for his doctor appointment at eight, six hours from now.* "I have to go now, though."

"Then dream of me holding you, Tracy," Robert said in caressing tones. "Of us falling asleep together. Goodnight."

Tracy murmured some kind of assent, then put down the phone with a shaking hand. Lying back on the bed, she closed her eyes for a minute, then opened them, knowing sleep was not going to come. She was too wired.

She had just had sex with a virtual stranger, literally. What had she done? What had come over her? What would her daughter think if she ever found out?

Tracy closed her eyes, pushed away the questions, and instead thought of Robert, of him holding her the way Shane had years ago. In a few moments, she dropped off into a deep, dreamless sleep.

T racy groaned, looking at her bloodshot eyes in the rearview mirror as she waited for the minivan to back slowly out of the parking space. *At least she had found a spot in the front parking lot, saving them both a long walk.*

"We're going to be late," her dad griped from the backseat.

"We'll be on time," Tracy replied, hoping like hell she was right. She slipped into the space and stopped the van, her father stepping out before she had shifted the van fully into park. Tracy gathered her purse and slammed the door, hurrying after her father. She'd learned the hard way that she had to be with her father at all times whenever they left the house. There was too much trouble he could get into with his failing memory.

Tracy and her father made the lobby with a few minutes to spare. After checking in, she cajoled him to take a seat, then got him a magazine to page through. He no longer read much himself for pleasure, but he always enjoyed the pictures, specifically of a certain blonde celebrity. Thankfully, this magazine was featuring a cover story on the woman. Her father took the magazine eagerly, flipping pages happily.

As she waited for his name to be called by the nurse, Tracy thought over the previous night. *What did it mean?* Yes, the phone sex with Robert had rocked her world. Yes, given the chance, she'd likely do it again. But there was a niggling feeling in her gut that didn't let her savor the moment. *Are you the kind of woman that does this?*

"Maybe" Tracy murmured aloud.

"What?" her father asked crankily, irritated at being disturbed.

"Nothing," Tracy said, savoring a secret smile.

Tracy waited the rest of the week for another phone call, but there was no word from Robert. Though Tracy had his phone number, she felt too shy to just call him up. *Rebekka would be bold enough to leave a message asking for more … or whisper sexily to Robert if he was "up for another encounter" if he did answer. But I'm not her.* Stymie —and more than a little frustrated at being stood up—she looked through her emails to find his email address.

How do I word this, so I don't sound like a groupie? Tracy began several emails, then deleted them, not liking how they were either too cryptic, or else too blatant. Who knew who answered Robert's email? His publicist, his assistant, or someone else? Hell, there was no mention of a wife on his website, but that didn't mean anything. Tracy had never asked him, though she remembered he had made a point to ask her. But maybe that was just to make sure when he'd called her that she would be receptive to his idea of recreation.

Don't beat yourself up. It wasn't like you had any warning what he was going to suggest. It was a lot of fun and sure did give you something new to write about. Plus, you're both consenting adults … and phone sex is probably just about the safest kind of sex there is.

Stifling a laugh, Tracy sat back in her chair, then closed down the computer with a reluctant sigh. Much as she wanted to contact Robert, she would wait and let him make the next move.

Tracy let out a breath and forced a smile. *Just smile for another two hours.* The two-day convention was almost over, and it had been a fair success. She'd sold some of her erotica, but also a fair number of her sweet romances, as well as several copies of an anthology that featured her first foray into paranormal "hot" romance.

Tracy smiled to herself. *How much of that is me finally feeling confident enough about my work to talk to strangers candidly?*

Tracy looked up at the figures passing by, catching sight of several more costumed characters. That was nothing new; people had been dressed up since the beginning of the convention as everything from Slave Leia to Groot. What had caught Tracy's eye was an imposing figure with a cape and cowl, finally striding down her booth lane. Batman. *Maybe no Christian Bale or Ben Affleck, but damn, he's hot.*

Tracy watched him come, heading for something past her booth. Seized by sudden inspiration, she grabbed her signing Sharpie and wrote quickly on one of her promo pens marked with her author name and web address. "Batman!"

The cowled figure turned, and stepped to her silently, his eyes hard to see within the cowl, his smile a faint line.

"Would you like a pen?"

The figure tilted his head, as if he was unsure.

"It's a feeling naughty pen," Tracy said brazenly with a sexy smile, holding the altered pen out with one hand. "Then you'll be naughty Batman." She winked.

Batman looked back at her, seemed like he didn't know what to do for a moment, then stepped right in front of her, reaching for the pen.

"I wasn't sure you had a spot to hide it in your costume," Tracy flirted. "Securely, I mean."

That finally elicited a smile from Batman, who took the pen, then lowered his head in a slight bow Tracy recognized from the movie. "I have a spot," he intoned in a deep voice. "Thanks." Then he bowed his head slightly again.

I can't tell if that's his real voice or not, but it's sexy as hell. He's sexy as hell. I just want to climb over this table and grab hold of him. Her sudden lust made Tracy flush, and she went for her phone, quickly unlocking it. "Can I take your picture?"

Batman gave another slight nod, then struck a smoldering Dark Knight stare. She quickly snapped a pic, and thanked him, then the moment was broken by two kids who ran up to him, asking for a picture. He moved off, heading up the row.

Later that night as she drove home from the convention, she chastised herself for her behavior. What had gotten into her? *You had no idea of what he looked like under his costume or what kind of man he was. What has Robert brought out in me?*

Another week passed, then two. Tracy's dreams became hotbeds of frenzied sex. She would awake horny as hell, unable to leave her bed until she had sated her needs. Yet falling asleep was harder than ever, as she would fight to stay awake, worried somehow, she would miss a late night phone call from Robert.

"Why are you letting one night get to you?" she said aloud crossly to herself, as she pruned the hedge in her backyard one afternoon, as her father lay inside napping. "It wasn't even real sex—"

"Hi, Tracy."

Tracy's first thought was *Robert!* as she turned, but instead it was her neighbor Matt coming across his lawn toward her, his easy smile familiar, his ice-blue eyes twinkling.

"Trimming the verge?" he quipped. "Isn't it a little late for that? It's close to dark."

Matt had always been a big Tolkien fan. "I have a little open time, and Katrina should be home soon to watch Dad," Tracy said. "I've got more than a little writing to finish tonight."

"Glad to hear it," Matt replied in a teasing tone. "I'm waiting for a sequel to Hot Stuff."

Tracy flushed crimson from her forehead to her waist. *Matt had read her erotica.*

"Sorry," Matt said quickly, his tone now unsure. "I just wanted to let you know I'd liked your work."

"I'm glad," Tracy mumbled, looking at the hedge, then the grass, then the sky in quick succession.

"Would you mind signing it for me, please?" Matt said, a shy tone she'd never heard in his voice before. "I can go run in and get it."

Get hold of yourself already! Stop acting like you're a teen and start acting like a professional author. "Tell you what," Tracy said, forcing a smile— and her gaze upwards from the scenery to Matt's face. "I've been meaning to bring you back some of your tools I borrowed this past summer. Let me just put my stuff away here and I'll be right over to sign your copy."

"Sure," Matt said, his smile genuine. "But there's no rush. Finish up here, then come over whenever you're ready."

Tracy went into the house, showered and dressed in record time, then called Katrina, telling her she was going over to Matt's and to come home earlier if possible. Her daughter assented in a preoccupied tone, then quickly hung up. Dismissing Katrina's odd behavior as irritation, Tracy headed over to Matt's house, his level and drill in hand, feeling slightly ridiculous. *Why did I borrow his tools? I should have just bought my own.*

Because you didn't know how to use even the simplest ones, remember? Shane always took care of everything like that, from hanging pictures to fixing the car. Matt's been a good friend these last few years, teaching you how to take care of yourself and your family. Vowing to show her appreciation more often, starting tonight, Tracy knocked on the door.

Matt opened it, then stepped aside. "Hi."

He looked wonderful, that light blue shirt setting off his blue eyes and blond hair. It was obvious he'd taken time to shower himself and put on fresh clothes. And was that cologne she smelled? Tracy awkwardly handed him the drill. "Thanks."

"I told you that you could keep it, remember?" Matt said, taking it and placing the case on the small hall table beside him. "Everybody— male or female—should have a drill."

Tracy shook her head, then gave him a sheepish look. "You're right, you did."

"It's alright," Matt said, handing her a copy of *Hot Stuff*. "I'm just glad to have an excuse to get you to come over. We haven't talked much since your dad became ill, hot stuff."

Tracy smiled, looking up with a quick retort to Matt, wanting to snare his gaze with her own as she said it. To her surprise, his expression was serious, and the look in his eyes right before he dropped them wasn't teasing; it was hungry.

Tracy almost lost her hold on the book, grabbing it in a death grip with both hands. She opened it to the title page, then bent over the table, realizing in that second, she hadn't brought a pen.

"Here," Matt said, handing her one from the table drawer. "I always keep a few in there to write phone messages on."

Tracy took the pen, even as her gaze lingered on the phone, thinking of Robert with a stirring in her loins. *Robert hadn't waited a second to go after what he wanted. Why should I?*

"Write, 'To Matt, for all his nights of sole wild abandon'," Matt teased.

Do it. Quickly, Tracy inscribed the book, then signed it with a flourish. "There you go," she said, handing it to him.

Matt opened it and read the inscription, his light tone turning surprised. "To Matt, in the hopes that your future nights of wild abandon aren't sole." He looked at Tracy, as if waiting for her to explain.

God, he looks great in those jeans, all lean muscle. "Do you want me to explain?" Tracy asked huskily. "It would be far easier to demonstrate … if you want to show me where your bedroom is."

Matt blinked once, then shut the book, setting it down on the table next to the drill. He locked the door, shooting the deadbolt with a heavy-handed bang. Then he was striding across the room, taking her in his arms and kissing her for all she was worth.

The shock of his mouth pressed to hers made Tracy's knees weak, and she clung to Matt, devouring his lips, only leaving his mouth to trail kisses down his neck, unbuttoning his shirt as fast as she could.

Matt let out a groan, then pulled away, taking her hand and leading her into his bedroom off to the right. He slammed the door, then turned to her. To her shock, his expression was unsure, even a little afraid.

"Tell me what you want," he murmured, taking her face in his hands gently. "I'll do it."

Tracy looked at him, then flushed. *He was worried he wasn't going to satisfy her, because of the erotica.* "You," she said, turning her head to kiss his hands, then sucked lightly on his finger, slipping the entire digit between moist lips.

Matt took a sharp intake of breath, then stammered, "I'm open to anything you want to do. I mean that, Tracy."

Tracy swayed slightly, drunk on the power he had just offered her. Tracy had never felt unsatisfied with her late husband. But they had never done anything beyond "regular" and oral sex. *Here with Robert was a chance to try out her fantasies, with no restraints …*

Tracy went still. *This is not Robert; it's Matt. Are you doing this for the right reasons?*

"I admit," Matt said huskily, slipping out of his shirt and tossing it aside. "I can't help but hope you'll fulfill some of my fantasies."

Tracy snapped out of her thoughts, looking at his tight abs and wide chest. "Such as?"

Matt flushed slightly, looking away.

Tracy bit her lip, then forced herself to stand up straight. *The first rule of being sexy was utter confidence. There was no reason she wasn't capable of fulfilling his fantasies, and hers as well.* She took off her shoes, then her socks. "Tell me what you hoped for, Matt. When you were having all those sole adventures in the dark, something tells me at least once, I was the one you visualized there with you. What did you fantasize me doing?"

"Seducing me," Matt said, his gaze locking onto Tracy as she shimmied out of her tight jeans. "Just like you're doing now, with that striptease."

This is nothing, Sweetheart. I can go so much farther. Tracy paused a split second, then opened the door. She returned a moment later with her purse, then took her phone out of it. She hit a few buttons, then stood it up near the lamp on the end table. She resumed undressing as the first strains of The Stroke broke the silence of the bedroom.

Tracy slid her hands over her hips, then upwards, pulling off her top and letting it fall to the floor. Her bra followed as she gyrated, rubbing her skin, her nipples standing firmly in the cool air. She cast a quick glance at Matt with lowered eyes; he was riveted on her, his clothing all off, his cock straining fully erect and purple with blood.

"Stroke me, stroke me ... "

Tracy sauntered over to him, then straddled his lap, making sure to sit just near his knees lightly. She grabbed each of his hands in hers, then slid them up her thighs as she swayed to the music, then upwards to cup her full breasts.

Matt gripped her flesh eagerly, rubbing the taut nipples, eliciting a groan from Tracy. She let go of his hands, slipping hers down to stroke his erection, rubbing the palm of her hand over the slick hot head as she circled the hot shaft with her other hand, sliding up and down as she squeezed.

"Stroke me, stroke me."

Matt jerked, then fell back on the bed, bringing Tracy with him. She climbed atop him, then settled down between his legs. Teasing the head of his penis with her tongue, she looked up at him with desire, then lowered her head and took his entire shaft in her mouth to the root.

"Oh, God!" Matt moaned. "Oh God!"

Tracy sucked gently, stroking his penis with her mouth and tongue, then slipped the hot flesh out of her mouth. She rolled off him onto her back, letting her legs splay open, turning her head to look at him.

Matt rolled on his side with effort, then hesitantly reached for her.

Tracy grasped his hand and brought it to her mound, then rubbed hard. Matt leaned in closer, then slipped his fingers inside her, a soft gasp escaping him as he felt her wetness, and his mouth came down on hers in a possessive kiss.

Then he was pulling back and fumbling with the bedside drawer. There was the sharp rubber snap of a condom being applied, then Matt was atop her, spreading her legs and thrusting himself in with a deep moan of satisfaction.

Tracy let out a shriek as his hot flesh slid inside her, clasping him to her, her head lolling back slackly as he thrust madly, his breathing becoming panting. But just as she thought he was going to come he stopped, then disengaged, rolling onto his back.

"Mount me," he rasped. "I want you to ride me."

Tracy maneuvered above him, sinking down with a fresh cry as Matt entered her to the root. She thrust down in long sure strokes, enjoying the feel of his large cock hitting her cervix, rubbing, the pleasure building with each thrust of her body on his.

"Stroke me, stroke me ... "

Matt grasped her hips, pushing down with each thrust up, his expression maddened almost to a snarl. A moment passed, as they strained in silence. Matt suddenly came, shouting beneath her, bucking wildly. His movements pushed Tracy into her own orgasm, her screams loud as she ground against him.

Their cries mellowed, then Tracy sank down on him. Matt hugged her, then gently rolled her off. He moved to the side of the bed, removing the condom.

Suddenly in the silence came the loud pounding rock music of Guns and Roses. Startled, Tracy realized her phone had gone through several songs since Stroke Me. She leaned over and grabbed the phone, clicking it off quickly. Matt gave no sign he'd heard, still attending to cleaning up.

Tracy waited in the silence, breathing hard. *Now what? Would he ask her to stay or leave?*

Matt did neither, to her surprise. He just took her in his arms and held her, hugging her tightly. Tracy looked at the clock, then closed her eyes, vowing that in a few minutes, she would make herself get up and go home. His quiet breathing at her side was comforting, even with its newness. It had been a long time since someone had held her. She gave a little sigh of happiness, then shifted slightly, checking the clock.

Katrina was home by now, so dad was all right. It wasn't as if the house was in danger of burning down; Tracy was right here next door. *So why do I feel so guilty?*

Because I came into Matt's house and practically seduced him. Okay, so there was no practically about it; it was plain seduction. And forget the why, because I can't blame this on Robert. It was because I wanted to. I wanted him, and I wanted to know if he wanted me, if he would take the chance if I gave him one. And now what? Where do we go from here?

Tracy slipped out of bed, then made her way to the bathroom. She turned on the light, then looked into the bathroom mirror at herself. *No signs of The Mark of The Slut. But I'm certainly becoming one. What's happening to me?*

Tracy found herself grinning. *If this were a novel, there would be some valid reason, likely supernatural in origin. Like a runestone, or some family curse, maybe even getting possessed. But I can't blame that. I think I have to chalk it up to good old-fashioned lust.*

Stifling a quiet laugh, Tracy shut the light off, then slipped back under the covers with Matt.

I n the morning, Tracy woke early. For a moment she didn't remember where she was. When she did, she sat up quickly, looking over at Matt. He was still asleep.

What she had laughed over and reveled in during the night was more than a little different in the harsh light of day. Mortified at what she had done, Tracy got out of bed, then dressed quickly. She snuck down the stairs, and hurried to the front door, grabbing her shoes on the way. She unlocked the door, opening it.

A piercing shriek of an alarm siren filled the early morning air.

Damn it, how had she forgotten Matt's house was alarmed! "No," Tracy squeaked frantically, pushing random buttons on the control pad. "Oh no, no, no!"

There was fumbling on the floor above coupled with loud swearing, then Matt came running down the stairs in his jeans. He punched in a code on the panel, then shut the door. He leaned against it, eyeing her. "Sneaking off?" he asked, his disappointment obvious.

"I'm sorry," Tracy said, flushing. "I just thought I should get back. Katrina's not used to me not being there at night and having to deal with my dad herself. He rarely sleeps through the night—"

"I understand that," Matt murmured, coming close to take one of her hands in his. "But why not tell me you were going?" He kissed her hand. "Didn't you think I'd want to say good morning?"

Tracy looked frantically at the floor, hoping for some kind of brilliant answer to come to her. But nothing appeared.

"What was this to you?" Matt said gently.

I don't know. An escape, maybe. Or maybe it's just that you're so much like Shane, and I wish to God he were here with me now, to help me with dad.

"I'm not trying to pressure you," Matt said a little more gruffly. "I just don't want this to be … I hope you don't think you made a mistake last night, is all."

I didn't think, is the problem. What kind of relationship can I offer you, when all I have time for is a night here and there, and dad needs me?

"Say something, Tracy," Matt persisted, squeezing her hand.

"I don't think I made a mistake," Tracy said, squeezing his hand in return. "But I'm not sure where we go from here, Matt. My family needs me."

"But what about what you need?" he asked. "Aren't you important, too? You deserve to be happy."

"I can't offer you more than what we had last night right now," she replied, hating the desperation of her words. "Is that what you want, Matt? To be snuck in between laundry, and my caretaking, to see me for brief moments, and spend the rest of the time alone? For me to stand you up, when they need me? Because that last is going to happen sooner rather than later."

"I want you to be happy," he whispered, hugging her close. "You are so much more than a caretaker, Tracy. I love your writing, honest to God. That wasn't a ploy to get you into bed." He kissed her forehead. "But I loved last night more."

"Even though I stayed away from the bondage?" she teased.

"Yep," Matt said, kissing her gently. "Though I'm game to follow wherever you lead me, like I said."

Yes, he actually just said that. "I'll keep that in mind," Tracy said, kissing his cheek. "I'll call you tomorrow."

She hurried out the door, before he could reply.

———

T racy let out a sigh that night, rubbed her eyes, then stared at her computer screen. The phone sex scene she'd written between Rebekka and her English professor neighbor had been much more detailed than she'd ever managed before ... and hotter, too. And that was a direct result of the interludes Tracy had shared with Robert and Matt. *Was this what real erotica authors did, hook up with new partners regularly for inspiration? That couldn't be true, could it?*

Tracy's phone vibrated. She looked at the text screen. It was Matt.

Hi. Hope your day was good. Talk to you tomorrow. Kiss, Matt

Tracy smiled, opened a text box to reply, then thought better of it. She still didn't know what she wanted from their relationship. She was going to have to come to some kind of decision tonight. Matt deserved that much.

Her phone vibrated again. Tracy glanced at it, sure it was just another text from Matt. To her surprise, the text was from Robert.

U busy?

Tracy's eyes narrowed. She wanted to text back no but UR SOL anyway asshole, but instead typed *no. why?* and hit send.

Want to come out and play? was his almost instant reply.

Maybe, Tracy sent, then deliberately waited.

There was no reply. She waited for several minutes, but Robert did not send any further communication.

Waiting for instructions, she sent finally.

I'm waiting for a yes. Or a no, he sent back.

"Okay, now I want to see you just so I can smack you upside your head in person," Tracy said aloud. Letting out an exasperated sigh, she typed, *yes. Now what?*

Be outside in ten was the reply.

Tracy blinked at the screen, then scrambled off the bed, lunging for her closet.

She shrugged into a crimson velvet blouse, tugged on some black jeans, then ran her fingers through her short curly hair. After hurriedly applying some lipstick, she headed down the hall, relieved that Katrina's light was still on, and her father's was not.

Tracy pushed open the door. Katrina was in bed, her tablet in her hand. She looked up, startled. "What is it, Mom?"

"I was going out to ... um, for an hour or so," Tracy said, trying hard not to blush. "I just wanted to let you know."

Katrina gave her a wide smile. "Matt need you to sign something again?"

Tracy bit her lip. "No, this is something else. Will you be okay?"

Katrina blinked at her. "You mean someone else, don't you? Who? You've never mentioned anyone else."

"It's not like that," Tracy replied with a forced smile, pushing down her guilty feelings. "Just a friend."

"A friend you put on your best blouse for," Katrina commented with raised brows. "And are those heels you're wearing?"

"It was the first thing I grabbed," Tracy retorted. "You know I look better in heels than I do in flats. I want to look good."

"Go ahead," Katrina said waving her off. "I'll be fine with him. But if you aren't coming home tonight, I want you to call, okay?"

"Of course," Tracy said guiltily, then shut the door and walked downstairs. *When had she and her daughter switched roles?*

She paced the front hallway for a few minutes, wondering if Robert would show, then paused, stopping to look at herself in the hallway mirror. The blouse had worked to show off her short reddish curls as it always did, bringing out the blue of her eyes and making her pale complexion rosy. The black jeans clung to her in all the right places, and the heels did their job, making her seem slimmer with the added height. *Would Robert like it?*

It doesn't matter if he likes it, remember? You just wanted to smack him in person. But looking to die for while you're doing that is important.

There was the sound of a vehicle pulling up to the curb outside, then a car door opened and slammed.

Tracy grabbed her purse and keys, opening her front door. A limo driver stood there on the stoop, an umbrella in his hand. Tracy looked at him in surprise.

He offered her his arm, even as he put the umbrella over her to shield her. "This way, Ma'am."

Tracy walked with him to the limo, preparing a smile. But when she got into the back, Robert was not there waiting for her.

"Wait," she called to the driver. "Where are you taking me?"

"To Brusettio's," he said. "Mr. Stranger is there waiting for you."

"Why didn't he come himself?" Tracy persisted, irked.

"He's entertaining someone, I believe," the driver responded. "Now please sit back and enjoy some champagne, if you like."

Tracy sat back with a determined expression, folding her hands across her chest. *I'm going to smack him.*

Brusettio's was an Italian restaurant, clearly fine dining but with a casual atmosphere, the other patrons dress ranging from slacks and sequin silk blouses to jeans and sweaters. Glad she looked good, Tracy followed the maître'd to a corner table, where a casually dressed Robert was deep in conversation with a ruddy-faced fellow who was dressed in a sport coat and slacks.

"Ah," Robert exclaimed, noticing her approach. "Gary, this is a friend of mine, Tracy." He rose from his chair, then held it out for her. "Please take a seat. I'm so glad you came."

Tracy smiled at Robert sweetly, even as she glared daggers at him, unswayed by the note of happiness in his words. *Being happy to see her didn't make up for his thoughtlessness of the last few weeks.*

Showing no sign he'd seen her angry look, Robert sat down in the chair next to her. "Tracy, this is Gary Brusettio. He's the owner of the restaurant, and a fan of our kind of work." He grinned licentiously. "I've been trying to convince him to let you sign here, maybe have a little coming out party for you, as it were."

Tracy's mouth dropped open, and she stared at Robert in disbelief. *He'd brought her here to just spring this on her, out of the blue? What on earth was he thinking?*

"Robert let me read your porn novel," Gary said to Tracy. "It was hot stuff. Got me going full steam. Or should I say full stream?"

He really just said that. "Erotica," Tracy said, straightening and holding fast to her dignity. "I write erotica, not porn."

"She's right," Robert said, shooting a cautioning look at Gary. "There is a technical difference between porn, erotica, and erotic romance, though the line varies depending on who you're talking to. But the market for her books would be like mine, predominately women who like a little romance with their erotic fantasies." He motioned to the waitress, who had brought a bottle of white wine and three glasses. She handed him the first one, which he handed to Tracy, who took it, eager to have something to hold onto.

"I didn't mean anything bad by it," Gary said, putting up his hands in a supplicant gesture. "Just complimenting your work, Tracy. In fact," he leered, "you might say I gave your story a standing ovation in several spots, until I left spots."

Tracy was simultaneously flattered on one hand, but also appalled at her new fan's descriptive language. Then she relented. *After all, wasn't the entire point of erotica to get the reader sexually excited? This man hadn't thought her sex scenes were faked at all.* "I'm glad you enjoyed my work," she managed finally, taking a sip of wine.

"Very much," Gary continued, as he took a glass of white wine for himself. "I was so thrilled to learn you were a local author. So when Robert said he could get you down here, I asked him to arrange this meeting. I had a question to ask you that needed to be answered, before I could decide if I should have that party for you at my restaurant."

What would he ask? It was sure to be something lewd. But she could handle it. Tracy forced a smile. "Which was?"

Gary reached into his pocket and produced a little metal figurine. It was a man cupping his hands over his genital area, from which protruded an out of proportion shining stainless steel corkscrew. "What's your gut reaction to this?"

"That I think that corkscrew fits you to a T," Tracy said dryly.

"Cock screw?" Gary inquired of her, as if she'd mumbled.

"Corkscrew!" she said, unable to stifle a laugh. "But sure, cock screw fits."

"You're right, it's really perfect for me," he replied, grinning bawdily.

"I've got to put it on Facebook. But I'm not sure what to say to introduce it, you know? 'Screw the wine' or something like that?"

"Screw the wine. Let's get right to the fucking," Robert said, leering.

Tracy rolled her eyes at him. "A bit much."

"She's right," Gary said, a tad regretfully. "Someone's sure to get offended. Just last week, a person was upset when I responded to a poll." He grinned. "The post asked, 'real or fake?' and I said, 'Real for trees and tits.'"

"Nice," Tracie commented mock politely. "I can't imagine why anyone was offended."

"I know! But I think you're right," Gary said, looking down again at the corkscrew man in his hand. "'Screw the wine' is probably the best caption."

"We should have used that for our bottle of wine," Robert said drolly, sipping from his glass.

"Too hard," Gary guffawed. "This is more of a novelty than a useful tool. You'd have to crank on the damn cork and then the wine would go all over." He gestured with his hands.

"But isn't that the point?" Tracie said to him, a sly look in her eyes. "To put forth a good long effort, with an ending resembling an explosion?" She smiled sexily.

"She's got a point," Gary said, nodding to Robert. "Go write some more erotica, Tracy. Then tell me a date when Hot Stuff 2 is coming out, and I'll throw you that party."

"I'll get right on it," Tracie said meaningfully.

"I'm liking what you're saying," Gary said, shooting her a smile as he left the table.

"Very good," Robert said in approval, clinking his glass with Tracy. "But then I knew you had the skills."

"I think you know very little," Tracy said, taking a big swallow of wine. "Like when you tell someone you're going to call, you should actually call."

Robert stared at her, as if he couldn't believe she had said what she had. "I got busy," he said after a few awkward moments of silence.

"So why not send me a message, or something?" Tracy persisted, softening her tone. "It's like saying you'll be right back, then not coming back at all for weeks."

"I wasn't aware that we were at that level," Robert said, his tone cordial yet cool.

"There is no required level for common courtesy," Tracy said in an equally cool tone.

"I set you up with a free promotion, likely the biggest you've ever had, and this is how you thank me?" Robert said angrily, his dark eyes flashing. "With a lecture about how I didn't call you?"

"That's right," Tracy said, finishing her wine in one long swallow, and getting to her feet. "Because I don't care what you can do for my career, and I don't care if it was the hottest phone sex I've ever had. I'm not going to take your shit." She grabbed her purse, then headed for the door.

By the time Tracy was at the door, she was regretting her hasty words, and hoping like hell that she could get a signal on her cell to access a local cab company. Calling Katrina to come and pick her up would mean a long explanation she didn't want to admit to.

Tracy opened the door, then stepped out into the night air, taking a deep breath.

You may have tanked your career. But damn it, saying it felt good.

Tracy opened her phone, then looked up the number of a cab company. She was dialing it when a hand grabbed her arm and spun her around.

Robert stood there. "I'm sorry I didn't call," he said. Before she could answer, he pulled her close, his mouth devouring hers. Tracy dropped her phone, her arms going around him, losing herself in his embrace, his kisses.

The sound of a car approached. Tracy opened her eyes and pulled back, as the limo ghosted to a stop near them.

Robert opened the door. "Want to come, with me?" he offered, the meaning in his words clear.

Tracy took a long shuddering breath, bent quickly to pick up her phone, then climbed into the limo.

The ride to Robert's hotel passed in a blur of kisses and murmured half-heard sexy innuendos, as the two of them grappled and touched in the back of the limo. They managed to get to the elevator, then embraced again, starving for shared heat. As soon as the doors opened, Robert was dragging her by the hand, his card key out and ready. He swiped it, then pushed her inside. She turned on the light and then she was in his arms again, kissing as they tore off their clothes.

"I can't wait, this first time," Robert said hungrily, as he pulled her blouse off. "I want to know what you feel like, Tracy."

Tracy dropped her jeans, kicked them aside, then grabbed his hand, pushing it down the front of her underwear to cup her pussy. "What do you think so far?" she said huskily.

Robert gripped her, sliding two of his fingers inside partway. "You're not a river," he whispered. "But then I haven't yet opened the floodgates, have I?"

Tracy paused, searching desperately for something to say back to him. *Maybe it should be done, not said.* She backed away slightly, pulled off her underwear, then leaned back on the bed, drawing both legs up to expose herself slightly. Then she sat up, leaning her elbow on one bent knee, the other bent leg flat against the bedspread. "Not yet," she drawled sexily. "But I have high hopes."

Robert stared at her, then laughed. He pulled off his shirt, and dropped his slacks, turning to face her. "So do I, Tracy."

Tracy went still, staring at his erection. *He hadn't lied about his size.* "So I see."

Robert stared at her, and brazenly stroked his stiffened cock. "Do you want me to wear a condom, or not?"

Tracy blinked at him. "Yes, of course."

"Did you bring any?" Robert asked, still stroking himself, the flushed skin of his penis glistening as he rubbed it. "I hadn't planned this, Tracy, so I'm not prepared."

Tracy stared at him. *Was he serious? Or was this more role-playing? He'd responded to her walking out of the restaurant. Was this a ploy to make her dominate him?* "Don't give me that," Tracy said angrily. "Earlier tonight was all just a prelude to this." She stood up, then walked to him, grabbing hold of his penis. Robert let out a grunt. She stroked his slick flesh, making him groan. "Now glove that and stop screwing around, so we can get to fucking."

Robert reached into his back pocket and took out a condom. Tearing the packet, he slid it onto his cock, then grabbed Tracy by her arm, pulling her back against him hard. His erection pressed to her buttocks, he reached down again, with his left hand, cupping her mound and sliding his fingers into her. With his right, he grabbed her short hair, pulling her head back to whisper in her ear, "You're coarser than I expected, Hot Stuff," he said roughly. "But I'm happy to give you just what you want." He pushed her to the bed.

Tracy stumbled, going to her knees against the foot of the bed with her arms outstretched to brace her fall. Robert was right there behind her, shoving her legs apart as he knelt. His cock nudged at her vagina, then slid inside in a long thrust as he pushed his hips tight to hers. Tracy let out a short cry, then her head was yanked back again by her hair, Robert's mouth muffling her sounds as his tongue delved into her in time with his erection.

Tracy was awash in sensation, enjoying his rough handling of her along with her submission. She felt her body's response, her juices flowing freely to lubricate their joined bodies.

Robert broke the kiss, holding still. "There," he said with satisfaction. "Now my dear, you are a river."

"Not yet," Tracy murmured defiantly. "Not until you make me come."

Robert chuckled, then suddenly withdrew. The shock of it made Tracy groan, then turn to see what he was doing. He got something from his duffel bag, then returned to her, some small pieces of metal and chain in his hand. "Stand up, my dear."

Tracy stood nervously. *It had to be some kind of sex toy. Handcuffs maybe?*

"Close your eyes and hold still."

Tracy stared at him, unsure.

"I'm not going to hurt you," he promised.

Tracy closed her eyes most of the way, peeking to see what he was doing. Robert sat on the bed, then began attaching something to her left breast. There was a cold sensation on her nipple, then a sharp pinch like a metal clothespin. "Ow!" Tracy exclaimed.

"Shush," Robert said absently, already at work on the right breast. After another pinch and another exclamation, Tracy had two small metal clamps affixed to her breasts with chains trailing from them. Robert linked the two chains together with a clip, then tugged lightly on the chain, eliciting another loud protest from Tracy.

Robert laughed, then sat back on the edge of the bed. "Come here."

He pulled down on the chain deliberately slowly. Tracy sat astride him, letting out another moan as she felt his throbbing erection enter her warm wetness for the second time.

Robert lay back on the bed, his slight tug on the chain enough to get Tracy to come with him. He said nothing, just took her hips in his hands, moving her in long strokes to receive his slow thrusts. Every so often he would tug sharply on the chain, always bringing a cry from her lips. Every time she let out a cry, he would spank her ass with his free hand, the light blow, always straightening her spine as she sharply exhaled.

Tracy was awash in sensation; her filled Corian an ocean of steadily seeping excitement. Pleasure at Robert's body's motion in hers, with hers as they coupled mingled with the pain of the nipple clamps, heightening her excitement. As she began to have the first stirrings of her orgasm, Robert suddenly bucked beneath her, his familiar roar of climax as loud as it was unexpected.

Tracy looked down at him in horror as he finished coming, her disappointment so total she was speechless. Robert looked up at her, then chuckled. "Don't worry, Hot Stuff," he said, sated. "I'm not done with you. Not by a long shot." He carefully eased her off him, removed the soiled condom, then wiped off his flaccid penis.

Tracy watched him stonily, then let herself be laid back on the bed. Robert parted her thighs, then she felt the warm press of his face on her inner thighs. Then came the warmth of his mouth on her engorged flesh, the shock of his tongue as it entered her dragging a scream from her throat as her back arched up on the bed. Another cry was torn from her, as he again jerked the chain, stimulating her already painfully erect nipples.

Robert explored her orally, his teasing and sucking sweet torture, his gentle licking then rhythmically tonguing her clit driving her wild, until sweat covered her naked skin, and her throat was hoarse from her cries. Over and over, he let her feel the first stirrings of orgasm, then with a painful jerk of the chain brought her away from it. Tracy began to plead as her frustration mounted, begging Robert to let her come. Finally he let her crest the wave, his tongue bringing her to climax as she clutched his head to her groin.

Tracy lay panting, shuddering, scared of the intensity of her orgasm. Then she felt a fresh shock as Robert undid the clamp on her right breast, the sudden release from pain masked as she felt his mouth close over her reddened nipple. Tracy cried out weakly, clutching him to her, but he gently pushed her away, loosening her left breast and quickly suckling at that. Without breaking contact, Tracy felt him pushing apart her legs, then sheer joy as she felt his erect penis slip inside her once more.

Robert teased her nipple with his teeth, then released it. "I put on another," he murmured. Then he clutched her in earnest, driving into her with abandon. Tracy reached up to grasp his pistoning buttocks, holding him to her, feeling the grind of his pelvis on hers. To her shock, the starting tendrils of another orgasm began again. Tracy embraced them, striving hard to meet Robert's thrusts, even as he began to shake above her.

They came together, Robert's roar joining Tracy's triumphant scream as she came a second time. They held one another, breathing hard.

Robert leaned up from her on his forearms. "Aren't you glad you came with me now?"

Tracy gave an exultant sigh, stretching her arms over her head. "Yes. An unequivocal, yes."

"Good," he said, kissing her nose. "Because I'm glad I came with you. Come here and let me hold you."

"That's a good line," Tracy commented, as she snuggled close to his chest. "You should put that in a book."

"Who is to say I won't?" Robert said loftily. "You just might read this in my next erotica sequel."

Tracy looked up at him, unabashedly curious. "Is that how you get your ideas?"

Robert looked down at her in silence for a moment.

Is he trying to decide how much to admit to me? And do I really want to know anyway? "You don't have to answer," Tracy whispered quickly, looking down.

"You wouldn't have asked, if you didn't really want to know," Robert said, tilting her chin up to face him. "The truth is that yes, I have sometimes written some of my true exploits into my novels. I think every fiction author does, to some extent. Haven't you?"

The scenes she had just written earlier tonight were a direct result of her recent adventures. "Yes," Tracy admitted, flushing. "But only a few scenes."

"Exactly," Robert agreed, hugging her. "It's the passion we feel in real life that gives us the momentum to tell the story in the first place. There's no crime in it, so long as you don't use someone's real name, or make it obvious that the scene you are describing wasn't one you dreamed up."

"Thanks for the pointers," Tracy replied, her tone genuine. "I'm sure you guessed by now, but I don't usually do things like this."

"I know," Robert whispered, his hold tightening on her. "You fabricated most if not all of Hot Stuff, didn't you?"

Tracy struggled at once, wanting to deny it. Robert held her tightly, not speaking. Tracy let out a long breath. "How did you know?"

"Because it felt like a fantasy that was untested," he answered. "A real experience with someone has that unknown factor, that slightly strange and unexpected added depth that gives the scene reality when it's included. The bitter truth is that sex is sex, and you're right, there are only so many ways to say climax. What makes the sex memorable isn't the platitudes that get whispered, the positions or toys that get used, or how many times the hero gets his rocks off. It's the heat that comes off the page; a heat any reader can feel. When it's there, it envelops them completely, arousing them even as it rivets them, holding them captive to the writer's will." He kissed her tenderly, the press of his lips a gentler touch than any he had offered previously. "When that passion is not there, the scene becomes just another sex scene, something you can take or leave."

"Then why did you do any of this with me, if you knew what I'd written was fake?" Tracy asked weakly.

"Because I saw the yearning underneath your words," Robert murmured, kissing her cheeks, her mouth, her forehead. "You wanted what you wrote to be utterly enslaving, to have that kind of power to move people. You just needed to be shown the way to grasp it."

Tracy hugged him, even as the confident arrogance in his words annoyed her slightly. "Thank you."

"You're welcome," Robert said happily, squeezing her. "And I admit, I was eager to find out if you'd accept my challenge, such as it was."

Tracy looked at him, confused.

"You could have simply hung up on me," he explained. "Or said no tonight, when I asked you to come out."

Like that was going to happen. "Did you really ever doubt we'd be right here?" Tracy asked pointedly. "You did come prepared, Robert, in spite of what you stated to the contrary."

He didn't answer right away, yet Tracy remained silent, willing herself to outlast him this time.

"I wasn't sure what you would do," he said finally. "Real people don't often do what a character in a book does. They're less willing to take chances." He rolled onto his back, then sat up. "It's easy to see the way a story should go when you're on the outside looking in. It's a lot harder when it's your own story."

Tracy sat up too, wondering if there was something Robert was trying to tell her. *Why not just ask?* "Are you trying to say something?"

"No," Robert replied. "Well, not in the way you mean, Tracy." He got up from the bed, moving over to the window to pull aside the curtain. He peered out, then let the folds of cloth fall back into place. "I just mean that usually there's a set path. In a book, you're not just writing for you; you have to think of your audience, and where they want the plot to go, what they want to see happen. There's an external pressure there that's absent in the real world."

Didn't he have family? Must be not, or he would know how wrong he was about external pressure. "I'm not sure I agree. Between my daughter and my father's expectations, my life is pretty well planned out for me."

"Then why are you here tonight with me?" Robert said, turning to face her. "I can surmise that I am probably not on their 'To Do' list for you."

"Because I wanted to come," Tracy answered with a shrug. "I wanted to know what it would be like to just say the hell with it and do something for me for a change."

Robert smiled, then nodded. "Good. I'm glad that you did."

Tracy shifted uneasily. Was this a dismissal? It sounded like one. If it were, there would not be a better opportunity for a farewell slap than on her way out tonight. "What did you want really, Robert? Why me?"

"Just what I said," Robert answered. He checked the door, then came back to bed, lying down beside her. "I guess what I'm trying to say is that I'm not looking at you as a character, or an experience, Tracy. I was … am glad to share tonight with you." He took her hand in hers and squeezed.

"But you don't want more than tonight," Tracy finished, crestfallen and hurt.

"From what you just said to me, you don't really have time for anything more in your life right now," Robert replied, kissing her hand. "But I'm not going to disappear out of your life, now that I know it upsets you so."

While his words were sincere there was something in them that seemed condescending. Or maybe she was imagining it? "Look, I'm not asking for a ring," Tracy said flatly, sitting up again so she could look down at him. "I just want to know how to act with you."

"How do you want to act?" he asked.

Enough games. "Is there someone else who might answer if I were to call your phone late at night?" Tracy said bluntly. "And would they mind me calling?"

"No to both questions," he answered, smirking. "Are you jealous?"

Pissed off, Tracy almost told him about Matt, but the guilt of how she had used her neighbor made her stay silent.

"You are, though I just told you that you have no cause to be," Robert continued. "Do you have feelings for me?"

No ... but saying that aloud seems so cold. "I can't just have sex with someone and not feel anything after," she said awkwardly. "It's wrong."

"Not that I don't agree," Robert said. "But whether that view is wrong or not is immaterial. What matters is what is right for you, and how you personally feel about it. You don't have anything to prove to me, Tracy."

Don't I? In the space of a few hours, you've basically called me a faker, and challenged me to write a sequel to Hot Stuff that sets everyone's loins aflame. "Alright," Tracy said slowly. "I'll accept that. But I want the truth right now, Robert. What do you want from me? You want me to decide a path. To do that I need to know."

"I'd like you to stay the night, if it's feasible," he replied. "And when I'm in town again, I'd love to spend my free time with you, like we did tonight. Do you want that?"

Tracy's first instinct was to agree instantly. But there was something unemotional about Robert's tone and choice of words that made her pause. "I'm not sure," she said. "But next time you're in town, give me a call. How does that sound?"

"Like a good idea," he said, hugging her. "Now will you stay?"

"That depends," Tracy said sexily. "Do you have any more plans for tonight?"

Robert chuckled. "Oh, I might have one or two more ideas, if you're up for them. I enjoy spanking, as I'm sure you noticed."

"I am if you are," Tracy said pointedly.

"Then let the games began," Robert said, drawing her down for another kiss.

T racy gave a long sigh as she settled into the back seat of the limo, looking at the early dawn sky above.

On the drive back to her house, she thought about the night with Robert, and what she wanted. No conclusion was forthcoming.

Robert had been his usual self this morning: polite, pleasant, and a gentleman. He'd let her have the shower first, then called for the limo to take her home after a goodbye kiss and an apology about an early morning meeting.

Tracy grimaced. The night had been the most adventurous of her life. Yet this morning she felt slightly disappointed and wasn't sure why. A direct and hard look yielded that it was because last night had been little more than a one-night stand, no matter what Robert had said. *But am I feeling bad because I wanted more than that … or because I'm supposed to want a perfect love to end all loves along with great sex? What do I want?*

Tracy was still musing on that as she hurried to her front door and opened it. *At least she had called last night, so Katrina wasn't going to be angry.*

Dropping her keys on the counter, she jogged upstairs and changed clothes, then went downstairs to make breakfast. As she was cooking eggs, her father came in, then settled down at the table.

"Hi, Dad," Tracy said automatically. "I'm making your eggs."

Her father didn't answer, but she knew he wouldn't. He would be engrossed in his tablet. For as much as the Alzheimer's was progressing, he still enjoyed surfing the Web and checking his email. His memory was getting worse as the disease progressed, but Tracy had had a local computer store adjust the settings on the tablet, so that there was no way her father could access sites like eBay or Amazon. His passwords were on a little cheat sheet that she had taped to the tablet, which helped with his access. Most days he spent on Wikipedia or other historical sites, indulging his love of history.

That had been the hardest part of his getting the disease, having to give up his teaching at the local community college. But at least with his pension, he wasn't in a home ...

"Good morning," Katrina said, coming in breezily. "And how was your night, Mom?"

"Good," Tracy admitted, blushing. "But you sound pretty happy yourself. Did you have a sleepover yourself while I was gone?"

Tracy expected a smart remark from her daughter. Instead, there was a sudden crimson blush as Katrina looked away, the bowl she'd been filling with cereal dropping from her hands to the floor. The sound of it shattering startled Tracy's father, who let out a cry, then half fell out of his chair to sprawl on the linoleum.

"It's okay," Tracy comforted, turning the oven off and walking quickly to his side, where he was trying to rise from the floor and failing. She got him back into his chair with effort, then looked over at Katrina. She had thrown away the broken bowl and was sweeping up the last shards.

"Why don't we eat?" Tracy said brightly. "We don't want anything to get cold."

Tracy's dad protested when she tried to take the tablet away, but she was adamant. He relented, letting her shut it off, and began eating his eggs. By that time Katrina was also eating, her eyes lowered.

Tracy made herself some cereal, toast, and fruit, devouring the meal. After getting her father settled in the other room with his tablet, she came back to the kitchen, where Katrina was cleaning up.

"I didn't mean anything by what I said," Tracy began. "I didn't mean to embarrass you."

"It's not that," Katrina said, not turning to face her. "It's just that when you called and said you weren't going to be home ... I did invite over someone to spend the night."

"That's a good thing," Tracy said, wincing, and wishing her tone was more supportive. "I mean, you haven't talked about someone special since you moved in, nor have you dated."

"I have, actually," Katrina said in a muffled tone. "You just didn't know."

Tracy blinked in shock. "But why didn't you tell me? You know I want you to be happy."

Katrina whipped around. "Even if I tell you the someone special is Blair?" she said in a quivering voice.

For a moment Tracy couldn't process the information. "Blair's your best friend," she said slowly. "You've been friends since grade school, and all through college—"

"More than friends," Katrina said, biting her lip. "Until Blair moved away." She swallowed hard. "But she emailed me she was moving back last month. And we … we kind of picked up where we left off, all those years ago."

Tracy stared at her daughter, trying to find the words. "You're gay."

"I'm not sure what I am," Katrina said, angrily wiping at tears. "I've had boyfriends, even some that were serious that I wanted to marry. You remember Pete, the college physics major? But through the years, I sometimes had feelings for others, too."

"Women, you mean," Tracy supplied. She stepped closer, opening her arms. "Why didn't you tell me?"

"Because you always made it seem like you were waiting for me to get married and produce a grandchild," Katrina wailed, dissolving into tears as she clung to her mother. "Like that was what was supposed to happen. I always felt like I was letting you down, that I didn't want that."

"Shh," Tracy whispered, blinking back her own tears. "You're not letting me down, Katrina. The only way that could happen would be if you did something that wasn't right for you."

"But I don't know what's right," Katrina sniffled. "I don't know what I want."

"Sometimes I think that's the only thing you can know for sure," Tracy whispered, hugging her daughter hard. She drew back. "I have to go in to work. Are you going to be okay?"

Katrina nodded, her half smile wavering. "I'm glad I finally told you. I wanted to for a while. But I kept finding reasons not to."

"I'm glad you did, too," Tracy said.

Later that night, Tracy sat on her back porch, working on some backstory for Rebekka. She was toying with the idea of bringing in a sibling for some added emotion but wasn't sure that would help her plot. *Maybe a step-sibling or a half sibling? That was done in a lot of books*

But am I going too deep into characterization? This is supposed to be a sex story, not a novel. She'd already added that Rebekka was a secret poetess, an outlet she'd used since childhood to battle her family's repressive behavior, pouring out all her shame and fear on paper before her choice of release became exotic sex. Tracy had even gone so far as to write a short sonnet to attribute to Rebekka, called Catharsis:

We bottle up everything until we combust into pieces,
    shedding shrapnel like old scales over everyone around us.
    My mother drank and smoked to release her emotions.
My father did the same plus drugs and sex. I come or cry
    instead with my partner of choice.
It's a much quicker release, with no bad health effects.
All my walls are instantly broken down to rubble.
My mind suddenly clear ... inspiration descends.
Is it any wonder I write my best sonnets in my bedroom?

Tracy frowned at her computer screen, then grimaced. *I can't tell if this is a brilliant thing to include ... or if I've entered the realm of the completely bizarre.*

"Hey, stranger," a male voice called out.

Tracy looked up to see Matt coming around the side of her house, a bunch of flowers in his hand. She rose, then went to meet him.

"For you," Matt said, handing them to her. "I decided that I would have to come to you."

"I'm sorry I didn't call," Tracy said, embarrassed. "I've got to stay here tonight and watch dad, I'm afraid. Katrina is out with a friend."

"You know I don't just want your body," Matt said in a low tone. "I just wanted to spend time with you."

But is that what I want? "Then come over and sit down," Tracy said with a smile. She peeked inside, but her father was right where she had left him, sitting on the couch, his tablet in his hands, his fingers touching the screen. He had his headphones on, so he was likely listening to music.

She turned back toward Matt. "Do you want a beer or a soda or something?"

Matt shook his head. "Just to see how your day was." He gave a sheepish grin. "I admit I've been watching my phone for two hours now, waiting to see if you would call."

"I would have called," Tracy said honestly. "I was waiting until my father went to bed, Matt."

"How is he?" Matt asked, taking her hand in his and stroking it.

"He's on the drugs, but they don't seem to be doing much," Tracy said with a sigh. "The doctors said his Alzheimer's is a slow form, though, so he'll be fine for a while."

"How are you?" Matt asked, concerned.

"Some days I'm fine," Tracy said, her tone losing its cheeriness. "Other days I think my life is on hold, waiting for him to get to the point where him living with me isn't an option anymore. Knowing I can't stop it makes me feel powerless. It's like some looming fate that's there in the shadows, waiting." She sighed. "I get tired of living from moment to moment. But there's no way to make any long-range plans, when I have no idea what my life will be like this time next month."

"I'm sorry," Matt said, squeezing her hand in his. "I just want you to know that if you need me to help, I'm here, Tracy. If you need me to watch him, or anything, just call, okay?"

And if I stop having sex with you will you still be so helpful? Stop that, Tracy, he's not like that. "Thanks, Matt," Tracy replied. "I appreciate that, really."

There was an awkward silence, then Matt rose. "I should let you get back to your writing," he said, then grinned. "Dare I hope that's the long-awaited sequel to Hot Stuff?"

Tracy nodded, laughing aloud. "Though I'm not sure how many people are waiting for it besides you."

"Lots," Matt insisted. "You're a really good writer, Tracy. I just wished you could see how talented your fans think you are."

"Thanks," Tracy replied, touched. "I appreciate that."

"Goodnight," Matt said, then turned to leave.

"Matt," Tracy called.

Matt turned back to her, his expression hopeful.

"How about tomorrow for dinner?" Tracy offered. "I can bring over a pizza or something?"

"You're on," Matt said, his relief palpable. "We can go in my Jacuzzi afterwards, if you'd like?"

"Sure," Tracy said with gusto. "I'd love to!"

He blew her a kiss, then sauntered off.

Tracy watched him go with a smile, then went back to writing her scene.

The pizza was a big success. But a larger one was when Matt produced a blindfold and used it on Tracy. He proceeded to feed her various chocolates, asking her to identify if the chocolate was white, dark, or regular. To her chagrin, Tracy couldn't tell one type of chocolate from the other, guessing wrong again and again. Finally they both collapsed laughing on the bed.

"So much for my sexy idea," Matt said, crestfallen as he removed the blindfold. "I planned to reward you if you guessed right."

Tracy grabbed his hand, suddenly inspired. "Maybe instead you should have punished me for guessing wrong?" she offered wickedly.

Matt stared at her. "What would you want me to do?"

It's a sure bet he doesn't have any nipple clamps lying around. But that doesn't mean we can't improvise. "Something to tease me, but not satisfy," Tracy answered. "That's at the heart of all domination games. Domestic discipline is also an option."

Matt shifted uneasily. "Like what?"

Tracy settled the blindfold back over her eyes. "Just wing it, Matt." She lay back on the bed, expectant.

A few moments passed, then she heard him leave the room and return. Then he was on the bed, and she felt something encircling her left wrist. Carefully, Matt proceeded to bind her, until she laid spread eagled on the bed.

"You're at my mercy," Matt whispered in her ear. Then his mouth found her breast, suckling hard. Tracy cried out, then fought against her bonds. They stretched but held her tightly.

Matt began playing with her body, caressing every inch of Tracy, massaging, and rubbing. She groaned in pleasure at his soft touch, even as she longed for him to take it further. She was relaxed and comfortable when the first touch of ice on her left nipple made her arch up off the bed in shock.

"Don't want you falling asleep," Matt whispered, sliding the ice down her breast and to her navel. Tracy started to giggle, then let out a yelp as he parted her legs and stuck the cube several inches into her vagina.

The sensation of utter cold and resulting involuntary shiver was so deep, it was like being dunked in a frigid tub of water. "Get it out!" she yelled, squirming all over, trying to contract her muscles to expel the intruder. "Get it out!" But Matt kept the cube in place, even as he began rubbing her clit with his hand. The stimulation was like nothing Tracy had felt before, even as she felt a new sensation of uncanny warming building at Matt's ministrations.

"That feels warmer, doesn't it?" Matt murmured.

Tracy moaned at the odd sensations. The ice was melting now, even as the cold flowed outward, numbing her inner channel. Yet her clit was unbelievably hot now, and tingling. *Some kind of warming gel.*

"It feels good, doesn't it?"

"Yes," she groaned, moving her hips. "God, yes!"

Matt kept stroking. As the minutes passed, Tracy began to pant, her pussy feeling as if it was on fire, the small nub of her womanhood swollen and protruding.

"Good," Matt murmured. "You're ready."

He undid Tracy's restraints, then took off her blindfold. Tracy felt a moment's disappointment that his teasing of her was at an end, until she felt cold metal around her wrists and the soft click of handcuffs fastening above her head.

"You've been a bad girl," Matt said sternly, administering a sharp stinging slap to her ass, then bringing her cuffed hands down in front of her. "Please me, or I'll have to punish you some more." He lay back, then moved her to straddle him. Tracy felt a moment of fear, then he placed her hands on his soft member. As her hands encircled it, she felt it flex beneath her hands, then begin to elongate and stiffen.

Matt pushed up with his hips with a sigh, sliding his cock against her buttocks, then again and again, grimacing and groaning as she stroked him, his erection becoming hard as rock, wet with his excitement as he rubbed his skin on hers. He shuddered, then moved her aside, slipping on a condom. Quickly he set her astride him sliding in with a grunt of possession.

After the overstimulation of the foreplay, the feeling of his cock stroking her was almost too much. Matt's penis seemed to be huge, stretching her to breaking as it entered and withdrew, even with the slickness of her desire lubricating him. And yet Tracy couldn't get enough of feeling him within her. She swayed above him, blissful.

Matt stopped mid-stroke, then grabbed the blindfold, putting it again over Tracy's eyes. The act of taking away her sight made the sensations she was feeling bigger. The orgasm built slowly, then crashed into her, making her scream as she felt Matt below hammering into her with gusto, then his own shout of orgasm as he came.

As her orgasm ebbed, she went limp on his chest. Carefully, he unlocked the cuffs, then snuggled her close.

"Did you like it?" Matt asked, satiated.

"Hell, yes," Tracy said, kissing his nose gently, then his cheek. "But you must have planned this."

"I went to the store that next morning," Matt said gleefully. "I've got a couple more items to try out, if you're not busy later this week."

"Day after tomorrow," Tracy offered with a smile. "I hope I can take a rain check for the Jacuzzi then, too? I'm too exhausted tonight."

"It's a date," Matt said.

The rain check was just as good as the previous time, with Matt producing some other items he'd bought on his foray to the local adult bookstore.

"You must have bought out the store?" Tracy questioned, as they relaxed afterward in the Jacuzzi.

"Some of this was online," Matt answered. "The local store only has a limited selection."

"You're going to be a regular sex toy connoisseur soon," Tracy teased.

"You mean we will be," Matt corrected.

Tracy leaned back in the tub, relaxing.

"We're good together, when we are in each other's arms," Matt said, after a moment.

"I agree," Tracy said leisurely. "I love our times together, Matt."

"Why can't you admit that it's more than that?" he persisted softly.

He was right, it was getting to be more than that, with them texting every night, or him calling or her coming over. And the longer it went on, the deeper her attachment was going to grow. Matt was right, it was time they talked about it.

"It is more than that now," Tracy said seriously. "I like you, Matt. I like our times together, and I look forward to the next one."

"I know," Matt said, an edge to his voice. "But are you ever going to want more?"

"I want more now," Tracy teased, batting her eyes at him.

Instead of his expected banter, Matt stared at her, then slowly shook his head. "I don't think you do," he said, regretful. Then he rose from the warm water, his skin steaming. "There's someone else, isn't there?"

Tracy looked away.

Matt grabbed a towel and wrapped it around him. Then without another word, he started walking toward his house.

"Matt," Tracy called. He didn't turn, going inside and turning off his porch light.

Tracy reached for her towel, only to find there wasn't one. Cursing, she rose from the water, folding her arms over her chest she went after him. "Matt!"

She went to the door, but he didn't answer. When she tried the knob, she found it locked. "Matt! Open the door! I'm freezing out here!"

"Mom!" came a child's shout from behind her. "There's a naked woman trying to break into Mr. Bannister's house!"

Tracy looked over with horror. Staring at her from one yard over was not one but two children. *And one of them had a cell phone!* She let out a shriek, then ducked down, running in a crouch back to the Jacuzzi. Grabbing a canvas deck chair, she sandwiched herself in the middle, then fled behind Matt's garden shed. Carefully, she hopped the fence, leaving the chair on Matt's side of the fence, and ran back to her house.

Breathing a sigh of relief, Tracy let herself in the open back door, then locked it. She tiptoed upstairs, then dressed.

Flopping on the bed, she thought over the events of the night. *That's what you get for showing up at his door in just a coat as a sexy surprise. Rebekka the sex goddess would never have been so dumb to be caught out naked at night.*

The more Tracy thought about it, the worse she felt. Was this who she was, a woman who cavorted naked on her back deck and took refuge from neighbor children behind the garden shed? Even if that was who she had been earlier tonight … it was not who she had to be, right? This was not one of her novels, and she wasn't Rebekka, whose life was one unending pleasure trip with a guaranteed happy ending. This was her life. The choices she made couldn't be unmade with a few added characters … or a plot twist that tied up the loose ends, making her happiness a surety. Robert had been right about that, at least.

I do like you, Matt. It would be easy to say yes, I want more. But until I'm sure, I can't. Why is that so hard to understand? Why do you have to push? That's almost as bad as Robert's distance.

Tracy sighed. *Was some of the reason she wasn't able to tell Matt yes because she was hoping for more from Robert?* She liked his way with words; there was a common ground they shared, no question. But there was a warmth about Matt that Robert didn't have, for all his sexiness. But Robert fit into her world better right now, precisely because he didn't make any demands on her, other than hooking up on the rare occasions when he was in town.

Tracy rubbed her eyes. Thinking about both of them was pointless. She had too many responsibilities to lose herself in anyone … or be anyone but who she was. As for exactly who that was, she'd figure that out as she went along. Matt clearly wanted some space, so she'd give it to him. That was a starting point.

Tracy lost herself in work, putting in extra shifts at the coffee shop. She avoided Matt. That lasted for two weeks, until he was sitting with Katrina on her stoop when she got home one afternoon.

"Hi," she said, dreading the confrontation. "Matt, I—"

It was then Katrina looked up, and Tracy noticed her red-rimmed eyes and tear streaked face.

"God, what happened?"

"Grandpa had a stroke," Katrina cried, running to embrace her mother. "I only went to the bathroom for a minute. The phone rang. When I came back he was on the rug, twitching."

Tracy took a hitching breath. "Is he—?"

"He's on his way to the hospital," Katrina explained. "It just happened, Mom. Matt saw the ambulance pull up, and he came over."

"Why didn't you call?" Tracy shouted.

"I thought you'd be driving," Katrina said stubbornly. "I didn't want there to be two disasters today." She looked to Matt, then back at Tracy. "We decided to wait here for you to arrive, then we'd all go together."

"I can drive," Matt said, rising from the stair. "I don't think either of you should be driving."

Tracy shot him a grateful look. "Thank you. I can pack a bag quickly, and we can go."

"I'll get the truck ready and be waiting," Matt said with a nod. "Just come out when you're ready."

"I want to call Blair," Katrina said, hurrying inside.

"We'll be right out," Tracy said to Matt, then headed after Katrina.

She raced upstairs. As she was throwing stuff into bags, her cell phone vibrated. She picked it up immediately, her first thought that it was the hospital. "Hello?"

"Hi, Hot Stuff," Robert drawled sexily. "Want to come out and play tonight?"

"No," Tracy said harshly. "My father's in the hospital, and I've got to go."

"I'm sorry," Robert replied quickly. "Another time?"

"Don't you have any feelings?" Tracy screamed.

"There's someone else, isn't there?" Robert said in a cool tone.

Tracy hung up on him, then hurried to finish packing. Darting down the stairs, she got into Matt's truck with Katrina, and they raced away.

Blair met them at the hospital, her expression upset. Katrina went into her arms at once, bawling, as Tracy tried to find out where ICU was, and if her father was still there. After presenting ID, they were finally told he was still being evaluated, and they would have to wait.

Hours passed while they waited, drinking bad coffee, and eating snack food. Then finally a doctor appeared. At his expression, Katrina burst into tears. Blair hugged her, nodding to Tracy.

Tracy went to the doctor, Matt following at a distance.

"Your father had a stroke, a bad one," the doctor said. "I'm sorry, but we've been monitoring for a good hour now with no result."

"What are you saying?" Tracy asked brokenly.

"That your father is on life support, but he's gone," the doctor said gently. "His brain is dead from lack of oxygen. The stroke was a bad one, as I've said."

"I should have been there," Tracy said, feeling the tears welling up.

"There was probably nothing anyone could have done," the doctor said gently. "I'm sorry, but I have to ask you if you want to be there when we turn off the machines. I saw your father's living will in his medical file."

"He had a living will," Tracy stated blankly. "It's at home."

There was the pressure of a hand in hers. Tracy blinked, then turned to find Matt there beside her. "Yes," he said to the doctor. "I think we all want to be present."

The doctor nodded. "Come in when you're ready." He moved away down the hall.

Tracy buried herself in Matt's arms, hugging him tightly. He said nothing, just held her as the minutes passed, the hospital chatter in the background fading to stillness.

There was sudden tap on her shoulder. Tracy looked up from Matt's shoulder to see Katrina and Blair.

"We should go in," Blair said hesitantly. "I'm sorry, but it's not going to get any easier."

Tracy wanted to yell at her, say it was none of her business, that she didn't belong here at all, that she wasn't family. But one look at Katrina let her know how wrong her feelings were. So she swallowed her pain and forced a smile. "You're right."

Tracy and Matt headed into the room, Blair and Katrina following.

Later that night, Blair stayed at the house with Katrina, and Tracy headed over to Matt's house. As much as she'd have liked to spend the time with her daughter this night of all nights, Tracy could see that it was Blair her daughter wanted to turn to when she was hurting.

Tracy sat on the couch, sipping some wine Matt had brought her, replaying the scene at the hospital again and again. Her father had looked two dimensional in the hospital bed, his body bony under the sheet. *When had he gotten so thin?*

"I'm sorry," Matt said, sitting down beside her with a bottle of beer. "I know that you already know that, but I wanted to say it anyway."

"Thank you," Tracy said automatically.

"If you need anything, I'm here," Matt continued. His expression tried for a smile, but it was so strained it came off as more of a grimace.

"I know that," Tracy said.

"Talk to me," Matt persisted. "Tell me what you're feeling."

"Relief," Tracy said. The moment she said it, tears welled up in her eyes, and she began crying. Matt grabbed hold of her and hugged her as she sobbed.

Tracy cried for only a short time before she began choking, her nose too stuffed to breathe. Matt grabbed a fistful of tissues and gave them to her, and Tracy blew her nose several times, then dabbed at her eyes.

"I know it sounds like I didn't love my father, to admit that," Tracy said in a cracked tone of voice. She blew her nose again. "But there was so much I kept preparing myself for mentally. I had read up on all the stages of Alzheimer's, to get ready. I had checklists for all the stages and plans for how I was going to handle him here at home. I'd even put him on the list for several nursing homes, just to make sure that everything was covered." She wiped at her eyes again. "I was prepared for everything but this."

"Like the doctor said, it was probably a blessing."

Tracy nodded. "I know that. But I feel adrift now, that so much that I planned for isn't going to happen. I'm guilty for all the relief, and I'm scared now, too."

"Scared of what?" Matt asked.

"That now I have to start living for myself, and not my father," Tracy said, blinking back more tears. "And it's been so long since I stopped living minute to minute, I'm not sure how to begin."

"You can start with me," Matt said lovingly, embracing her.

Tracy hugged him back, not answering.

E arly that next morning, Tracy began making arrangements with Katrina's help. Her father's body had been donated to science, so there was only the question of whether to hold a service or not, and to put something in the paper. With only a small discussion, Katrina and Tracy decided to do both.

As Katrina wrote the obituary with Blair's help, Tracy began cleaning the house, readying it for guests. As much as her father hadn't had many friends in his later years, some of his students would show. He'd been too much of a beloved teacher in the thirty some years he had taught.

"Mom," Katrina called. "We're going to take this over to the paper, then stop to set up some arrangements for a get together for friends and family."

"Okay," Tracy said, wondering if the get together had been Blair's idea. "When?"

"This weekend, as it's Monday. That way no one will have to get off work to come. And it will give us time to get together some photos of Grandpa to have for display."

Tracy nodded, feeling better about the idea. There should be some kind of memorial for her father, for all the good he had done in his life. "That sounds great. Sure, tell me the details when you get home. Try to make it for later afternoon, if you can?"

"All right," Katrina called, then there was the sound of the front door slamming.

Katrina would probably be fifty, and she would still slam the front door every time she left. Tracy chuckled, then began vacuuming. After she finished, she sat down at her father's tablet. Using her own email password, she logged in, then began compiling a list of friends and family to let them know the sad news.

The phone rang.

Who could that be at 10 am? Tracie hurried to the phone and picked it up. "Hello?"

"Hi. Is Jake Daniels there?"

"No," Tracy said curiously. "Who is this?"

"Who is this?" the woman asked her.

"Tracy."

"Oh yes, you're Jake's niece," the woman said in relief. "I'm so glad I caught you. I've been calling for hours."

"Sorry, I was vacuuming—" Tracy began.

The woman talked right over her. "I've trying to get ahold of Jake. I haven't talked to him for three months, not since he had to go into therapy after his surgery."

"I think you must have the wrong number," Tracie said, bewildered.

"Isn't this 17 Parkview Rd?"

Tracy began to feel uneasy. That was the address of her father's old house across town. "No. But I don't understand. Who told you that a Jake lived here?"

"Jake did when we met online more than three years ago. He's a wonderful man, but you already know that. He loves to go to the opera. He used to be a musician himself, you know. He sent me clippings." The woman laughed. "But I'm going on about him, like my kids tell me I do—"

"The last three years?" Tracie said in a dry voice.

"Yes. He's been watching the house for his sister, Amanda."

Amanda had been her mother's name. This was weirder and weirder. "And you say he's been a friend to you?"

"More than a friend, at least in spirit," the woman said. "We've been sort of an online couple for the last few years. We Skyped every night until he had to have that surgery. And now I'm worried because I haven't heard anything from him in the last eight months."

It had been eight months since her father had been diagnosed with Alzheimer's. Right after Tracy had started making plans, the first of which had been moving her father in and putting his house up for sale. "How old is Jake?"

"Thirty-seven, just like me. He sent me pictures."

The walls felt as though they were caving in on Tracy. *No. My father couldn't have done this, pretended to be someone else with a whole life that didn't involve me. No. This woman has to be crazy.* "Pictures?" she echoed.

"Yes," the woman said, sounding irritated. "And other little presents. We love sending each other little presents, Jake and me."

This has to be a joke. This can't be happening! "I'm sorry," Tracy managed. "But I didn't catch your name."

"Lily," the woman said, her tone peeved. "I'm surprised Jake didn't tell you about me. I used to send him a monthly package of treats for his rescued greyhound. How is Tandy?"

Tandy had been in the same car accident that had claimed her mother's life close to a year and a half ago. Her dad had lied to this woman, built a fabricated life out of half-truths. *This is real. This is happening.* Tracy couldn't say a word.

"I'm sorry to break this to you," the woman said, after a moment. Her tone was apologetic. "But things have gotten quite serious for us. Jake had planned to move out to be with me, as soon as his sister Amanda comes back from Europe. Because of that, I felt it was all right to call." She paused. "It took me a while to find this number through information. I'm so glad to finally talk to you, Tracy. I've been so worried, not hearing anything for so long—"

Tracie swallowed hard. *Tell her the truth and start now. Damn you, Dad.* "I think you'd better sit down, Lily. I've got something to tell you."

Tracy luxuriated under the shower, letting the hot water wash away everything. She had no choice but to tell Lily the truth. The woman had been inconsolable, raging at her at first from keeping her from her love, and then shattered to find out the depths to which she had been lied to. But there had been no other choice.

Why did you do this, Dad? Was it the beginnings of the disease? I want to believe it was. If Lily's telling the truth, then you began with her while Mom was still alive.

Tracy got out of the shower, dried off, and sat down. It was hard to do anything but replay the hours long phone call in her mind, wondering if she had handled it right.

Could it have been a scam?

Tracy opened her father's tablet, then used the little cheat sheet on the bottom to log in to his email with his password.

There were no emails in his inbox. *But the computer techs had blocked just about everything, like she'd asked. Dad hadn't emailed at all in the last few months, that she knew of.*

She looked in sent mail. There were only three emails from the last few months, the first from her father letting all his friends know that he was moving, and his diagnosis. The second was one she had sent from this email, cancelling her father's one valid online account with

Amazon. The last was an email to an unknown address. Tracy opened it.

My dearest Lily,

I'm sorry, but I'm going to have to have surgery, and the prognosis is not good. I hoped for so much for us, but I know now that it's likely not going to happen. This will likely be my last communication to you, darling. Please know I love you, and that will never end.

Love, Jake

Tracy clapped her hand over her mouth, swaying slightly. *It hadn't been a scam. Lily had been telling the truth.*

Tracy went back to the inbox, then looked in the Trash. Here were dozens of emails from Lily, some angry, demanding Jake answer her. Others professed her love, her devotion, her hope that everything was okay. The last was dated two weeks ago.

Reeling, Tracy closed down her father's email. For a moment she sat still, knowing that moving one inch would break her. Slowly, in small increments, she came back to herself, gathering her courage back around her.

Katrina can't know. What would be the point? In fact, it's better if no one knows. If even one person knew, that would make it real. Right now, Tracy wanted just to forget the phone call, forget what she had found, pretend it had never happened.

Get that email out, then go over to Matt. He can help you decide what to do. And he won't tell anyone, either.

Biting her lip, Tracy went back to her email. She finished the list, and got the email ready, then realized she didn't know the place or time for the weekend memorial party.

With a sigh, she went into her inbox, deleting ads, and leaving some friend's emails with drafts as a reminder to write them back. As she was finishing up, an email appeared from Robert, with an attachment whose title Tracy recognized as his newest series release, due out in a few months. His only note on the email was *Is this real enough?-R*

There was something odd about the formality of the letter. *Maybe he felt bad about his insensitivity, that day he had called? Was this an apology?*

"Mom!" Katrina called from below.

Tracy got up and went downstairs. Katrina was there, looking more cheerful than she had. Tracy renewed her resolve to say nothing. "Did you make arrangements?"

"Yes, five to eight Saturday at Brusettio's," Katrina said. "I had no idea you knew the owner, Mom."

Tracy swallowed hard. *Why hadn't she told Katrina not to book that particular restaurant?* "Yes, he's a fan," she said weakly.

"A big one," Katrina assured her, even as she and Blair began to unpack groceries. "He offered us a big discount."

"That's good," Tracy murmured. She helped unpack, then went to go upstairs.

"Tracy," Blair called hesitantly.

Tracy stopped, then looked back over her shoulder.

"I hope you don't mind if I take you both out to dinner tonight," Blair said. "I know you don't know me that well, Tracy, and I'd like to change that."

"Maybe now isn't the best time for that," Tracy said, uncomfortable.

"Then how about Katrina and I don't want to cook, but we need to eat something and so do you," Blair replied, undaunted. "You don't need to be here kicking around in this big house on your own tonight."

"I can call Matt," Tracy said automatically, then winced again.

"He's working tonight, to take off Saturday," Blair answered. "Now come on, before I drag you."

Tracy stared at Blair in surprise, then laughed. Blair laughed too in response.

Katrina came out of the kitchen. "What's so funny?"

That something I wasn't sure I could embrace might be this family's saving grace. "Nothing," Tracy said. "But I'm ready to go if you are."

Tracy hugged both her daughter and Blair goodbye, then closed the door as they walked to their car.

She's assured them that she would be okay tonight on her own. *Maybe that's something I'm going to have to get used to again.* At dinner, Blair had been obviously much in love with Katrina ... and vice versa. While it lifted her heart to see her daughter so happy, Tracy also admitted that it likely meant that Katrina would be moving out soon to live with Blair.

I'll be on my own again. I wanted that so much when all this began. I felt crowded. Now the house seems too quiet.

Tracy watched some TV, then went upstairs. To her surprise, her laptop was still up, not closed.

I never sent that email. Shit!

Tracy filled out the party information, then hit send. Then she finished all the emails to friends, finishing up after midnight. Then she looked at Robert's email, considering.

I can just read a little and finish the rest tomorrow. After screaming at him on the phone, it's the least I can do.

She opened the attachment and began to read.

Two hours later, Tracy read the final words, drew a hitching sob, and reached for the box of tissues, letting all of her agony spill out of her in a hot rush of tears.

The story was an erotic love story of the pagan woman Kiyra and her latest conquest, a pirate who rescued her from a sinking ship, made her his sex slave, then finally set her free at her original destination with a bittersweet romantic farewell. In short, it was the kind of erotica that Robert usually wrote, complete with exotic locales, steamy sex, and more than a touch of romance. But buried in the pages was his own pain at losing her, scenes and bits of dialogue from their few shared moments together grafted seamlessly throughout the story, complete with the pirate's utter heartbreak when he finally set Kiyra free.

He meant me to see this, so I would know what I meant to him, knowing that once he had, I'd be unable to walk away.

Tracy glanced at the clock. *God, it was 4:45 am.*

He knows I check email last thing before bed. He knew that I would read this. And he is likely there dozing with the phone by his side, waiting for me to call him.

Tracy grabbed for the phone, trying to punch in the numbers, blurry through her tears. She did it successfully, then waited, shaking, for him to answer.

"Hello, Tracy," he said gently.

"I read your story," she said haltingly, hating how her words wavered and broke.

"Did you like it?"

Tracy swallowed hard. "You know I loved it."

"What did you like about it?" Instead of the expected warmth, his tone held only cool casual interest.

Tracy wavered, feeling as if her heart were breaking, unable to bring herself to pour out her feelings when he was being so cold. "That I felt like I was the one losing the person I loved," she said slowly. "It shattered me, Robert."

"Take a moment, Tracy," he said soothingly. "I'm very glad you liked it, but I didn't mean to upset you."

Didn't you? "How could you think I wouldn't be upset? This hits home, Robert."

"All my works do that," he said gently. "Please don't be upset. It's just a story."

Just a story. Tracy closed her eyes, trying to hold onto herself, to not break down and cry, to not call him a bastard and slam down the phone.

"Is it?" she whispered. "And is this just fiction too, that I'm here talking with you?"

"No. I'm real. And so are you. And so is what we shared."

His words were gentle, but empty of emotion. Suddenly Tracy felt like the biggest fool ever. "I have to go," she said swallowing. "Goodnight."

"Goodnight," he said softly.

Tracy put down the phone and dissolved into tears. That was where Blair found her an hour later.

The woman came and hugged her, then offered her a tissue. Tracy took it gratefully, then took a long deep breath. "Thanks."

"Do you want to tell me?" Blair asked.

"No," Tracy blurted. "I don't want to tell anyone." Then she burst into tears again.

"You need to tell someone, clearly," Blair said, handing her another tissue.

With only that impetus, the whole tale of Robert, Matt, and 'Jake' came spilling out. "I just don't know what to think," Tracy said bleakly, her tired eyes red rimmed. "How can everything really be this way?"

"Because people usually aren't just bad or good, but something in between," Blair said, handing her yet another tissue. "Everyone has feelings, even when they act as though they don't. Everyone wants to love someone and be loved in return. But it's hard to ask for that love, especially if it's expressed in non-traditional ways. No one wants to make themselves vulnerable or be the one left alone when the one they love walks away."

"I just wish I knew what to do," Tracy said.

"Katrina told me a wise woman once told her that sometimes the only thing you can know for sure is that you aren't sure," Blair said.

"Ha ha," Tracy said drolly, making a face. "Not one of my better witticisms."

"That doesn't make it wrong," Blair insisted. "No one is saying that right now, today, you have to know what you want for the rest of your life."

"But I should, shouldn't I?" Tracy said weakly. "I'm not young anymore, Blair. I should know who I am by now."

"Why?" Blair countered. "Life changes people. Where is it written that you have to stay the same?"

"If you marry someone, you're supposed to stay that person for them, to keep your promise to always love them."

"But sometimes you can't, and that promise occasionally gets broken," Blair said gently. "That's why we have divorce, Tracy. I know you must think that your parents were in love. But it's a real possibility that if your mother hadn't died—and your father hadn't gotten Alzheimer's—that he would have left her for this Lily woman."

"But he lied to Lily, told her he was forty years younger!" Tracy exclaimed. "Their romance could never have been real, only virtual."

"People can accept a hell of a lot for love," Blair said. "Maybe you're right, that it wouldn't have worked. Maybe it was just your father's disease. We won't ever know for sure. So believe what you need to in order to accept this and get past it."

Tracy nodded. "Will you tell Katrina?"

Blair nodded. "Yes, just in case this Lily person shows up sometime. Technically, your dad committed fraud. Katrina needs to know."

Tracy put her head in her hands. "I didn't even think of that."

Blair hugged her. "I'm sure she's hurt and only wants to distance herself from all of this. But Lily went to a hell of a lot of trouble to track your father down. We need to be prepared."

Tracy sat back, grabbing another tissue. "And Robert? Any words of wisdom on him?"

"Only that he took offense to your saying he had no feelings," Blair said, after a moment. "And that the time you shared must have meant something to him."

"He never told me what he wanted," Tracy said absently. "He was careful not to."

"Then accept that, too, and move on," Blair said. "Matt is solid, and he's not afraid to express himself."

"Are you cheering for him?" Tracy said with a smile.

"I think he's a good guy," Blair said. "He deserves to know if you want more than you have now, don't you think? Aren't you doing to him exactly the same thing Robert did to you by not answering him?"

Blair was right. I just never saw it that way. "You're right," Tracy said, abashed.

Blair got up from the couch, then brought over the garbage can with a grin. "Let's clean up the evidence." Tracy tossed in her used tissues, then hugged Blair again. "Thanks for listening. I just didn't feel there was anyone I could tell."

"I've felt like that more than a few times," Blair said. "I hope we can be good friends, Tracy."

"So you're not going to call me Mom, too?" Tracy joked.

"Sure, if you want, Mom," Blair laughed, a new lighter tone in her voice. "But I had better get moving. I was here to find some extra clothes for Katrina. She's going to be staying at my house a few days."

"Good," Tracy said, meaning it. "I'm glad you two got together. I haven't seen her so happy—or so in love before, Blair."

Blair said nothing. But her expression turned radiant with joy, and her short parting smile was dazzling before she hurried upstairs.

Tracy called into work, saying she would be off the rest of the week. After dealing with a lot of other busywork, she headed to Matt's house.

There had been a list of things she planned to say when she got there, like apologizing for her behavior, followed by yelling at him for leaving her naked in his backyard. But when he opened the door, Tracy just blurted, "I'm sorry," and threw her arms around his neck.

Matt embraced her, then shoved the door closed, and began kissing her.

Unlike their times before, there was no special toys, no kinks, no tricks, and no soundtrack in the background. Tracy said nothing, and neither did Matt, as they undressed and made love.

When it was over, they lay in each other's arms, clinging to one another. As she lay there, it came to Tracy finally what she did know for sure.

I don't know what I want … except to look like Blair did, to be that happy again. Now that my life is my own again, it's time I spent some time discovering what will make that happen. Overcome, Tracy blinked her filling eyes rapidly, then took a quick deep breath.

"It's okay," Matt said gently. "I'm here."

"I know," Tracy said, holding him in her arms. "And I'm here for you, too. I'm sorry I haven't said it until now."

"But you can say it now?"

"There's not a lot I'm sure of," Tracy said. "But I want you in my life, Matt. I want more nights like these, and dinners together, and talking with you."

"Then marry me," Matt said lovingly. "We can have all that, Tracy."

Yes, he really just said that. Tracy pulled back slightly, staring up at Matt.

"There's nothing to stop us now," Matt continued. "I'm sorry to say it so bluntly, but that hell you've worried about and dreaded is over now. And Katrina is going to be happy with Blair—"

"You know?" Tracy stammered.

"I'm not blind," Matt said, irked. "I was surprised, yes, but they seem very happy together." He hugged her. "As happy as we could be, Tracy."

Tracy bit her lip, feeling like she was sinking in quicksand. "I'm not ready for that," she said sadly, then moved away from him, sitting on the edge of the bed.

"Why do you always pull away from me?" Matt said, the first touch of real anger in his tone.

"Because I'm not sure if I want forever with you," she said wiping angrily at her eyes as she reached for her clothes. "I'd rather hurt you by saying that now, then say yes and not be able to follow through on my promise. I need time to figure out what's right for me."

She thought that Matt would stop her, call her back, something. But instead he only watched her as she dressed, then walked out the door.

T racy spent the rest of the week handling her dad's remaining affairs. In spite of all the prep she had done, there was still much to do, including attending the reading of the will.

Blair, Katrina, and she were present as her father's attorney read the words they expected to hear, telling them of a few charitable donations her father had arranged. Then came the clincher.

"I hereby leave the remainder of my estate to be split equally between my granddaughter Katrina, my daughter Tracy, and my good friend Lily Pechard."

Blair hugged Katrina, then shot eyes at Tracy as if to say *See? This is why Katrina needed to know.*

After signing the necessary paperwork, the three left the lawyers office. All of them walked to the sidewalk, then stood there.

"I expected something like that," Blair said, lighting up a cigarette.

"I didn't know you smoked," Tracy said politely, hoping she hadn't evaluated Blair the wrong way.

"Only in times of dire stress," Blair answered. "Like today."

"It makes it better," Katrina said in a small voice. She was looking at the ground. "At least we know he didn't do what he did to be mean, or just for fun. He really cared about Lily. That's something."

Not nearly enough. He owed us all some kind of explanation. Tracy nodded, biting her lip.

"Hopefully it will be enough for Lily, too," Blair said, taking a puff.

Tracy stared out in the distance and didn't answer.

B rusettio's was hopping Saturday night. Far more people had turned out to celebrate her father's life than Tracy had expected. She lost count of all the former students that had come up to shake her hand and offer their condolences. She smiled at each one, thanking them, even as she longed to scream at them that the man they were remembering wasn't who they thought he was. *What would be the point? They would never believe her anyway. And for them, her dad had been what they needed: a teacher, a mentor, a coach, and a friend.*

Katrina was holding it together, with Blair by her side. Gary had been a big help, his normal lusty boisterous behavior turned to solemn politeness. Any other time Tracy might have been grateful for that. But after all of the events of the last few days, she just wanted him to be the happy letch he was, not some polite stranger.

As the steady flow of people turned to a trickle, Tracy excused herself for a moment. Matt had still not shown up. *Would he stay away?*

Tracy went to the bathroom and splashed some cold water on her face. She emerged, pasting a smile back in place, then scanned the room. Abruptly, shock flooded her.

Robert was standing there, talking to Blair and Katrina. As Tracy watched, she saw Katrina point to her, then Robert's slow turn in her direction. He shook Katrina's hand, then headed toward her. Blair and Katrina were both watching closely, obviously eager to see what would happen.

Not in front of my daughter. Tracy ducked though the nearest open doorway, into the bar area, and waited just inside the door. Robert came in a moment later. Tracy just stared at him.

"My condolences," he uttered sincerely. "Gary told me about your party, so I wanted to come and tell you how sorry I was."

"Now you have," Tracy said brusquely. "Have a good night."

"Have I offended you in some way?" Robert asked.

"Yes, in just about every way possible," Tracy retorted. "I'm not sure what you hoped to accomplish by coming here, but—"

"What one usually hopes to accomplish by attending a memorial," Robert said right back, clearly annoyed. "Conveying sympathy to the surviving family."

Tracy bit back her intended diatribe. *What was the point? Make some polite conversation, and then he'll leave, and you never have to see him again.* "I'm glad you came," she said, keeping her tone cool. "I'm overwrought. Excuse my upset."

"That's normal," Robert said soothingly. "My apologies. I'm not very good in times like these."

"No one is," Tracy said dryly. "Except those that make their business running funeral homes."

Robert chuckled. "I'm glad to see you're still you, Tracy. I've been worried about you."

"I'm okay," Tracy replied. She didn't expect the words to be genuine, but to her surprise they were. "Or I will be, in time."

"Good," Robert said. "I want you to be happy, Tracy."

I didn't get resolution with Dad. Damn it, I am getting some kind of resolution with you before this is done. "Do you?" Tracy said coolly. "You wrote me—or rather us—into your story, used it to finally show me your feelings. Was it just a story with a few well-crafted kernels of truth? Or were you jealous, and wanted to use it to bring me back to you?"

Robert stared at her. Then he shifted slightly, nodding once. "I am a little jealous," he said. "But it's not what you think."

"Then what is it?" Tracy demanded.

"When I saw you there at that signing, it was easy to see you weren't happy, but that you were trying hard to fake it," Robert said. "You could barely bring yourself to admit to writing erotica, much less considering experiencing it."

"And you wanted to show me everything I was missing, is that it?" Tracy said icily.

"I wanted to show you that you were missing out on something in your life," Robert explained. "That it's not only the twenty-something's and virgins of our fictional worlds that can be swept away, Tracy. We can too, no matter how old we are, or what we've been through. Why do you think my heroine gets older in my series? To make that point, that love and complete satisfaction doesn't end the moment you turn thirty. That happiness isn't settling for less than you deserve. That pushing boundaries is a must, from your first breath to your last."

"For a bestselling author, your speech is convoluted," Tracy said scathingly. "Don't tell me that night we shared was about teaching me that exotic sex was still possible for a woman my age. Or that it was some teachable moment. All it was to you was research for your next novel."

"No," Robert said, his eyes narrowing. "I wanted to feel something myself, not just give you a moment to remember. I thought you could make me feel something again, and I was right. Tell me I'm wrong, Tracy. Tell me that whomever you're with now and whatever you have isn't because I rekindled the fire inside you, and made you believe you could be and do anything you wanted."

He wasn't wrong. Without Robert as a catalyst, I'd never have opened the door with Matt ... or dared to do any of what we did together.

Tracy leaned back against the wall, weary to the bone. After a moment, Robert leaned back beside her.

"I'm sorry," Tracy said.

"So am I," Robert said, taking her hand, and squeezing it. "I never meant to hurt you, just help you. I never expected you to have so much fire that I'd get singed helping release it."

Was that all it had been? It was likely all he would admit to. Tracy forced a smile. "Friends then?"

Robert nodded, a small smile on his lips. "Friends." He laughed. "Maybe more than friends, if your new boyfriend doesn't work out." He raised her hand to his lips and kissed it. "Let me know, okay?"

Tracy nodded, biting back her sarcastic remark. *Never say never.*

Robert leaned in and kissed her cheek. "Goodbye, Hot Stuff." He gave her a last smile, then left.

Tracy watched him go, then turned to leave the bar area, and ran smack into Matt.

"Who was that?" he growled.

"A friend," Tracy said honestly. "One I needed to close some doors with. Thanks for coming, Matt."

"Can we talk?" he asked.

If you're not going to propose again. "Sure. Go ahead."

"I'm sorry I pushed last night," Matt said earnestly. "I'm just scared that I'm going to lose you."

"Why are you so scared?" Tracy asked pointedly.

"Because in all the stories I've ever read, that's always why the girl breaks up with the guy, that he doesn't tell her how he feels," Matt said. "I'd rather overshare than have you wonder where you stand."

"Okay, that's honest," Tracy said. "Now let me be honest, too. I don't want to be a woman who has to get married to enjoy sex with someone I care about," she said her voice gaining strength with each word. "I need to be the woman I want to be, even if it means I'm not what others think

I should be. I don't want a husband right now, and I don't want a lover who's here one night and gone the next. Part of what I was looking for was someone to lean on." Tracy paused. "When all along I could handle what I was going through. I just needed to be strong enough to try ... and to reach out to my loved ones when I needed strength."

"Being strong isn't just handling everything that comes your way. It's letting others help, and reaching out to them," Matt cautioned.

"Yes," Tracy agreed. "But it's also saying that no one can make me happy but me, Matt. I went through something and it's changed me, changed the direction of my life. I'm not who I was for most of the time you've known me."

"Good," he said lovingly. "Because that's the woman I want to be with, seeing as I'm already in love with her."

"Are you sure?" she teased.

He nodded. "But are you sure you want me in your life? I'm probably going to push again, though I'll try not to."

"Yes," she said happily. "Because I'm fully capable of pushing back, Matt."

He grasped her hand in his. "I know that, Tracy. You're not the only one that's changed."

"We're not done changing, either," Tracy said, squeezing his hand. "But I do want a future with you, Matt. We'll figure it out together, one step at a time."

"I agree," he replied, then gave her a little smile. "But I do have one thing to confess."

"And what's that?"

"A fantasy I have, that I hope you can help me make come true."

Tracy laughed. "I'll do my best. What does it involve?"

"A costume."

She laughed again. "What do you want me to dress up as?"

Matt shook his head. "The costume's for me." He rummaged in his pocket. "This is all you need." He handed her a pen, one that was very familiar.

Tracy took the pen, her mouth falling open as she read the familiar hand-printed words on it, her shocked expression changing to one of awe. "You're...you're Batman."

"Yes," Matt intoned in his Dark Knight voice, giving her a slight incline of his head and the little smile coupled with an intense stare. "And I want a different ending to that scene we had so many months ago."

"You're on," Tracy said, taking his hand. "I'm seriously thinking about doing a little role-playing myself, actually."

"Really? As whom?"

"A dominatrix who focuses on couples instead of a partner, helping them to get the best out of their passion for each other by encouraging them to expand their sexual horizons. Someone who helps them to discover that they don't have to be afraid of what they truly want, or who they truly are, in or out of the bedroom. Do you think there's any way I could really do that?"

"Like a sex coach? I'm sure that there's a need for that. You'd have to contact the local adult bookstore, maybe some of the erotic websites, see if you could set something up. I think it would be hard to get it started, but I know you could do it, Tracy. What are you thinking for a costume?

"Platinum hair," Tracy said slowly, fingering her locks. "And maybe contacts to make my eyes a riveting blue. I'd have to look the part."

"And you'd need a name, too. Any ideas?"

"Yes, I've already thought of the perfect one."

"What?"

"Sin."

THE END

THANK YOU FOR READING

Did you enjoy this book?

We invite you to leave a review at the website of your choice, such as Goodreads, Amazon, Barnes & Noble, etc.

DID YOU KNOW THAT LEAVING A REVIEW...

- Helps other readers find books they may enjoy.
- Gives you a chance to let your voice be heard.
- Gives authors recognition for their hard work.
- Doesn't have to be long. A sentence or two about why you liked the book will do.

ABOUT TARA FOX HALL

Tara Fox Hall's writing credits include nonfiction, horror, suspense, action-adventure, erotica, and contemporary and historical paranormal romance. She is the author of the paranormal action-adventure *Lash* series and the vampire romantic suspense *Promise Me* series. Tara divides her free time unequally between writing novels and short stories, chainsawing firewood, caring for stray animals, sewing cat and dog beds for donation to animal shelters, and target practice.

www.tarafoxhall.com

ALSO BY TARA FOX HALL

With Satin Romance

Novellas
Night Music

Anthologies
Her Frozen Heart in Frozen
One Perfect Moment in Propose To Me
A Love For Michelle in Second Chance for Love

With Melange Books

Unhallowed Love Series
A Good Year
Year of the Demon (available 2019)

Promise Me Series
Promise Me
Broken Promise
Taken in the Night
Taken For His Own
Immortal Confessions
Promise Me Anthology
Her Secret
Point of No Return
Lost Paradise

Dark Solace

Eye of the Storm

Tempest of Vengeance

Sundown & Serena

Hope's Return

Fate's Prison

Web of Memory

Forever

Freedom: Elle's Story

Immortal Reckoning

Novellas

Return To Me

Surrender to Me

The Oath

Anthologies

The Origin of Fear in Spellbound 2011 Anthology

Night Music in Midnight Thirsts II Anthology

Partners in Midnight Thirsts II Anthology

Kink in Wicked Christmas Wishes Anthology

The Oath in Wicked Christmas Wishes Anthology

Make Me Behave Anthology

Latham's Landing, An Anthology